# Unburied

A Collection of Queer Dark Fiction

Edited by Rebecca Rowland

www.DarkInkBooks.com

First Published by *Dark Ink Books*, Southwick, MA, 2021

*Dark Ink Books* is a division of *AM Ink Publishing*. *Dark Ink* and *AM Ink* and its logos are trademarked by *AM Ink Publishing*.

www.AMInkPublishing.com

Dedicated to those who were brave enough to stand up to the monsters

and those who continue to sharpen their swords

"Drink," I said, presenting him the wine.

He raised it to his lips with a leer. He paused and nodded to me familiarly, while his bells jingled. "I drink," he said, "to the **buried** that repose around us."

"And I to your long life."

He again took my arm, and we proceeded.

-Edgar Allan Poe, *The Cask of Amontillado* (1846)

# Contents

Sweet Dreams · M.C. St. John · 1
(supernatural horror)

Night Follows Night · Greg Herren · 9
(psychological horror)

Flawed · Felice Picano · 25
(dark fantasy)

When the Dust Settles · Sarah Lyn Eaton · 41
(science fiction horror)

I Can't Wait to Become a Man · Thomas Kearnes · 59
(psychological horror)

Open Up and Let Me In · Laura DeHaan · 87
(paranormal horror)

The Red Candle · Louis Stephenson · 103
(dark fantasy)

Razor, Knife · Elin Olausson · 113
(psychological horror)

The Procedure · Daniel M. Jaffe · 129
(science fiction horror)

Moi Aussi · Christina Delia · 143
(ghost story)

The Other Boy · Laramie Dean · 151
(psychological horror)

Cut Off Your Nose to Spite Your Race · J. Askew · 169
(science fiction horror)

For The Gods · Robert P. Ottone · 183
(dark fable)

Some Kind of Monster · Azzurra Nox · 215
(supernatural horror)

1,000 Tiny Cuts · Veronica Zora Kirin · 223
(psychological thriller)

Blessed · George Daniel Lea · 249
(dark fantasy)

# Sweet Dreams
## M.C. St. John

It was well past midnight, with a sickle moon sailing through gray clouds. The streets lay in quiet lines on the face of the town below. Each house was dark, save for the occasional reflection from a window catching the streetlight when the wind rustled through the trees.

One house did not even have that. It was wrapped up in the night and dreaming. Clocks ticked softly in its rooms. For some, sleep came easy in that steady, reliable movement of time. But not for everyone.

Down the hall, past the framed photographs of a baby boy, then a toddler, then a little league shortstop, came a voice.

"Dad?...Dad...?"

Silence. Then again, more frantic:

"Daaa-*uhd?*"

In the master bedroom, Luke turned on his reading lamp. He rubbed his eyes, yawned, and poked the mound of blankets next to him.

"Stanley," he said, "wake up. Harold's calling for you." The next time he shoved. "Stanley, the house is on fire. We're being robbed. A flying saucer landed on the roof. *Wake up.*"

"Wha-at, what? What's wrong?"

"That you sleep like the dead. And Harold wants you. He's calling for Dad, not Daddy."

Stanley squinted at the clock on his nightstand and groaned. He pulled back the comforter and swung his feet out of bed. The nubs of his spine stood out in stark relief in the lamplight. Grabbing a shirt, he said, "How long will he keep doing this? He's almost seven."

"It's a phase. You had nightmares as a kid, too. Everyone does."

Stanley paused halfway through putting on his shirt, the collar pulling back the skin of his face. It hurt. "I didn't," he said. "He shouldn't have strawberry ice cream before bed."

"I happen to love strawberry ice cream *and* sleeping all night." As if to prove it, Luke's breath slowed, curling in on itself. He started to drift. "Go help our little boy," he whispered. Then he was out and lightly snoring.

"*Daaa-uhd...*"

"On it, on it," Stanley said. He put on his comfortable pair of wool slippers and shuffled down the hall.

Along the way, the thought did pass through his sleepy mind that maybe this time, just *maybe*, someone else was there. He paused at the top of the stairs, listening to the spaces between Harold's calls. The house was quiet. Stanley had grown accustomed to the tone emitted from the rooms, a sort of muted hum. He heard it now. No one else was there except the three of them.

To be sure, he looked down to the foyer. Luke had wanted a mirror hung next to the coat rack so he could check his outfit before leaving for work. Stanley now used the reflection to see the opposite wall, where the key code panel of their security system was. He was proud of this little discovery. From his vantage point, he could see a green light, meaning the doors and windows were locked and the alarm was set.

Still, though. He rubbed the back of his head, feeling unsure about something that he couldn't quite place. He craned his head to the dark ceiling. His eyes moved from the crown molding, an air vent register, a crack in the plaster. He saw these details without any of them sticking. Did he need to check anywhere else, except the obvious, which was on his son? He didn't think so, and yet...and yet and yet and yet...

*You need sleep, and so does Harold.* That was true. He was exhausted from getting two to three hours of sleep at a stretch before hearing—

"Dad?" Bedsprings shifted, sheets moved. "Is that you, Dad?"

"Yeah, bud, it's me." Stanley went to the bedroom door where taped up on display were crayon drawings of dragons and robots. He gave it a nudge and peeked in. "Are you doing okay? What's wrong?"

"I heard something."

"You remember what we talked about."

"This was different, Dad. I swear."

Stanley came in and clicked on the boy's nightlight. He knelt next to the bed. His boy. His sweet, sweet boy. Harold sat cross-legged in the middle of the tangled sheets. His eyes were wide open, but Stanley saw the blue-purple rings around them and thought, *This is one of the rough nights, he's been up for hours.*

He rubbed the boy's back and said, "It was a bad dream, that's all."

"No, it was real."

"Harold."

"I mean it. Don't you believe me?"

"I do think you heard something. This is an old house, and it can make funny noises. At night, they can seem like more than what they are. But they aren't."

Stanley thought what he had said made sense, but the words felt half-formed falling from his mouth. He was so tired, physically and emotionally drained. How many times, and in how many ways, would he have to explain away the bad things?

Many more times, it seemed. Harold wasn't buying it. The boy's face was solemn. He was so pale that Stanley could see the fine blue veins at his temples.

"It wasn't the house that woke me up. It was her," he said. "The Underbed Witch."

"We've been over this. She doesn't exist."

"Then how can I hear her? She has claws for hands. She scratched the floor to wake me up. To let me know she's here." Then Harold shivered, a genuine ripple of gooseflesh that ran from his neck on down. Stanley felt the skin pebble beneath his own hand. *Correction*, he thought, *this is the worst night yet.*

For many near-sleepless weeks, Stanley had heard about the Underbed Witch. Each night when Stanley came to comfort him, Harold had a new detail about her to report. Heaven help any police sketch artist who would ever need to draw her likeness. Like many other boogeymen before her, The Underbed Witch was legion to a young kid. She went by many guises, and no two of her shadows were the same.

One night, Harold ranted that she was at the foot of his bed, perched like a gargoyle with sharp grinning teeth. Another night, he claimed she slithered across the floor and up the wall, only to rest on the bookshelf near his door (a convenient explanation, Stanley thought, as to why Harold couldn't get to the bathroom and wet the bed that night). Sometimes she whispered ugly things to him, just loud enough for Harold to hear, about how she wished the boy was bigger so she could have more to eat.

And one time—which made Stanley pause and consider the power of his son's imagination—Harold swore he only *felt* her in the room, and when he peered over the edge of the bed, he was met with a nasty surprise:

only the top half of her face poking out from underneath the mattress, her black eyes as patient and deadly as a crocodile's. She had been waiting for the boy's curiosity to get the best of him. Waiting for the right time to attack.

That was, if she were real.

"So you're saying she now has claws?"

"Uh-huh."

"Why can't we hear them now? Is she afraid to use them? Let's find out."

"No, Dad, don't. *Don't.*"

"Remember what we said about deep breaths, right? You know I have to check. If she lives up to her name, she should be down here."

The boy's bed was a single-sized mattress on stubby wooden legs. Stanley had to get on all fours to get low enough to see. He had a momentary image of himself and, though he was tired as hell, he couldn't suppress a smile: a grown man in polka dot boxer briefs on his hands and knees, rooting around for nightmares. As far as he could tell, he was only catching cobwebs. The bed shifted as he scooched farther underneath.

Harold did not find it funny. He skittered from one end of the bed to the other. "She can get you, Dad. She told me if I ever got close to the edge, she could grab me, and no one would hear me yell when she did. Dad. Daaaaa-*uhd...*"

From beneath the bed, muffled, Stanley said, "There you are."

"Is it her? Is she *there?*"

"Hold on."

The bed reared up on two of its legs and dropped. Stanley swore under his breath and continued to wriggle out of the tight space. In the process, his underwear rode up the crack of his ass, and one of his slippers nearly popped off. Finally, he was free. He sat up and smiled.

"I found her."

"You did?"

Stanley nodded. "Just not the one you're thinking of," he said, and brought up what he had found. A stuffed hippopotamus sat on the bed. Dirt and dust bunnies clung to her, but as Stanley wiped all of that away, she regained her familiar shade of bright purple. "Petunia was under there the whole time."

"I thought she got lost when we went to see Uncle Danny."

"Guess she didn't like Wisconsin and decided to stay with us. For a hippo, she sure can hide in a small space." Stanley pointed to Petunia's face, which was tilted enough to make her look quizzical. "Look at her eyes," he said. "They're big and black. Do they look familiar? Could they have been the ones you saw a few weeks ago?"

"Maybe..."

"They're also made of glass, see? They click against a hard surface. I found her lying facedown on the air register. If you were moving around on the bed—like I know you have been—those glass eyes could click on the grate. I bet if the AC kicked on, the air would get her to make that sound, too. Do you think that could make a sound like claws?"

"I guess so."

Stanley took Petunia by the scruff of her neck and walked her across the sheets. In his best hippo voice, he said, "How could you be afwaid of me, Hay-wold? I'm your fwiend fwom way back when. I only wanna snoogle."

When he nuzzled Petunia into Harold's neck and the boy laughed, Stanley knew things would be all right. Harold took the stuffed hippo in his arms. The dark circles were still there around his eyes, but the expression in them now was of sweet relief. He was seven again, and free. The bad dreams were at bay, at least for tonight.

"Thanks, Dad."

"Any time, bud."

Still on his knees, with his arms resting on the bed like a big kid, Stanley watched his son. It was nice to see him happy. "You've got a big imagination," he said, "and you can make great things without even knowing. Some of them get loose, but there are some you can hold on to. Make sure they're the good ones. Do you understand what I'm saying?"

"I can let the Und—you know, *her*...go."

"That's right. Can you try for me?"

Harold nodded, holding the stuffed hippo tight. "Petunia's gonna help. Aren't you, Petunia? That bad lady will *never* come in this room again."

"Good. Now let's all go to bed...what? What's that look for?"

"Can you wait, Dad? Just a few more minutes?"

Stanley agreed. He tucked Harold in and—as a promise, just this last time—waited for his son to fall asleep. Eventually, cocooned in his blankets and hugging Petunia, Harold did. Stanley could only hope it was a dreamless sleep.

He turned off the night light and tiptoed out of the room.

The house lay quiet, dark, still. Stanley went down the hall, his body taking him along the way as it always had. The photographs on the wall, gray shadows behind glass. The railing leading downstairs. The mirror. The security panel, floating in the murk. No intruders here. The nagging feeling he had had before was still there, but it was lower in its urgency. His son was safe. That was what mattered.

*Luke's right*, he thought. *It's a phase for most people, being scared of the dark.*

He made it to the bedroom and went to his bureau in the corner, his moves automatic. The slippers came off. He set them next to the register, just like the one in Harold's room, where a hippo's eyes could click against the grate. He took off his shirt and draped it on a chair in the corner. In the dark, he found his way around this familiar room, this familiar life. His body wanted what his body wanted, which was more sleep.

*People build up their defenses against it. Night lights. Stuffed animals. Prayers. All of these charms and rituals for the dark.*

He walked over to his side of the bed and paused. He knew that underneath his mattress were shoeboxes, storage tubs, and gifts for Harold from Santa this coming Christmas. There was hardly any room under the bed as it was. Nothing else could be under there. But Stanley stood there just the same. Then he poked his bare foot below. His big toe touched the corner of a cardboard box, probably the one filled with tax paperwork. Nothing out of the ordinary.

He got into bed and nestled in the covers. He felt the delicious warmth coming from Luke, and he spooned up alongside him. The clock ticked and the room hummed and his mind started to drift. He thought about Harold, how the boy banished his bad dreams from his bedroom. It was a phase, yes, but maybe soon, it would come to a close. There was nothing to be afraid of. Everything would be okay for Harold.

"I took care of The Underbed Witch," Stanley whispered, and snuggled in for a kiss. He was the hero tonight, after all. "We won't have to worry about her bothering Harold anymore."

"That's good, dear," Luke said.

Only it didn't sound like Luke. No, whoever Stanley was in bed cuddling with sounded older. Much, *much* older. Beneath his hand, the one holding what he thought was Luke's hip, Stanley felt a body shift and ripple. And grow.

"But what about you?" the thing asked. "How are you sleeping?"

No one heard Stanley reply.

Down the hall, Harold was fast asleep with Petunia in his arms, a slight smile touching his lips. It was the best sleep he had had in months. Nothing could wake him. In the dark house, among the soft ticking of the clocks, the boy slept like the dead.

## About the Author

M.C. St. John is the author of the short story collection *Other Music*. His stories have appeared, as if by luck or magic, in *Burial Day Books*, *Coffin Bell*, *Hybrid Fiction*, *J.J. Outré Review*, *Oddity Prodigy Productions*, and *Wyldblood Press*. Aside from the worlds he's dreamed up, he can be found in Chicago, where he attempts to outread his partner Jamie and their cat Queso. See what he's writing next on www.mcstjohn.com and follow him on Instagram under the handle @MC_StJohn.

# Night Follows Night

Greg Herren

Zane parks his wobbling shopping cart next to the island divided in half. The side he parked beside contains cantaloupes, separated by a partition from round, green-striped watermelons beneath a sign reading *Red Seedless Personal Watermelons, $3.99* The cantaloupes are cheaper, per the sign casting shadow on the stacks of melons below. He glances around. There's an older woman, rooting through the baking potatoes like a pig hunting truffles. A younger woman is inspecting the rubber-banded clusters of green onions. Two men in uniforms are building salads at the salad bar, scooping things into Styrofoam boxes. Three people are waiting for their orders at the deli meat counter, their backs to him.

No one is paying him the slightest bit of mind.

He picks up one of the cantaloupes and does what he's seen others do. He sniffs it where the vine had been attached, holds it up to his ear and thumps it with his thumb. He doesn't know how it should smell or sound if it's ripe or not, but he's too self-conscious to not go through the same motions everyone else does when selecting a melon. He's terrified someone will notice him not thumping and laugh at him, mock him for his stupidity, point out he doesn't belong in this big modern supermarket with its aisles and aisles of bounty. He's always afraid someone, *anyone,* will notice he doesn't know how to do a simple task every other shopper seems to know how to do instinctively, something so incredibly simple his failure will be like an enormous neon sign announcing to the other shoppers in their yoga pants or tennis skirts that he doesn't belong here.

*One of these things is not like the others.*

*Stop thinking like that,* he scolds himself as he puts the cantaloupe back with the others. *You belong here just as much as anyone. Who knows what secrets these other shoppers might be hiding?*

He closes his eyes for a moment, hears his heart thumping rapidly in his ears. It's too fast, but that isn't anxiety or stress, it's because he just taught back to back spin classes, it's why his legs are tired and why he's in the produce section of the Rouse's Supermarket on Tchoupitoulas Street, listening to melons while wearing a black tank top drenched in sweat and tight bike shorts under looser-fitting cotton ones and shivering in the air-conditioned coldness.

*If anyone's staring at me it's because of what I'm wearing, that's all.*

"And besides, you're so good-looking," he hears Richard's voice in his head, "people can't help but look at you, so just get used to it, Zane." Richard had laughed then, kissed his cheek, ruffled his hair. "No one can look at you and see anything but an incredibly sexy young man. That's why they stare at you, not because you don't belong."

*Vanity is a sin. Mirrors are tools of Satan.*

He shrugs that thought away like it's an annoying mosquito and reaches for another cantaloupe. He holds it to his ear, ready to thump it with his finger, when he notices a man watching him, standing over by the bins holding onions and potatoes, a clear plastic bag in one hand, a red onion in the other.

There's something *familiar* about him...

Their eyes meet. The other man quickly looks away, like his retinas have seared. He shoves the onion into the plastic bag and wheels his cart away into the wine section, near the whites. He's wearing dirty-looking camouflage shorts over skinny, white legs and a black T-shirt with the Confederate flag on it. His long, graying-brown hair hangs down his back in a ponytail.

*A man's strength is in his hair. The Lord gave Samson strength as long as he didn't cut his hair.*

The man disappears down the aisle. Zane only realizes he's holding his breath when he lets it out with an audible gasp.

*I've seen him before.*

But where?

His stomach clenching with fear, he almost drops the cantaloupe.

*No, don't think that. It's been years. You don't have to worry about it anymore. That wasn't him. It couldn't be. You're being silly. If they were going to come for you, they would have years ago. This is New Orleans. Everyone looks familiar because it's a small town and you've seen him somewhere else before, is all.*

He opens his eyes, carefully places the cantaloupe in his cart, next to the probably unripe honeydew melon, the seedless red grapes, the bag of kiwis. He steps away from the cart and picks up one of the small watermelons. It's heavy in his hands. He holds it up, goes through the thumping process again before nodding his head slightly and adding it to the cart. He's making a melon salad for dessert, something cool and light and sweet, perfect for a sultry July evening in New Orleans. Chunks of melon, with little balls of fresh mozzarella and cherry tomatoes, tossed in olive oil and balsamic vinegar, a little hint of fresh basil.

*If he isn't from the Compound, why did he run off when I noticed him?*

*He isn't. He can't be. Stop doing this to yourself. He didn't run away. He just went down the white wine aisle.*

He sighs and pushes the cart down the aisle, the wobbly right front tire swinging back and forth and squeaking. It never fails: he always manages to get a defective cart, like they each have a kind of homing beacon drawing him in every time. He goes around the corner—

—and sees the man again, but now he's standing at the seafood counter. The young woman behind the counter is wrapping up fish in butcher paper; she tapes it shut, hands it to him over the counter.

Zane gets a good look at his face.

*No,* he thinks, *I've never seen that man before.*

He's overreacted again.

*He wasn't staring at me. He's shopping like everyone else. If they haven't come after me by now, they're never going to, and you know that. Get over it. Just get over it right now.*

*They don't know where you are.*

At least this time, he didn't have an anxiety attack in public.

He pushes the cart into the next aisle, trying to move as fast as he can without looking like he's hurrying. He keeps his eyes down. The wheel keeps squeaking and wobbling. He passes bottles of ketchup and barbecue sauce and vinegar. Almost in tears, he grabs a jar of the hot-and-sweet jalapeños Richard likes and stares into his cart.

This jar is round. He fits it into the cart's back corner, placing bottles of salad dressing around it to square it off. He crosses *jalapeños* and *salad dressing* off his list. He always needs a list, to write things down. He never remembers everything they need, and the last time he came without a list, he flashed back to—

*No. Don't go there.*

He grips the cart handle hard, wheeling around the next corner to the aisle with beans and soups and vegetables. He stops in front of the big plastic dispensers for the cans of Campbell's soup and massages his temples.

*I don't remember taking my pill this morning. And like Dr. Rivers said, if you don't remember taking it, you probably didn't.*

He needs to stop taking the alprazolam.

But the anxiety attacks are so awful! That sense of his mind racing out of control, the entire time being aware it's out of control, his emotions raging out of control and the whole time he—he *knows* he's acting and thinking and being crazy but there's nothing he can do about it.

Yes, alprazolam is addictive, but addiction isn't the worst thing that could happen to him. *Being dragged back to the compound would be THE worst thing, wouldn't it? Nothing worse than that.*

He grabs cans of cream of mushroom and French onion soup, stacks them neatly across the back of the cart. The price has gone up since last time. He frowns, crosses them off the list, fitting a can of baked beans next to the soup cans as he starts pushing his wobbly squeaking cart again. Rice and egg noodles and spaghetti sauce, check, check, check. A couple of jars of gravy, check. He reaches the end of the aisle—

And the man is there again, his back to Zane, using tongs to fill a plastic bag with fresh shrimp from a pile of shaved ice on an island display. The sign on top reads *FRESH GULF SHRIMP $1.99 PER POUND,* written in black marker.

From behind, he looks like—

*No, it can't be him. It can't be. It's just a coincidence, it has to be.*

Of all days not to have slipped the little brown pill bottle into his backpack just in case, why today? Why today? How could he have been so stupid?

He won't forget again.

*Your mind's playing tricks on you, that's all. It can't be him.*

It *can't* be him, he knows that, but Zane's hands are still slick with sweat as he pushes the cart hurriedly around the endcap and down the aisle with foreign foods and coffee and boxed meals, the wheel shrieking and wobbling, calling attention to him. He stops in front of the K-cups and closes his eyes and takes some deep breaths like Dr. Rivers taught him.

It works…sometimes.

*It's not him, of course, don't be silly.*

He looks at his little yellow notepad. Coffee is on the list, and *it's on sale!*

Small victories always make him smile, make him feel better, like he's won some skirmish in the eternal war between bank balance and groceries.

He fits boxes of Folger's Black Silk coffee pods into the cart and frowns. The cart doesn't look neat. He walks around to the front of the cart and tilts his head.

*Sloppy work is a sign of a sloppy mind. You need to do better.*

He rearranges things. There, better. The stupid round jars always cause problems. Their roundness causes wasted space, but there's nothing he can do about that. Round jars just don't make sense. They waste shelf space and—

"Is everything all right? Do you need some help, sir?"

It's a young man wearing a Rouse's vest, smiling at him, a gold tooth winking in the light.

"I'm fine, thank you for asking," he replies automatically.

*Always thank people. You know who doesn't thank people? Sinners who are going to hell. Do you want to go to hell?*

Zane smiles back, wondering why the clerk singled him out, what about him could have made the clerk concerned enough to approach him?

*He knows I don't belong here.*

*One of these things…is not like the others.*

He pushes the cart, stomach lurching, hand dipping into his backpack again, fumbling around, hoping against hope he'd put the bottle in there after all.

It's not there, of course. He left it on the bathroom sink.

*You can get through this, just follow the list and you'll be done.*

The next aisle is "foreign foods." He slips some easy Asian microwave meals on top of the soup, a packet of taco seasoning, a pack of hard taco shells. Richard likes tacos, and Zane eats the leftovers for lunch when he finishes cleaning the house, before watching *General Hospital.* He's lucky, he has to keep reminding himself sometimes. Luckier than so many, like his mother and his sister.

He'd gotten out of the compound and was never going back.

He just—must be *vigilant.*

*When you're a part of the family, they never let you go.*

*That isn't true*, he thinks as he slides pouches of Albacore tuna between the cans of soup, filling space left by their roundness. He'd left the compound over ten years ago, when he was eighteen, hadn't he?

*You can run away but we'll always find you.*

A backpack full of clothes strapped over his shoulders, and with slightly less than five hundred dollars (*stolen from Daddy*) in his pocket, he'd walked through the front gates and down the lonely red dirt road through the woods to the interstate, hitching a ride to New Orleans from northwest Mississippi. He'd only been to New Orleans before with groups from the compound, with their signs and hats and T-shirts about sin and hell and how the unrepentant would burn. Daddy always had the bullhorn, shouting at people to repent or face hellfire. The sinners always jeered and mocked them, and sometimes men would stand in front of Daddy and kiss while the crowd cheered, and Zane felt something inside move.

He was a sinner. He couldn't stop those images from popping into his brain, the way his loins stirred, always terrified someone would notice.

He prayed but God never answered.

He always pictured heaven to be something like New Orleans. Whenever they prayed or sang hymns about heaven, he closed his eyes and imagined Heaven looking like New Orleans.

But the reality had been nothing like Heaven, not for an eighteen-year-old boy with no experience.

*No, don't think about that. You're happily married now, and you don't have to dance in your underwear for dollars and let dirty old men touch you anymore.*

He needs to take a pill when he gets home.

Maybe more than one.

The memories are coming back. And that isn't a good sign.

*Focus, Zane.*

He checks his list again, sees he hasn't crossed off things when he picked them up, which isn't like him, the man watching clearly throwing him off his routine, and scribbles them out so hard, he almost tears the paper. He grips the cart handle with both hands, trying to breathe in and out the way Dr. Rivers tells him will help. Sometimes it does, not always. He closes his eyes, pushing out of his mind memories of that awful club he'd worked at and the older memories of the compound—

*like the squeaking sound the hinges on the door to his bedroom made at the Compound*

—and instead, thinking of the sound of waves on the shore, white sugary powder-like sand, the sparkling emerald water closer to shore and the dark blue sapphire water in the distance, the cool breeze coming in with the waves, the smell of salty, fishy sea air, the house they'd rented right on Destin beach the previous summer for a week, playing in the surf and sleeping late and letting the sound of the waves—so much louder and stronger after sunset—lull him into the deepest sleep.

Destin beach is his happy place.

So different, so nice.

Maybe there are guys cruising around, looking for young boys to pay for—

*No, no, no. Green water, white sugar sand beaches, waves against the shore.*

He skips the next aisle, heading back to where meat is stocked on refrigerated shelves against the back wall. The man is gone, and he smiles at a pretty young woman in a tennis skirt and a matching T-shirt without sleeves, skin smooth and tanned, eyes hidden behind sunglasses and blonde-streaked hair pulled back into a ponytail too young for her years, a diamond bracelet glittering on her petite wrist. The woman doesn't smile back, doesn't acknowledge him.

*Well, screw you, too. Bet you never had to worry about—*

He puts packs of low-fat ground sirloin (ninety percent fat-free!), a pack of chicken breasts, and a pork tenderloin into the cart. He moves on to the chips-and-soda aisle—

And there the man is, coming up the aisle from the other direction.

There's a resemblance. He isn't imagining it.

*It's been ten years. He'd look different now.*

Zane freezes, unsure whether to turn and run or brazen it out, lock eyes, see if he is from the family.

*You're being ridiculous. If he's from the family, he wouldn't come for you in the grocery store, would he?*

*Why wouldn't they? Didn't they track Leah down at—*

He stays frozen in place, turning his eyes to the wall of chips (so many different kinds to choose from!) like he's just shopping, nothing out of the ordinary, *normal,* although his heart is pounding and hands are shaking and sweat is forming in his armpits despite the frigid temperature in the store. This end of the aisle is where the canned peanuts are and the multiple varieties of flavored Pringles, and he grabs a couple of cans from the bottom shelf even though he doesn't care for them and neither does Richard. He could always remove them from the cart when he's safe—

*Safe? Have you completely lost your mind, Ezekiel?*

*Zane. My name is Zane now.*

Ezekiel.

Ezekiel was a million years ago, a different life, a different world, his name in the family, as part of the Compound, the name they'd given him when he was born with no idea who his father was. The idea, the premise of everything they believed, was that Daddy was everyone's father, spiritual if not genetic, and every other man in the family, in the Compound, served as role models, (*sperm donors,* his older brother Gabriel scoffed once) doing the heavy work in the fields while the women mothered and nurtured and home schooled the young. Women did women's work, men did men's work, and children were for the glory of God, educated in the Word and taught to honor Daddy and—

*Stop that.*

He can hear the hinges squeaking as the door opens…

His forehead damp with sweat, he fumbles for a tissue from his shoulder bag and blots it, aware his heart is racing, and he needs to calm down, he needs to—

*You can't get away forever, Ezekiel. God knows what you've done.*

The last words his mother ever spoke to him.

"You can run away," his mother, Rebekah, had said, standing in the doorway, wiping her hands on her apron, watching Ezekiel—*Zane*—put some clothes into his backpack. "But you can't hide from God, Ezekiel. And what are you going to do for money? You need money in the outside world."

"I'll be fine," he replied, not looking at her, unable to look his mother in the face any more then than he'd be able to do since—

*We'll always find you. You can't hide from God.*

He closes his eyes, squeezes them shut, forcing the memories back into the dark cobwebbed corner of his mind where everything he remembers from the Compound, from his life before he met Richard, is kept safely behind a locked door. They don't rear up very often, rarely in public, but there's always a first time, isn't there? And now that it is happening—

*I need to carry the pills in my backpack.*

Yes, that would help in the future, wouldn't it? Keeping the extra bottle in his bag for emergencies like this one, in the cold air-conditioned grocery store with an old Judy Collins song playing through the speakers, boxes being torn open and the shelves being restocked, other shoppers pushing carts, checkers scanning and bagging groceries before credit cards are swiped, carts going back out into the bright sunshine—

*Get a grip, boy.*

He exhales and opens his eyes.

There's no sign of the man. He's gone.

It wasn't him.

It couldn't be him.

He imagined the resemblance because he hadn't taken a pill, that's all.

He tries not to smile as he pushes the wobbling squealing cart down the aisle, stopping to place six-packs of plastic bottles of Coke in the front of the cart, where he's left room for them. He likes arranging his cart neatly, like a game of Jenga or Tetris, neat and orderly, everything arranged by size and to fit.

*Sloppy work is the sign of a sloppy mind, Ezekiel, and God doesn't like sloppy minds.*

His cabinets are the same way at home. It's a holdover from the Compound, but Dr. Rivers doesn't know that, no one knows, not even Richard. It's a secret he keeps, something small but precious and his own. He just likes things that way, doesn't think it matters, and it's such a small thing, really.

Not everything from the Compound is bad, after all.

Just some things.

*I was only eight the first time Daddy came to my*—

Beaches. Sand. Green water giving way to dark blue in the distance. The sky, the cry of gulls, waves against the shore.

Better. So much better.

But he's definitely taking a pill when he gets home.

Maybe two.

He smiles at a young woman struggling with a fussy child in the basket of her cart as he steers around the corner to the cracker aisle. They need saltines: Richard loves them, would eat them with practically anything, goes through a box a week. He frowns at the bottled water; he forgot to get a case of Pellegrino at Costco over the weekend, so he grabs a bottle with each hand, peering into the cart to figure out where they'll fit. He puts one down, shuffles a couple of things around and *voila!* there's a spot for them in the back. He hums as he starts back up the aisle, placing a box of crackers on top of the cereal boxes he'd put in the cart sideways, anticipating the need for a shelf for the cracker box. He rolls out of the aisle and around a cooler filled with discounted, about-to-expire things he doesn't even give a second glance.

*There had been a time when he wasn't so food-proud, after he'd left the Compound and when he was working at that bar on St. Louis Street, climbing onto the laps of old men with five dollar bills clutched in their clammy hands—*

He shivers. The refrigerated aisles are always too cold, and in shorts with his arms bare…

He checks a carton of eggs for cracked shells before putting it in the basket, leaving space for the bread. He'll put the English muffins and the bagels on top of the green egg carton.

Another harried-looking young woman with two small kids, a diamond tennis bracelet flashing on her tanned wrist and her black pleated tennis skirt swinging, crosses directly in front of him, not even seeing Zane because she's too busy fussing with her kids. Zane smiles and winks at the kids, who just stare back wide-eyed. Unconsciously, he puts a hand over his flat stomach.

*You have such a beautiful stomach, Daddy always said.*

He stops.

Well, there's *another* juicy little nugget hidden away inside his brain.

A wave of nausea washes over him.

*He'd been brainwashed.*

Dr. Rivers hates when he says brainwashing.

"Conditioning," he always corrects Zane with a slight frown and a small shake of his head. "You were conditioned from birth to believe Daddy was your personal savior, that Jesus was going to come back and take you all up in the Rapture. It wasn't your fault, Zane."

*No matter where you run, you can't hide from God.*

He reaches for the skim milk, checks the date, places it in the cart in the spot he left for it when he got the sodas. The loaf of bread goes into the space for things that need protection from crushing—he doesn't know what it's called, it's just kind of there and exists to be used and might have a name but he doesn't know what it is—and some blocks of sharp cheddar cheese and some pepper-jack, a little container of sour cream and some half-and-half and a little pint of heavy cream for the macaroni and cheese he wants to make tomorrow for the neighborhood potluck. He's never been to one, but Richard think it's time for him to meet some people, maybe even make some friends.

He checks everything off the list and smiles. That's everything. He tears the page off the notepad, crumples it up and puts it in his bag, turning the cart around and heading for the check-out lanes. He hears a woman laughing behind the bakery counter, resists the urge to put a fresh loaf of French bread in the cart—*always stick to the list, never buy anything not on the list*—and gets into line. He glances around idly, not seeing the man, wonders if maybe he imagined the whole thing. He feels calmer now that the shopping is done, everything on the list in the cart, soon enough he'd be swiping his credit card and loading the groceries into the back of the car, and then safely home, inside with the cat and able to relax with a well-deserved glass of wine.

*I almost had a full-blown panic attack right here in the store. That would have been awful. I'd have to start shopping somewhere else, and this Rouse's is just so…so convenient.*

He starts putting things on the belt, in order, the way he wants them bagged. He won't be able to watch the bagging process. He'll want to correct the young man shoving things into plastic bags for the woman in front of Zane, to make him see how much better it would be if he would just do it *his* way. He'll have to handle the rising irritation when he puts the bags into the back of the car, but once he's done all that, he'll be home free, ready to relax, ready to sit with his cat in his lap and watch *Judge Judy* before starting dinner. Carefully, he arranges things on the belt, square boxes and rectangular ones fit together neatly, no space between them with black conveyor belt showing, fitting the Cokes and the milk and the cartons of other dairy behind, then starting with the round things, cans and melons and finally the fresh vegetables, all as the belt creeps forward. The woman in front of him is using those reusable bags—

*Maybe I should start using them? Does it look funny that I don't?*

—but a quick furtive glance at the other lines shows other people having their purchases put into plastic bags, so he's still like everyone else, like the majority, nothing different there. The woman in front of him finishes loading her bags and the checker, Latasha, starts scanning Zane's items, smiling and saying hello. This is the worst part, waiting for the cashier to finish, so close to escaping the store and out into the bright sunlight and open sky of the outside. A few aisles over, a baby starts to cry—

*and he flashes back to a night at the Compound, a baby crying woke him up. He was maybe ten? Eleven? He couldn't remember, he never can remember, but he woke up in his bed and wasn't alone, which wasn't unusual, he always slept with his older brother Jedediah, but Jedediah wasn't there sometimes, and he wasn't there this time, but someone was in the bed with him, and he smelled sour wine and stale tobacco and MAN, you couldn't mistake the smell of man for anything else, and a deep voice was whispering to him not to cry, not to say anything, it was God's will and he was breathing hard—*

"Sir, are you all right?"

Latasha has stopped scanning things, looking at him with concern, her braids hanging heavy from her head. Zane forces a smile on his face and lets go of the cart with an effort and manages to say, somehow, "I'm sorry, my mind wandered off for a moment" and Latasha gives him a tentative smile back before looking at the young man bagging, and something passes between them, and the bagboy looks down and goes back to bagging as the scanner starts beeping again, and Zane wonders what is happening to him.

*You'll be back!*

His mother screamed after him as he walked down the driveway, shifting his backpack onto his shoulders, not looking back because he knew if he looked back he wouldn't have the courage to go. Lot was told not to look back, but his wife did, and he didn't want to be a pillar of salt. He ran once he was around the curve, kept running after he went through the gate, ran all the way down to the interstate, only stopping when he realized he had nowhere to go, didn't know what to do, didn't know what the rest of his life would be like. But he couldn't stay there anymore. He promised not to tell and never had. But there was a place in New Orleans he could go, he'd heard about, he just had to find it.

"$122.37."

He pulls out the gold Mastercard, swipes it, follows the directions on the little screen, takes the long receipt and smiles thanks at both Latasha and the bagger—his nametag says Antwine—and pushes the wobbling cart along to the electric doors, smiling at the woman who tells him to have a nice day. He goes out into the heat, pushing the cart to where he parked his little car next to the cart corral so he can just put the cart there when he's finished putting the plastic bags of groceries in the back of the car.

*Economy of motion, every movement useful and not a waste of energy.*

He opens the hatch and starts putting the bags in, lip trembling, eyes filling with tears as he tries organizing the bags in the hatch, trying to put them in some sort of order. He knows he didn't take a pill that morning, because he'd wanted to try to make it to the grocery store just once without chemicals; just once, he wanted to try out the little tricks and details that Dr. Rivers tried teaching him but he was making a mess and trying not to care but he could conjure the sight of the beach and the sound of the waves and he could feel—

*he could smell the smoke, the stale smell of Daddy as he lay hands on him, and they kept telling him it was a blessing, Daddy was showing him divine favor and it was a blessing, not all the boys and not all the girls were blessed with Daddy's love the way Zeke was and this meant he was going to go straight to Heaven when he died, wasn't he, and he should be grateful and stop crying and let Daddy do what he pleased because he was the voice of the Lord, he was a PROPHET and everything was ordained, wasn't it, and who was he, Zeke, to question the will of God, the word of the Prophet, even though they drove down to New Orleans three times a year with the signs and the bullhorns to try to convince the homosexuals to give up their sins but it was different, somehow Daddy was different…*

"Don't I know you?"

He spins around, the bag in his hand tearing, the cantaloupe and avocados scattering in the hatch, his eyes wild, his heart pounding.

*It's the man, oh god oh god he was right, the man had been following him, he'd been watching, and it's HIM, he knew it, he could smell him—*

In his mind, Zane sees the door to his room opening, that telltale smell.

"Get away from me," he says, his voice low, his eyes darting back and forth, wondering if he should scream. But no one would come help him, would they? They knew what he was and they knew he was a sinner. God had marked him, hadn't He?

"Ezekiel." The man is smiling, getting closer, and a white van is coming up the parking aisle, slowing, and the side panel is sliding open.

*It's him, oh yes, it's him, oh my God, it's him, he can smell him, he knows that smell, he remembers it, and the door is creaking open, and he's only ten and it's him, it is him, and he is going to take Zane back, and why oh, why hadn't he brought his gun? Both Richard and Dr. Rivers saying he doesn't need it, he is being paranoid, it doesn't matter.*

The man—*Daddy*—grabs him and the van is now beside them and someone reaches out and grabs hold of him, too.

And they shove him into the back of the van, the panel sliding shut.

"You can never get away from the Family," Daddy says.

And Zane—*Ezekiel*—starts to cry.

# About the Author

Greg Herren is the award-winning author of over thirty novels, over fifty published short stories, and has edited twenty-two anthologies. His most recent novel, *Royal Street Reveillon,* was a Lambda Literary Award finalist (his fifteenth time making the short-list, with two wins). He has also won an Anthony Award, several Moonbeam medals for childrens'/young adult mystery and horror, and been nominated for a Macavity Award and a Shirley Jackson Award. His short fiction has appeared in *Ellery Queen's Mystery Magazine, Mystery Week, Mystery Tribune,* and in anthologies such as the critically acclaimed *Florida Happens* and *New Orleans Noir.* He lives in New Orleans.

# Flawed

## Felice Picano

I'd be amazed if the little shop were still there. It's not really convenient to go back and check, so I'll probably not know for a while. But back then, even that scuzzy part of San Francisco was giving in to the gentrification that had begun taking over the city.

At the time, the shop was surrounded by small, ethnic, counter-top diners, a tumbled-down tailor shop and a cigarette store cum tiny grocery for the cripples and drunks and layabouts whenever their monthly welfare benefits arrived.

The only reason I even looked in the shop window was the owner, an oversized man, with ginger mustachios almost out to his ears and ginger whiskers down his front, with a shiny bald head, dressed in black leather, heavy with chains and gewgaws, including one dangling skull and crossbones earring. "A club act" I would call him if I'd noticed him while alongside my friend and she would smile. He was striking: meant to be as colorful as possible. Typical in the city. Less so as an antique store owner.

I was also drawn by the profusion of mirrors.

It was unclear whether this was a mirror shop or an antique shop. I stopped at the window after getting the opera house tickets and figured I'd amuse myself for ten minutes by going in. The owner ignored me, involved in a conversation on an antique puce Princess phone, adding up invoices on a pocked, old IBM desk calculator.

To my surprise, it wasn't just a store front; smaller rooms extended deep into the block, where surrounding shops still had living quarters.

I ended up looking around in the room furthest from the front door. Suddenly, Mr. Black Leather arrived, stuck out a meaty hand, and said, "Hans Olthen." Just then, we both heard jangled bells signaling someone entering the front door. "Back in a sec," Hans offered, flirtatiously adding, "Anything or one particularly interest you here?" Before I could answer, he pointed to three floor-model mirrors I'd stopped at and said, "Half off, half off, and don't bother with that one, it's flawed." He flounced off to the front of the store and I heard "*Ach, Gretel! Wunderbar!*" followed by rapid German.

So, of course, I looked at the three mirrors.

Looking glasses is more like it, since they appeared to be vintage 19ᵗʰ century. Two were faux-Federal style, late in the century with obvious attempts at copying the more prized earlier style with its distinctive architrave top. The third was a puzzler. It, too, had the faux-Federal style of arched top and double wood sides, but it also had what seemed to be East Asian carvings, finely done, almost hidden on the very dark wood of the two sides. I couldn't make out the wood used. The other two mirrors were maple and cherry, but while dark as mahogany, this was grained wrong for that and so, enigmatic. It was also larger: almost seven feet by four feet wide and leaning right on the floor, while the others had doubled bottom pieces and one had lion-claw legs.

The discounted two were placed direct to the passing viewer, and their glass was clear if a little blurry at the beveled edges, but without any crazing. The third, larger one, was faced away from the viewer. They were all surrounded by Craftsman-Era, fake zinc-shaded lamps set on brown-as-dirt matte ceramic bottoms, which rested on out-of-the-70's four-foot high, stereo speakers. I had to twist myself into a corner to get a good look inside the supposedly flawed mirror and even then, I made out nothing at all. No reflection, never mind a flawed one.

Wait! There it was! A dull reflection of the doorway behind me and my body in the camel-hair overcoat I'd unbuttoned in the warm back room. Despite the lack of sharp reflection, I didn't see a flaw until I looked closely, top corners first, then down, and left corner, all of them fine, but wait! there it was. A twist or turn of the glass? In the lower right.

When I knelt to look to see if it was the fault of the glass, suddenly it was clear, quite clear, but instead of reflecting back the closet door like the rest of the glass, it was reflecting green: light green, medium green, even a few deep greens, and as it clarified in front of me, it was *reflecting* green leaves, branches, portions of a bush and in some motion, too, as though it were a video or live action film.

I almost fell over. I did stumble into the closet door. When I crept forward and looked again, the flaw had spread. The entire right side third of the glass was reflecting what looked like part of a forest.

I was trying to make up my mind to call Hans and discuss this with him when he burst into the room and said, "It was nothing," shaking his head, then added, "Silly woman. She can see, no, how completely Gay Gay

Gay I am! Interested in the womankind not one bit." He'd spun about with his words and landed even closer to me than I found comfortable. "But you!" he added. "You, I have definitely seen before."

"I don't believe we—"

"No. No. Don't tell me. You were not so well dressed as this, I think. So maybe that is what off me throws." He touched his large pink brow as though to recall. "Black or navy blue tee and maybe, yes, it vas motorcycle boots."

"You must be kidding."

"No, no, Hans, that is incorrect," he lectured himself. "But somewhere…I am so sure."

"I am not that kind of—"

"No insult intended. I have nothing but respect for—"

"This mirror!' I interrupted him by changing the subject. "Unlike the others, it has no price on it."

"Because it is flawed."

"Then, the price…out of curiosity's sake," I explained.

"I told you. It is flawed and haunted, yes?"

"Yes. Well, as least about the flaw. I see very fine markings here. What's the provenance?"

"Provenance is very fine. From upper Nob Hill. Very large house next to Spreckles mansion. Well, on same street. Estate sale. All quite legal."

"I meant before that? Is it Asian or what?"

His big meaty hands came out and folded in space. "Wish that I knew."

"Because it might easily go with the dark wood colors in the library of a lady I know."

Hans peered at the delicate stylized chrysanthemums, and was that an open fan pictured too? "Cannot help. Hans takes notes at estate sales. Not this time. Siamese?" he hazarded.

"Or Javanese. And the flaw?" I turned to touch it on the right side. "Where's the flaw?"

As I looked at it, the green vanished and the glass was clear and shining, too.

"Is there!" Hans asserted without even looking. "Take my word. You bring it to that lady. She throw you out the door!"

"It's been months, maybe years since Diane has looked so well. She's positively glowing."

We were in the lobby of Davies Hall during the interval. MTT was conducting Mahler, a specialty of his, so it was full. I was just beyond the main floor bar, speaking with a blonde of a certain age named Conchita with seven last names, most of them, my friend, Diane, had intimated, husbands she'd divorced or outlived.

"She's a lovely woman," I agreed. "Lovely tonight. As are you."

"Do you think?" she preened. "It's vintage Balmain. I can't pull off those new designers. What do they always say, the older, the softer the lines and darker the skin, the more pastel the hues? Back to Diane. May we hope that there will be an announcement soon?"

"An announcement?" I asked, flummoxed.

"No announcement is forthcoming, Conchita, except the symphony will begin, now that we've had the overture and song cycle as appetizers and a bit of bubbly."

Diane slipped a beringed hand through my arm and smiled with her eyes at me, so that we were sharing something at the older woman's expense.

"But really, Diane," Conchita began, aggrieved. Then we all heard the chimes.

I wasn't sorry that Diane began to lead us away.

"But wait, darlings. You haven't told me yet that you'll both be at Keith and Enrica's?

Diane waved. We filtered through the orchestra crowd to our fifth-row center seats.

"Don't pay attention to Conchita," Diane lightly urged. "Listen only to me."

"Don't I always?"

We sat and the first violinist appeared on stage, and Tilson Thomas himself appeared and the audience settled down. That haunting post-horn motif tore through the silence with its plangent call from afar. I thought about what they had both said. I had made more progress than even I'd expected.

I turned to Diane and she to me and we smiled at the sonic wonders to come.

"What did you mean when you said that the mirror was flawed *and* haunted?"

"Is that what I said?"

"Yes, exactly those words."

Hans was wearing a variant of his usual dead cow: a vest covering his torso save for his very hairy nipples and his equally hirsute navel. He was certain I'd come to see him and my asking about the mirror was an excuse. He played along or at least pretended to do so.

"Specifically, what did you mean when you said it was haunted?

He had a feather duster and was dusting all around himself, reminding me of those balletic hippopotami in *Fantasia.*

"The mirror was wrapped in canvas sheet when I saw. Someone, I don't remember who, a servant or housekeeper, said it was kept wrapped many years. Wrapped tight and bound tight with cord. No one unwrapped since it was delivered. I think she said it was of danger." He shrugged.

"Because it was haunted?"

"It's superstition, is it not?"

"It was of danger if it fell on your toes, because it's so heavy?" I asked.

He emitted what romance novelists term a "mirthless laugh."

"What is important, is distorted. Because of flaw."

"And yet I like it very much," I said. "If it is so awfully flawed and distorted why not sell it to me at a discount? As damaged goods?"

"Well. . . I haven't put it up for sale yet."

"Does that mean you wish me to name a price?" I asked.

"That would be too much of a disregard. Is how you say it?"

"Insult, I think you mean? Too much of an insult?"

"Yes, insult is the word I look. But why talk of flaw things when there are so many perfect things?! For your lady friend, you said." This last phrase spoken so archly, I could have struck him for his insolence!

"Now you are insult. Subtleties I am aware, yes, but do not exactly understand," Hans admitted. "I still believe we have met before. Other circumstances. Yes! I believe."

"I *don't!* Now, shall I look into the mirror today?" I asked.

He didn't protest.

"Where exactly is this confounded flaw of yours?"

He danced a little on tiptoes. "Now you *not* see it," he said, pointing to the lower right-hand corner.

"When *do* you see it?"

Hans shrugged.

"Have *you* seen it?"

Hans shrugged again.

"And the haunted story? Fake, I suppose, to jack up the price."

He handed me a small pad and a chewed-up looking stub of lead pencil he kept in his vest pocket. "You make price you want here. Put it on desk when you leave."

That's when I knew he hadn't paid much, or perhaps anything, for it. It likely had been part of a general sale of furnishings.

I wrote a price and put it into my pocket.

As though in synch, the front bells jangled and he excused himself and exited. From where I stood, I heard his greeting. "So, Antony. What shall it be today? Perhaps this *escritoire* they say from Fontainebleau?"

I looked at the mirror again, and there was that green I'd seen before.

I wedged myself in such a way that I could look at it directly and touched the mirror. I'll be damned if the entire mirror didn't then clear enough to show that scene. I could make out forest, tropical, perhaps even Amazonian, given all the orchidaceous flowers and lianas. All the while, I was thinking, "I can see it, yet Hans couldn't? Or did he not even try?"

The leaves moved and sometimes a twig or branch jerked. As I stood entranced, I began seeing not so much movement as the tiny consequences of small, invisible things moving. I remembered there was a magnifying glass for sale a room away and longed to get it. At the same time, I was afraid to move away from this extraordinary sight for even a second.

I heard sounds coming too, faint at first, what might have been the far-off cries of primates or birds. I'd just absorbed that when a hummingbird darted into the scene. It went for the inside of an orchid-like bloom of cream spotted with red, hovered and sipped nectar; in profile, so that I could make out its bronze and green throat and front feathers. It was about to move out of the picture when it suddenly turned full face and stared.

"It can't possibly see me, can it?" I asked.

Perhaps in reaction, it darted forward, right to where I thought was the front edge of the glass. Astonishing. I was even more astonished when it darted forward another inch and I would swear its beak—nothing else but the beak—broke that indelible surface.

I must have gasped out loud and fallen back because faster than the eye, it darted away and out of sight. I fell into the wall and struck the side of one of the other mirrors there and had to move quickly to keep it and myself from falling.

"Are you okay?" I heard a voice. A distinguished looking African-American man—Antony?—must have been in the room next to this. He rushed forward to aid me. I thanked him.

"Oh, my!" he said and looked around. "He's been hiding these from me."

I moved in front of the "flawed" looking glass but he only had eyes for the smaller ones. "Hans!" he called, then smiled at me saying, "That scamp!" I could hear him saying as he went toward the front, "Hans, you naughty, naughty man! You've kept these lovely Federal mirrors from me," the voice diminishing as he went away.

I checked inside the big mirror and thought, I have to know for sure, and closed my eye and stuck a hand in. I opened them to see my fingers right at the branch end of some flowering bush. I grabbed it and snapped off the end. Hearing the other two approaching the room, I pulled my hand back, just in time to see the scene in the mirror beginning to dim again. I stashed the bit of foliage in my coat side pocket and strolled as casually as possible toward the front.

I met Hans and Antony coming at me. As they passed, I turned and said to Hans, "My offer will be on your desk."

"You're all right with all this, aren't you?" *All this* was the open front courtyard of the Legion of Honor set up with café tables and chairs, portable torch heaters, a string quartet playing, delicious food, and Mumm's and Prosecco served by waiters so smooth they might have been on roller-skates.

I might have answered satirically. Instead I said, "You're joshing, right? I *love* all this! I love the place. I love the Vlaminck and Derain exhibit inside. What's not to like?"

She smiled. "When we met, I wasn't sure you were as much of a culture maven as I am. God knows, Harley wasn't."

Harley: her dead husband. Worth who knew how much, exactly. Diane didn't.

"I am as much of a culture maven as you are. I just haven't been able to afford it like this before. You know, front row seats at the symphony, boxes at the opera, fund-raising galas with five-course dinners…"

"That's the other thing I have to ask you." Diana suddenly sounded serious. "Are you all right with someone else. . . you know, treating you to it."

"I'm fine with it. I'm delighted with it. But only because it's you—and not anyone else—who is doing the treating. I feel like we are in this together."

"We are! We are!"

She became pensive.

"You won't suddenly get all masculine proud on me and feel vulnerable about it?"

"I don't think so. Did Conchita say I would?"

"Several of my women friends have had more . . . more experience in these things, to be completely honest. I've always been sheltered. By my parents. By Harley. So I'm reduced to having to ask. So, no qualms?"

"My only qualm is what your friends think of you bringing me everywhere."

"Do you care?" Diana asked.

"Me. No. Not really. I know that makes me a terrible person."

"Me either. And, no, it doesn't make either of us a terrible person."

"I think it helps that we're not too different in age," I offered.

"It helps even more that you are well-read, knowledgeable, and intelligent on most of the subjects my friends are likely to—"

"Quiz me on?" I tried.

"Now you are being terrible."

"But yes, thank you." I agreed. "Except, of course, finances. I'm not very good at that."

"Thank the Lord," she laughed. "That's all Harley *thought about*, finances."

A *Romanza* by Schubert originally written for the piano was now glittering over our conversation, just as the dessert, a towering Bananas Foster, arrived.

"I couldn't possibly eat that monstrosity, could I?" Diane said.

To the waiter I suggested, "Why not leave *one*. We'll share it."

"You really are a mind-reader," Diane said. "I'll taste yours. But no more."

"Well, maybe *two* tastes!"

Just then, the transplanted-from-Atlanta heiress named Alexis-something-or-other flowed into one of the recently vacated chairs, followed by her far-too-young new husband.

"Well, darlings. Did you discuss it?" Alexis said, stealing sips of the other guest's bubbly.

"We were working our way to it." Diane tried shooing her friend away. "Go away!"

"Working our way to what?" I asked and gulped what seemed to be too much dessert.

"The round the world trip!" Alexis said.

"Come with us!" Paul, the new hubby, said to me. "It'll be fun."

"It'll be terrific fun if the four of us go," Alexis agreed. "You know it will!"

"Well, now that you've opened your big mouth, Alex darling, and let the feline out of the Prada," Diane said humorously. "You two had better go away and let *us* discuss it. Before the poor man chokes on his bananas and ice cream."

As they were leaving, Paul turned and I saw his lips move to "Say yes!"

Diane began. "I always wanted to go. Now Alexis has tickets. There's an itinerary at my place. Nice hotels. Super cruises. But we'd be gone a year and two months. I've always wanted to go and never could with Harley. We'll have separate rooms all the way, because well, we're just good friends, right? Don't want to spoil anything by being anything more than that."

"Will Alexis and Paul have separate rooms?" I asked before I could stop myself.

"Given how poorly she sleeps. I'd say yes. I'm sorry to spring this on you!"

I thought of Paul, so handsome, so young, so apparently willing. I thought of luxurious week-long cruises up the Nile and two weeks down the Danube. I thought of four-star hotels in Monte Carlo and Biarritz, Cartagena and Shanghai and all of it with this charming, sophisticated lady. Could I possibly bear it? You bet I could! "When do we leave?!" But before she could do more than be radiant in response, I added, "But I've got a gift for you, for your house actually. For that downstairs billiard room that no one has used since 1918. You cannot say no."

"Then I'll say yes," and Diane leaned across the arc of table laden with crystal and porcelain and sterling candlesticks and set a perfect little kiss on my forehead.

"Now I'm off to the Ladies. I'm grabbing Alexis on the way so we can scream like twelve-year-olds over how happy we are. Why don't you sit with Paul and keep him company?"

The flower I'd picked out of the forest was *Licula*, from the Ingei Forest outside of Sarawak. The leaves I'd grabbed belonged to another flowering plant, *Thrixspermium Eryhisbron*, again from that forest in Borneo. At least, that was the conclusion of the researcher at the Botany department at Berkeley I'd brought them to. He'd been "thrilled" to see them and so I left them with him, taking only his detailed report, which added, "This forest contains over 1,175 species of flora and fauna, much never seen elsewhere. Both of these plants grow near the so-called pitcher plants, *Nepenthes*, also known as the Venus Flytrap."

My next step was the most daring: to go through the mirror all the way.

I guessed it led only to that forest. I'd seen nothing indicative of a building or construction of any sort, and so I would need a knife or sharp edge to mark exactly where the entryway lay in the forest. Prepping for that meant dressing down from the formal clothing I'd worn whenever I went into the shop—to be able to say to Hans that he didn't know me and had never known me.

It was a lie, of course. He knew me from my bartending days South of Market in one or another motorcycle bar. Or from my work before that as assistant manager at a sex club. "Manager with extras," my friends called it. Meaning I visited clients' rooms for pay. True, I looked different. Gone was the long hair, the full beard, the eternal brown glass aviator glasses, though I'd kept souvenirs, especially the leather vests I'd stretched across my tanned, muscled, at times oiled, torso. My hair was short now and salt and pepper, my face bare of hair; gone now, too, were the small tattoos on my neck. And, I was always clothed now. More than clothed, *well* clothed, thanks to a friendly woman at a certain snobby Episcopal church donation room who had a maternal interest in me and so saved nicer things for me. It was there I'd encountered Diane, who saw me in good clothing and who'd assumed I was donating, like she was. That led to chat. Chat led to a coffee date. That led to a dinner date and…

But Hans could still screw it all up, so Hans must be dealt with. This meant I would have to make certain he was out of the way before the trip around the world began. For that, I needed to go in.

Hans closed early on Thursday. I slipped in when he was busy over-gesticulating and secreted myself in the back room of the shop behind the mirror. As soon as he locked up, I turned to the mirror and touched it to clarify. Shortly, it did. Same scene as before. The broken twigs were those I'd taken. I took many deep breaths, then tried a finger, a hand, an arm, and as I stepped through and spun around, took out the knife and marked the four upper and lower corners of the way I'd come through onto tree trunks and by arranging twigs on the ground. It was astonishing: I really was there. I needn't cut too much ahead to get out of this copse. Perfumes and odors assailed me. But the immediate area became quiet, noting my arrival. I kept turning to mark my path back, cutting many landmarks.

Ten minutes of walking ended when I heard voices. Suddenly, above me there was a whoosh and the cry of an animal. I saw the little monkey struck by the arrow fall to the ground. Three young male New Guinea natives wearing only penis sheathes and headdresses hustled into the area and picked it up, celebrated with each other, and took off again. They were too excited by their prey to stop and look around and perhaps notice me, crouching, silent, half terrified. Seeing them was all I needed to know.

I found the mirror re-entry only after some searching and some panic. What if I couldn't get through again? Or only later? It hadn't been long. Maybe twenty minutes.

I found it, and closing my eyes, I pushed a hand through. Yes!

Then, I went about destroying those careful signs I had made to find it and stepped through to the other side. It was dark in the room where it had been twilight before and I held my hand out before myself to ensure I didn't crash into anything. I let myself out and locked the shop door behind me.

"Aren't you glad you listened to me and put the mirror up for sale?" I paused for effect. "You're a hundred dollars richer and you got rid of something you never expected to sell." Before Hans could reply, I said, "Here's the address I want it shipped to. It's up Nob Hill a few streets from where you found it. By the way, since I did pay for the shipping, they'll be here in a half hour at the most to wrap it and take it. I'll remain, if you don't mind."

Hans still looked surprised as he pocketed the cash I'd given him and marked the bill *paid*. "I don't understand why you want." He sounded aggrieved. "It's flawed."

"I happened to discover it's flawed in a particular way. Which makes it marvelously valuable. Would you like to see?" I teased.

He followed me to the back room and together we took hold of it and faced it forward. Antony-Whatever-His-Name had bought one smaller glass, so there was room now to maneuver.

I knelt. "See! Right here!" I touched the surface and as I did, it began to clear, and then become green. I heard Hans grunt in surprise behind me. "Now look closely!"

The surface gradually cleared and it was the same New Guinea forest scene from before.

I heard him grunt again behind me. "But what is? A painting under?"

"Better than a painting, Hans. It's a doorway."

He grunted again. I touched the surface and my hand went right through.

"This cannot be!"

"It gets better!" I said in my best Abracadabra voice. "Watch!"

I stepped through the surface into the forest. He made a loud noise. When I turned, I could see him dimly, fallen against the far wall. I swatted at an insect and plucked a *Licula* off its branch and then stepped through into the shop again.

"It's trick of some kind!" Hans asserted.

"You don't believe me," I said, waving the pink and white flower at him.

"It cannot be."

"But it is. And now the wondrous magical mirror belongs to me."

He hesitated then he reached forward and touched the surface and watched his finger go through. He turned to me with a childlike grin on his face.

"Go on. Why stop there?"

"Oh, no!" He backed away.

"Suit yourself," I said, unconcerned. "But when the deliverers come… This really will be your last chance."

"You have gone through? It continues?"

"I have gone through. It continues. I've stayed an hour already. But once I have it for myself, no one else will be able to go in."

He'd been slowly inserting all five fingers and then a hand through. By this time, his hand had reached a twig. He snapped it off and pulled it through. There was wonder on his face.

"It's real."

"Of course it's real." I began polishing the wooden frame with a dust cloth I'd carried in my overcoat.

"So….Maybe I can go in for one minute?" Hans asked.

"It's now or never."

It took him a while to get up his nerve, then he cautiously entered the mirror. He found himself on the other side and suddenly, there were hummingbirds all around him. He was like a child again. He moved forward, then turned and could see me dimly, and went further still.

When I could barely make him out, I touched the mirror at its top right corner as I'd learned to do and swept my hand down through on a diagonal to the lower left. And then from the lower right to the upper left again, until it was solid glass again.

Then I took the hammer out of the inside pocket of my coat and slammed the mirror as hard as I could.

I expected it to smash. Instead it rang like a giant bell. At least in the little back room it did. I don't know what noise it made on the other side. But the mirror didn't shatter, as I'd hoped. Instead, it fogged over completely.

Not a minute later, the front bells jangled and I went to let the shippers in. I'd already begun wrapping the mirror and they took over swiftly and efficiently. They wrapped it tight, sealed it with tape and carried it to the truck. I went with them and met Diane's housekeeper at the door, and we placed it in the downstairs game room.

Nineteen months later, after our trip—and our official engagement, Diane suddenly had to see "her gift." I was afraid she would be disappointed. I was prepared to make excuses about the shippers' mishandling of it.

It was unwrapped without ceremony and before I could step to the front to go look, I could see utter delight on Diane's face. "It's a beautiful painting, Darling! Remarkable! Almost three dimensional. I feel like I could reach out and touch one of those hummingbirds!"

"Wait!"

Before I could stop her, she did touch it. She touched glass. She touched solid glass.

"It's too nice for this dingy room," she said. "Let's put it upstairs. But where?"

"How about above the mantel in what we are now calling my library?" I suggested.

"Perfect. Then I can visit it every day!"

That meant I can look at it every day.

I do.

Sometimes I think I see a hummingbird wing flutter. At other times, I've almost convinced myself that I can see the very edges of Hans's ginger mustachios behind a clump of *Thrixspermium* bushes.

# About the Author

Felice Picano is the author of more than thirty-five books of poetry, stories, novels, novellas, memoirs and non-fiction. His work is translated into seventeen languages. Several titles were national and international bestsellers, and four plays have been produced. Picano's first novel was a finalist for the PEN/Hemingway Award in 1975. Since then, he's been short-listed and/or received awards for poetry, drama, short stories, and novels. An adjunct professor of Literature at Antioch University, L.A., he founded and taught at three West Hollywood Public Library Writing Workshops. He lectures throughout North America on LGBT Culture, Gays in Hollywood, and Screen Writing. In 2019, *Justify My Sins: A Hollywood Novel in Three Acts* was published. Felice's latest book is *Songs & Poems*. His novel, *Pursuit: A Victorian Entertainment*, will be published in 2021, as will the re-publication of *The Book of Lies*. The first of his sci-fi trilogy, *Dryland's End*, (2004, 2020) will be republished, to be followed by *The Betrothal at Usk*, and *A Bard on Hercular* in 2021. His strange stories are his special love and have been in *OMNI*, *Twilight Zone*, *Best New Horrors*, in many magazines and anthologies, and in three collections. Find him at FelicePicano.net.

# When the Dust Settles
## Sarah Lyn Eaton

Tara was dreaming of earthen creek beds and moss-covered stones, of mudslides and tortoise shells, of stone giants that lived on planets too close to impossible suns. The landscape was all red and wet and fleshy. *Only in a dream could those contradictions be comforting*, a comfort soon disrupted by blinding light and overlapping voices that poked at her with needles.

She floated above it all, riding the line. The giantess of her dream world filled the empty space in her small room. Figures in blue wearing masks and carrying scalpels walked through the stone deity but she didn't seem to mind.

*No.* Tara shook her head. *That was last time. That was before.*

*Before what?*

She opened her eyes in the dark. She sighed, rethinking the body's need for water. It was seven steps to the toilet. It was seven cavernous steps to the toilet.

She blinked hard and the low light came on. A voice called out to her.

"Miss Everhill, do you require assistance?"

"No," she replied, rolling her eyes. The only thing less helpful than a disembodied voice was an overly cheerful night nurse.

"We'll be with you immediately," the voice said as Tara sat herself upright in bed. Her bladder clenched tightly.

"I'm fine," she waved her hand dismissively.

"Are you certain?"

"Yes."

"Cancelling order."

Tara sighed. That line between one reality and the next slammed her in the face every time she woke up. She eased her legs over the side of the bed. One was more titanium than flesh, biting into the top of her thigh. Before, she would have peed and been back in bed already.

"Bend," she said, yelling at her right knee but it did not listen. *Yet*, they promised her.

The right arm was better. She could swing it and bend it and mostly she could keep the fingers closed. At least they moved when she wanted them to. She grimaced as her bladder contracted again. Her arm wasn't going to get her to the bathroom. She knocked on her thigh.

"Come on, roomie. Work with me."

They also promised that eventually the circuitry in the metal leg would allow her sensation of when it was touching objects. That was also not working yet. She used the rail of the bed to stand.

There was weakness in her left leg, the one she referred to as her human leg. The right leg felt like they had set her torso on a stump of wood and she was supposed to trust it would hold her up. And then she was supposed to move it with the power of her mind.

*One step to the door. Just one step and I can grab the open edge of the bathroom door.*

"Miss Everhill? Your levels are showing signs of distress."

"Working on it."

"Calling for assistance."

Tara shook her head. Her arm was shaking. Her left leg trembled. It was just one step. She tried to swing her right hip but the leg attached was lead. She remembered hitting the ground before she was falling.

*No. That was before…Before what?* She couldn't hold onto the memory.

She hit the ground again just as her pod door slid open. Her bathroom need was forcibly relieved. Her pod was one of a hundred rooms in the Medhab, a floating hospital owned by The Company. Two nurses found her on the floor.

She let their hands lift her. She let them fuss over her. Tara even let them set her on the toilet. They retreated to her room to clean the floor, freshen up her bed, and give her some privacy.

"Accident?" the first nurse asked.

"One of the miners," the other replied.

The new implant in her ear picked up their whispers as if they were shouting. She didn't mind that they were talking about her. No one on the rehab floor had any secrets so she didn't mind them talking about her. She just wished they'd talk about it more.

She couldn't remember what happened.

There were others on the floor from the same accident. She knew them. They worked in an ore mine on an asteroid-in-transit. She was less than halfway through a sixteen month contract. She stared at her leg.

Now, she was damaged, but she was damaged goods, with an emphasis on goods. She was still under contract. Her new limbs belonged to The Company, too. At least until her contract was fulfilled. They were going to let her keep them when she left in sympathy for her suffering.

If she lived that long.

"Damn it," she said. Her body felt heavy.

"You all right in there?" the first nurse asked.

"Yes," Tara said. It wasn't true. She couldn't get herself out of bed or off the toilet. And until she could, she couldn't work. And as long as she wasn't working, she was not fulfilling her contract. She didn't know what that would mean.

She swallowed the thought down.

The nurse stood in the doorway in her green gown. She was one of the older women who had worked the MedHab Facility her entire career. "Your walker would be more helpful to you if you kept it by the bed."

"It would be easier to use it if I didn't have to drag this piece of scrap metal along with me," Tara retorted with a scowl.

It was her own fault. She'd skimmed the contract before signing it and she had failed to read it. She had not checked off the anti-robotic-measures. Some people cited religious reasons. Hers were just personal. She'd never liked the feel of metal. She could live in the tin at Perthe Camp. She could travel on ships. She could work in a mine on an asteroid and live in a tin can to do it. But she didn't want it grafted into her body. It was just a lump of dead weight. She gazed at it glumly.

"Your brain is resisting," the nurse said. She wet a washcloth in the sink.

"I understand that." Tara wiped down her thighs.

"How quickly you heal is in your hands."

"Yet only one of them is still mine." Tara flourished her good one.

"How perfectly you make my point about resistance," the nurse took the washcloth back. "Do you want to be here forever?"

"With such plush accommodations? I mean, the food—" Tara managed a weak laugh, thinking of the bland protein-packed drinks she looked forward to slurping down. "When I get my robo leg in working order, you'll be hard-pressed to evict me."

"There's a cheerier perspective. You done?"

Tara nodded. The nurse pushed the walker into the bathroom at her. "Might as well work on some physical therapy."

"Brilliant," Tara said.

"Word on the ward is that you took a header trying to get to the head."

"Morning, Bruce," Tara said, as he laughed at his own joke. It echoed across the gymnasium.

Bruce was a jovial worker at the mine, with a handful of kids and multiple wives waiting on him planet-side. He'd lost both legs and both arms and one of his eyes. His implants had taken better than hers. He climbed the stair unit beside the one she was parked at.

"You look all right," Ellen said from the weight bar. She had lost her dominant arm but had opted against replacement. She was working to strengthen her orphaned limb. She had chopped her blonde hair short recently.

"I've taken harder hits to the head," Tara said. She was sporting her own half-shave from the cochlear surgery. She looked around. "Quiet this morning."

"Warren's in for another surgery," Bruce said. "His new wang needs some adjusting."

"Mind that talk around him," Ellen bristled. "And be thankful your prick wasn't crushed."

Bruce threw his hands up. "Hey, I'm a little mindless but not insensitive."

Tara laughed at that. Bruce grinned. Ellen lifted weights with her weak arm. Tara's therapist came over from the main desk.

"Let's go, Tara," Gwen said, pointing at the stairs. "You'll never climb them sitting down."

"I haven't managed to climb a single one. And I had a bad fall this morning," Tara said. Just looking at the small three-stair unit gave her vertigo.

"I heard," Gwen said, bending low. She always smelled like saltwater. It reminded Tara of Earth. "We'll go slow. We're still programming your leg. We're not actually going to climb today. We just have to connect the wires between your leg and your brain."

"I'm not a robot. My brain is not a machine. It's soft tissue." Tara turned her head away.

"Your body is soft tissue but it is a soft tissue machine." Gwen waited. "I know you know that."

"So we have to poke the dead nerve endings and make them remember their job." Tara gripped the sides of the wheelchair and pushed herself up. She could feel Gwen's hands ready to catch her. It gave her courage. She stood in place for a moment.

"Ready?"

Tara nodded. She stared at the first rise and visualized stepping onto it. She recalled every time she had ever climbed a stair. She did this over and over until she broke out in an even sheen of sweat. She willed all of that muscle memory into the top stump of her thigh. Her hip twitched but the leg did not move.

"That's good," Gwen said. "That's progress. Next step."

Tara picked her leg up and bent the knee. The titanium joint swiveled. She rested the leg on the step and visualized the sensation of pushing up and off it.

"Switch direction."

Tara imagined stepping backwards off of the step. She lowered the leg down to the ground. She gripped the rail.

"Good job."

"It feels like I'm strapped to a steel beam."

"It won't always feel that way," Gwen said. Her long hair spilled over her face. "The neural interface will integrate."

"What if I don't want it to?" Tara knew the staff was frustrated with her. But she was equally frustrated. And equally tired.

"I'll get you some water. Rest a minute."

"I'm going to stare at the step some more," Tara said. She didn't believe it could be that simple. They said the leg was fine, that once she got the muscles working in tandem, the biomechanics would respond and the line between flesh and machine would be fluid.

That terrified her.

"We'll be back on shift in the mines again in no time," Bruce said flatly, coming up beside her.

"I heard someone's coming in from The Company to evaluate us," Ellen said, lifting ankle weights.

"That'll be fun," Tara responded just as blandly. She looked over for her water. Gwen was standing with the other physical therapists, speaking lowly to the floor nurse at the front desk. Tara focused in on their voices but there were too many overlapping for her to hear clearly. She caught Warren's name. The nurse looked tired and pale.

Tara lowered herself into her chair. "Something's wrong with Warren." Gwen caught Tara's eye and she whispered one word that Tara's implant heard clearly.

"Unresponsive."

Tara wilted in her chair. "He isn't waking up."

"Shit," Bruce said. Ellen turned away. Two of their other work mates hadn't made it. Now it might be three.

A scream erupted in the hallway.

"That's Warren," Tara said.

"No way," Ellen said. She shook her head. "That wasn't human."

Tara tapped her implant. "I can hear him."

She wheeled across the room into the corridor. She pretended not to hear Gwen calling after her. She could hear too much already.

Warren was still screaming.

People were running towards Warren's pod.

"He's having a flashback!" Tara shouted, wheeling down the hall. She could pump with her new right arm but she relied on her left to steer. An aide slammed into her from the side and she careened into the wall, spilling out of the chair.

She couldn't move her leg to turn onto her back. She tried to crawl but she couldn't pull herself forward. She couldn't move.

She was pinned down and Warren was screaming.

"Ellen!" she yelled, choking on the rock dust. Ellen had been near her on the line. The walls were still shaking. She knew how much tonnage of rock sat above them. She couldn't feel her body but she was breathing.

The lights were out. The tunnel was dark. But she was breathing.

"I can't move!" she screamed.

The lights blared back on, blinding her as Warren staggered out of his pod like a mountainous bear. There was blood everywhere. She shook her head. They weren't in the tunnel. And she wasn't pinned beneath a rock. She turned her head and saw the metal leg was caught in the foot rest of the wheelchair.

Warren was screaming and he was holding his own leg in his hand. The nurses shrieked as he hit the floor. He was staring at Tara. He was crazed. Blood pooled around him and he used his free hand to dig into the metal floor and pull himself towards her. He didn't blink. He didn't look away. He didn't stop screaming.

The pitch of his voice was a hissing steam pipe. It crawled beneath her skin. Her implant picked up words that bore deeper into her brain. Ice washed through her.

*We're all guinea pigs*, he was screaming under his pain. His eyes widened in relief when he saw Tara react to them. He was still screaming in her mind after his body went limp. A nurse in a green gown leaned over his body.

"He's dead."

"Are you all right?" Gwen asked.

They were all sitting in the gymnasium in loose solitude. Bruce and Ellen looked sad. Tara frowned. She felt fuzzy, far away.

"I don't know how to stay here," she said. Her voice sounded strange. Ellen glanced up with sad eyes. Tara nodded. "He looked at me that way. Just then."

"They gave you some sedation," Gwen said measuredly.

"Warren's dead," Bruce said.

"She knows that," Ellen snapped.

"There was blood everywhere," Tara said. She couldn't hold onto it.

"There still is," Ellen grimaced.

"He was saying something," Tara said, but that memory was just as slippery.

"He was screaming," Bruce frowned.

"There were words," Tara said, shaking her head. "They were important."

"Don't try to find them," Gwen said.

"He was screaming," Bruce repeated.

"Just like in the mine." Ellen curled in on herself in her chair.

"You remember that?" Tara asked. Ellen turned her head away.

"Some things are hard to scrub away." Ellen pulled at the ends of her short hair.

"Oh," Tara said. Her gut felt hollow. "He ripped his own leg off."

"Fucking a—" Bruce buried his face in his hands.

"His prosthetics rejected," Gwen said softly.

"He ripped his own leg off."

"Wasn't his leg," Ellen said. She stared out into the hallway. "It was theirs."

"I feel like shit," Bruce groaned. He was itching at his legs. The matte metal limbs were strangers infiltrating their bodies, trying to force a relationship with them.

"I never asked you to move in," she said out loud to her leg and arm. Ellen giggled hysterically.

"I'm going to get you something to help you even out," Gwen said. She looked around at all of them before leaving.

"I'm going back to my pod," Bruce said. He wheeled away slowly.

"Let Gwen help you," Tara spoke thickly. She couldn't see that Gwen had already left.

"I got you." Ellen sat herself beside Tara.

"You don't have a robo limb," Tara pointed out.

"You didn't read the contract before you signed it," Ellen countered.

"I did not." Bubbles floated in her mind. "If we're just replaceable labor, why did The Company bother giving us replaceable parts?"

"To squeeze every last drop of life from us."

"Don't cry," Tara said, patting Ellen's arm.

"I'm not crying," Ellen said, taking her hand. "You are."

"Oh," Tara said. She rubbed her cheek and her hand came away wet.

"It's okay. Sink in. I'll sit with you."

Tara felt herself falling into the undertow. Space didn't have a sound. The MedHab did. It was a low thrum, not even enough pulse for a heartbeat. Tara laughed at that. The ship had no heart. She laughed again. She started out living in tins and she'd become half tin herself.

She chortled as someone leaned over her. A needle pierced her skin. She surrendered to the dark silence.

*Fuck.* She was in her own bed again, her body fuzzy and tired. *Why is recovering so exhausting?*

"Is he tucked in?"

Tara paused. There was a voice on the other side of the wall that she didn't recognize.

"He'll be out for hours."

"Didn't expect you in today."

"Supervisor begged me. We're short now."

"She didn't make it?"

"No."

"Another nurse down. How out is he?"

"Pretty gone. Just like the woman next door."

"Can you imagine the pain they're in?"

"Nothing compared to what's coming."

Ice crawled through Tara's bloodstream. The second voice laughed. The room spun around her. Her heart raced. Her walker was by the door. She was trapped in her bed, trapped in her body.

"What about the guy down the hall?"

"He's not doing so well."

"Hopefully it will be faster than the last one."

*Bruce? Are they talking about Bruce?*

A voice rang out in her room. "Miss Everhill, you are showing distress. A nurse is coming shortly."

Tara's heart surged. "NO!"

"Miss Everhill, it is necessary. Please wait."

Tara shook. She was not going to lay in her fear and wait for whatever badness was coming for her. She needed to make sure Bruce was all right. She needed to find Ellen. They couldn't be the only ones left.

"I don't want either of the nurses from next door," Tara said.

"Miss Everhill?"

"You heard me." Tara tried to sit up but her muscles were weak.

"There are no nurses on the floor just now. There are no other patients at the end of the hall. Just you."

Her heart quickened. She was flooded with the impulse to run. "That's not possible."

"Someone is coming."

"What's your name?" Tara asked.

"Pardon?"

"Which nurse am I speaking to?"

There was a millisecond pause. "Someone is coming now."

Tara's heart fell. Of course it wasn't a person. The skeleton staff existed because so much was automated. The desk nurse was another program, just like her new limbs. Which she was constantly being reminded she should be lucky to have. Just like the job in the mine. Working ten hour shifts for shit pay was literally winning the lottery for someone from the Camps.

Tara had grown up in the Camps. Her people had no home. She was told her people had never had a home. And the Camps were not home. But there they had lived wide open in a small space where no one owned anything. And then she signed with a company who now owned her. She could taste the stale air recycling through the tunnel as they worked in sections separated by heavy doors.

"Tara?" Warren asked with a hand on her shoulder. He offered her a small roll. She nodded thanks and took it. Warren's family had shared the tin next to hers though he was quite a bit older. He had fancied her older sister. But she had died of a virus that swept through the Camps. She couldn't remember which virus had taken her sister and which her father. There was always a new one storming, though.

That was another life. The lights in the mine tunnel were brash and hard, meant to evoke happy toiling. They only back lit the clouds of dust. Beneath the strange outer rock were bits of ore The Company desired.

She was nervous. She'd done plenty of labor over the years, doing whatever construction and paving work came through. But she had always returned to her families' small tin every night. Now she was all that was left of them and their tin had been turned over to another family who had been waiting and living in the tents. And her name had been thrown into the lottery.

It was a starting over that felt utterly final.

"Tara?" Warren asked. His hand was still on her shoulder. She tasted the ore of the asteroid in her mouth. His hand glinted metal.

"Warren?" she squinted through the cloud. The asteroid began to shake. The lights flickered. Warren looked up and pushed Tara backwards so hard she flew through the air and slammed into another body moments before the ceiling began to collapse.

She couldn't move. She was trying to run. She could feel some of her flesh pulling away. Everyone was screaming.

"Tara?" Ellen asked. She tilted her head and frowned. "You're crying again."

"Sorry?"

"And you're walking." Ellen looked around. "How'd you get out here?"

"I don't know how to walk anymore," Tara said. But she looked down and sure enough, she was standing without a walker or crutch at the far end of the ship corridor. She waited for the waking thought to topple her, but she stayed upright.

"You look in a bad way," Ellen said. "Let me get someone."

"No!" Tara's heart fluttered. Ellen hesitated. "Please." She looked around in the empty corridor. "I heard something I don't think I was meant to hear."

"What are you talking about?"

"The nurses know why this is happening to us. I think Bruce is in danger."

"Bruce is dead," Ellen said flatly. "Five minutes ago. I was coming to tell you."

"Did he rip his leg off?" Tara asked.

Ellen shook her head slowly. Tara noted the green cast to her face. Ellen frowned and looked up at her. "He shoved his metal fingers into his ears while we were talking. And he just kept pushing until something popped." Ellen blinked. "I thought I'd find you dead, too. Not suddenly walking towards me like Laz'rus."

"They know why this is happening."

"What makes you say that?" Ellen asked.

"I heard the nurses talking about how what was coming was worse than what's happening." Tara reached out to touch the wall. She needed to touch something real.

"Which nurses?"

Tara faltered. "I don't know who. I couldn't see them. They were on the other side of the wall."

"In the next room?"

"Yes."

"But no one's in that room."

"No. The other one. The further one."

"Tara, no one is in either room. They kept the rooms on either side of all of you empty, so why would there be nurses in there?"

Tara was dizzy and sweaty. "I have to find Gwen. I don't trust the others."

"Gwen?" Ellen grabbed Tara's arm tightly. "That's the second time you've said her name."

Tara scowled. "She's our physical therapist."

Ellen bit her lip. "No, she's not."

"She smells like saltwater," Tara said insistently.

"She worked with us on the asteroid," Ellen said. "Gwen doesn't work here."

Ellen kept talking but the corridor lights flickered and Tara couldn't catch her breath. She needed to get outside. She needed some space. She needed some fresh air. Her chest was tight. She could taste her dead skin cells in the air.

The dust was thick in her mouth as Tara slammed into another body. The lights went out and everyone started to scream. She was praying that the outer tunnel doors held. Their outer gravity suits were all in lockers in the changing room between tunnel doors. She didn't want to die that way.

She wasn't thinking about being buried alive. Maybe because it was happening and her brain hadn't caught up with real time. She was thinking about Warren and how he saved her when she landed on the dirt, the small roll still clutched in her left hand. She couldn't feel her right hand. She couldn't feel the rock holding her to the tunnel floor.

She couldn't feel anything but absolute horror as she stared into Gwen's face. Gwen, who slept in the bunk beneath hers and sometimes shared hers. Gwen, who was buried up to her neck beneath a pile of rocks. Blood obscured one of her jade green eyes.

The light had already left it.

Everyone was screaming. Everyone except Gwen. Gwen would never scream again.

"Tara?" Gwen asked in the corridor of the MedHab.

Tara yelped and jumped. She was in the tunnel. *No.* She shook her head. She was in the corridor. *Right.* The MedHab was real time. But Gwen wasn't.

"How are you here?" Tara asked tearfully. "You can't be here." She reached out with her right hand. Not with *her* hand. It wasn't her hand. There was an itching in her shoulder. She wanted to scratch at it the same way Bruce had been scratching at his thighs.

"Tara!" Gwen said, backing away. Her scalp was bleeding. Her mouth started to open wider and wider and a chasm lay inside it trying to get out, trying to find purchase, trying to find a new home in Tara. She could feel that desire tugging at the base of her skull.

*Let me tell you what to do*, it said.

"You can't be here!" she screamed. Everyone was screaming. She lunged with her arm, wrapping her hand around the thing masquerading as Gwen's neck and squeezing. Everyone was screaming. Gwen was screaming. Tara was screaming.

Ellen was screaming.

Tara blinked and the corridor came into focus. Ellen's right hand was bloody, clawing at Tara's new limb. Tara couldn't make the fingers release. She recoiled, trying to pull away but she just dragged Ellen with her.

"No!" *No.* She rammed her shoulder into the wall over and over as Ellen turned colors. Tara slammed herself into the wall until she saw stars and the metal hand released its hold. Ellen fell to the floor sputtering and gasping for air in shuddering notes.

Tara stumbled backwards along the wall. She backed away from Ellen, away from the nurse picking Ellen up off the floor, away from the security aide entering the corridor, away from the eyes staring at her. And the whole time she backed away, her arm resisted her.

She pressed the door for the inner airlock. It shot open and she threw her arm into it, leaning into the jam. She could do this. She'd been through it before. She pressed again to close the door but it stopped at the biometric touch of her skin. It was a Dead Man's protocol. It could be overridden. She leaned out and made sure the door wasn't touching any soft tissue, just titanium. Her hand touched the button one more time.

"Oh my god! What is she doing?!"

"Miss Everhill!"

Tara heard them but she did not listen. She couldn't trust they were there, even though they had touched her. Gwen had touched her, too. Was any of it real? Was she still pinned beneath the rock in the mine? Was she listening to Warren and Bruce die? Was Gwen lying beside her in the mineral dust? Were they all dying together in the tunnel on the asteroid, twinkling out of the world like distant starlight?

Her hand hovered over the button and the nurses kept their distance. They were talking but she wasn't hearing them anymore. Rocks were falling and voices were screaming and if she was going to die, she was going to write her own ending. And she sure as hell wasn't going to let a robotic arm be the last note.

It was twitching in the air lock, trying to find purchase to push the door pinning it closed. She watched the door creep open in panic. The right leg had wedged itself in the door, pushing it open.

Tara concentrated on stepping backwards until the thigh muscles in her stump twitched backwards and the leg came with it.

*I finally did it!*

She sighed and closed her eyes and hit the override. The nurses screamed as the inner door slammed shut with a metallic crunch and snap.

The unwanted arm fell to the ground inside the air lock. Tara was sure it was still moving. Her leg started to jerk as she was tackled to the ground.

She smiled as she fell.

Tara's mind was a jumble of adrenaline and sedative and she startled groggily awake. She was lying in her bed in her pod, swaddled in bandages and warming blankets.

"Good morning, Miss Everhill. A nurse is on their way to your room. You have experienced a trauma and have undergone surgery."

"Oh," Tara muttered. "The ceiling nurse is talking again." Her throat was rough and raw. Her body was numb. She felt more aligned with the air in the room than she did her arms and legs.

*But what else is new—*

She tried sitting up with a jerk but every muscle in her body resisted. She had two arms and two legs.

*How?*

A nurse in a green gown entered the pod, followed by a tall woman in a dark suit Tara had never seen before. They were accompanied by a security aide.

"So," Tara gasped, staring at The Company representative. "What happened?"

"I can tell you that unfortunately, due to circumstances out of our control, a batch of replacements parts meant for disposal were inadvertently sent to this medical facility from a sister company. These parts were not able to be reprogrammed from their previous usage."

"That's why you couldn't connect to it," the nurse said. "You were right. It was never going to work for you."

"What was its default usage?" Tara asked. The stranger gazed at her. Tara raised her eyebrow. "It tried to kill me."

"No worries," the nurse said low, patting her arm. "Both bad appendages were removed."

"I think I helped with one of them," Tara said. She sighed. "My ear implant?"

"There was nothing wrong with that," The Company woman said, "but we gave you an upgrade free of charge."

Tara frowned, staring at the lumps under the blanket. "I have four arms and legs."

"In compensation for your suffering, we went ahead and fitted you with state of the art limbs from our parent company." The woman leaned in conspiratorially. "Honestly, only the military get to bid on these parts. We've had one hundred percent satisfaction with the neural integration of these units. You'll be back to work in no time."

There was a fluttering in her ear. She reached up to scratch and the arm responded swiftly and easily and lightly. She scratched at her face with her right hand. It was seamless and sleek and looked like white flesh rather than metal.

"Isn't that wonderful?" The nurse in the green gown gasped in delight. In weeks, Tara hadn't managed to do nearly that much with the robo arm.

Tara's face burned. The hand was still scratching. The nail dug at her skin. The company woman gasped and the nurse grabbed at her arm. It did not stop scratching. The security aide raised his gun.

Tara screamed.

# About the Author

Sarah Lyn Eaton is a queer pagan writer who is surviving a near death by fire. She lives quietly in a city with her wife and cat, where two rivers meet in the foothills of mountains. When not focusing on her recovery, she spends time with nature taking pictures of birch tree eyes, bodies of water, and whatever fungus she finds on the forest floor.

Sarah Lyn loves Star Wars, apples, and collecting rocks like tiger eye, labradorite, smokey quartz, and petrified wood. She also talks to dead people with regularity. Sometimes they talk back.

You can read about her spiritual connection to Ancestor work and other genealogy mysteries on her page Walking with Ancestors. Sarah Lyn's published stories can be found in the anthologies *Of Fae & Fate*, *On Fire*, *Dystopia Utopia*, *Fracture: Essays Poems and Stories on Fracking in America*, and *What Follows*. Her work has also appeared in *Pantheon Magazine* and, most recently, *parABnormal Magazine*.

Find her on Facebook @sarahlyneaton, and at her blogs, sarahlyn-eaton.blogspot.com and walkingwithancestors.blogspot.com.

# I Can't Wait to Become a Man

Thomas Kearnes

He needed more furniture. Chairs and end tables, however, might invite dismay. With no men to sit in such chairs, no men to make use of such end tables, Wes would be forced to confront a more treacherous stripe of solitude. This solitude, to be sure, imparted a mean, hard dismay—chairs and end tables were merely its prologue. Solitude and dismay. His spartan ground-floor one-bedroom could resist them, provided he never acknowledge their menace.

Brock wrote, *You never told me about your interview this morning.*

Moments later, *I've waited so long to be proud.*

These states, Wes pondered. His trick might wonder why California, New York, Florida, and the rest were each condemned to needlepoint, every state relegated to its own dollar-store dark plastic frame the size of a snapshot. Should they fan out, forming an arc above the hopeful sofa? Or did the knickknacks deserve a more decisive display—perhaps a tight, geometric cluster above the twin bed, its hopeful air even more pungent than that of the sofa? Whatever he might decide, the absence of Arizona would persist perplexing him. His bedroom, too, felt bereft of more incidental furnishings. Surely, solitude and dismay might find themselves stymied by his Dallas Cowboys quilt, draped atop his precisely pleated beddings.

Amarillo was too many hours removed from Dallas for Wes to recall the exact distance.

Brock deposited a new framed needlepoint saluting whichever state compelled him, too early each Monday for Wes to spy him through the window. Wes, during these last three months, had committed to memory his ex-lover's rigid routines. He made sure to avoid the front windows whenever Brock arrived or departed. Their pact, made those three endless months ago, remained one of the very few certainties aiding Wes' negotiation with the world.

Brock wrote, *These are my words. Remember my voice.*

He added, *Listen to me cross the room above you.*

Wes met his trick, Frederick, two evenings ago on Grindr. Gay men were so sparsely scattered amid the meager, dust-doomed city, hookup apps offered their only, albeit illusory, sense of community. His profile pic sparked within Wes long-faded fantasies of campus cads seeking sex with a side of sleaze. Surely, Wes wagered, his prospect was at least two decades his junior. His profile left no doubt what specific sex acts he sought. Wes felt a weary kinship. He, like most men forced onto the cruel stage of middle age, had come to doubt the sincerity of any man's desire—his own included. Frederick was due by seven that evening.

Wes stretched upon his bed, limbs stiff. The furniture that seemed unwise, the needlepoints with no real home—he'd decided nothing. Solitude and dismay, however, had failed to intrude.

Brock wrote, *You can triumph, Wes. Please don't leave me alone on this.*

His ex-lover—now his upstairs neighbor, forever unseen—didn't send texts in hope of response. At least, no instant response. Wes liked to keep count of the phrases stacking atop one another on his iPhone. How long could he stall the inevitable reply, how long before what must be articulated buckled his back? Wes texted Brock during morning's most blameless hour. He was asleep, Wes told himself. Whenever Brock opened his eyes, Wes was certain, he listened.

Simon spent most of his visits merely observing his little brother. Wes didn't mind playing host—he so seldom had the chance. Knowing, however, that Simon spent their times together preoccupied by a third party would liberate his host, somehow satisfy this duty that condemned him to disappoint. The most reliable way to elude his brother's judgment, he'd discovered, was to never acknowledge it when in flux.

"Did the manager let you know when to expect a decision?"

"He'll be here soon," Wes blurted. "It's tonight, you know. My date."

"My friend told me about your interview," Simon said, blatantly fishing. "Said you did well."

"Just as long as I'm not killing the animals myself."

"Don't fret, good man. They make the Mexicans do that."

Wes winced at the endearment. *Good man.* He'd been seated in the warm bathwater, the bubbles attempting liftoff from the water's surface. His LEGO fire boat quivered atop that same surface. Next to the tub, someone pissed into the commode. He'd been standing there, and Wes, the afterglow of his eighth birthday now dissipated, had decided to look.

The older brother crossed his legs, perched in the living room's sole recliner. They were much alike, Wes and Simon Wink, in the realm, at least, of surface characteristics. Throughout their shared childhood, distant relatives sighed and clicked dentures marveling over the boys' identical noses, the steep and smooth slopes that terminated in pert, bulbous nostrils. The wide and generous mouths seemed too irresistibly ripe for those same distant relatives to refrain. Both boys sprouted a whole two grades before classmates, and never quite stopped. Wes stood at just under six and a half feet. Simon's height gave him a slight advantage over his little brother, yet the older man insisted on wearing ornate cowboy boots with heels that elevated him higher still.

Simon had dropped by Wes' apartment unannounced—a call or text rarely preceded these "friendly" visits. He had his own key. He'd insisted. Wes had needed him to cosign the lease.

The scuffle of Simon's key penetrating the lock had caught Wes flat-backed upon his twin bed, that hopeful air now stagnant. *Where had he hidden his supplies!?!* This was his juvenile lingo for dope. It was one of the more common slang terms among his Grindr grunts. Wes was sometimes careless with the dope after his spiked dopamine convinced him some vagrant good luck would remain at the ready.

Throughout Simon's unrequested domestic banalities—family gossip, news about his three sons, fretfulness over the latest forecast—Wes could focus on nothing but the perverse victory he felt as his brother interpreted his silences or grunts as polite assent.

Wes, however, failed to return a verbal volley that plainly required multiple syllables. "I'm sorry." He looked startled. "I drifted, I guess. I wish you'd let me get some rest before tonight."

"We're circling the same bullseye. Good." Simon's fingertips met, five to five, a tent upon his lap. Wes couldn't help thinking of the old children's rhyme: *and here is the steeple: open it up and there are the people.* "You haven't told me much about Freeman—"

"Frederick!"

"Good man, I respect your privacy. I do. But reputation in a town this small can be a real house of cards." The hand tent collapsed, his fingers, now nothing but bone and flesh, jumbled in his lap. "I promised Dad. I promised to watch over you."

"Frederick will be here in half an hour."

"Please, Wes, behave yourself."

He remained on the sofa as Simon let himself out and dutifully locked the front door after shutting it. Wes felt too drained to speculate on his brother's last capricious gesture. Nobody fucks morose, middle-age men— not even other morose, middle-aged men.

Montana! He'd Scotch-taped the tiny plastic baggie behind Brock's needlepoint of Montana!

While listening for Simon to start his pickup, that blessed rumble informing Wes his mind and actions were once more his alone, he debated whether a quick snort was a truly a good idea. Frederick had never specified when he assured Wes he liked to "amplify" his sex. If Frederick hadn't been referring to speed, Wes would feel obliged to spare him the sordid truth. He didn't notice the scrape and click inside the front door's lock.

"Since when do you root for the Cowgirls?"

Simon carried a ballcap, the Dallas Cowboys logo accompanied by a single glittering star, navy blue, printed above the brim. The solution was simple: Brock had misplaced his cap. Wes, however, knew better than to indulge his brother with candor. He left the Montana needlepoint untouched among the other states, and approached Simon.

"It's my neighbor's. Where did you find it?"

"The lawn, not far from the porch."

"Probably the wind."

Wes reached for the cap, but Simon withdrew it. Wes knew if he pursued with even mild aggression, there would be more questions. And Frederick, Frederick arrived very soon.

"I thought you didn't know your neighbor. How do you know it's his?"

Wes chuckled. He knew its sincerity hardly mattered. "This is a duplex. Process of elimination."

"I'll knock on his door."

A cloudburst of panic erupted above Wes. He wasn't worried about Brock's reaction, but the imperative befell him at once: he must correctly quantify whether Simon's memory was sharp enough to spark a whole new grief. At The Journey Home, Simon had participated in Family Night and indulged the counselors' invitation to unleash all those years of bitterness and rage while the addicts sat in mandatory silence. Wes had introduced Brock to his brother. It had been at least six months since, but Wes firmly believed miniscule risks, taken in stride, too often heralded disaster.

"My neighbor's very private. He wouldn't answer the door for a stranger."

Simon was halfway to the door. "I'll tell him I'm your brother."

"How? Shout it from the welcome mat?"

"Unless his door is soundproof, I don't see the problem, good man."

"Goddammit! You never listen to one damn word!" He reached again for the cap. He refused to simply swipe it. No, unless Simon relinquished it, willingly, there'd be no proof Wes had been heard.

Grunting, Simon surrendered it. "Let me know when the slaughterhouse calls about the job."

Wes promised to call. Simon left. This time, however, his little brother loitered in the doorway until his battered white Chevy turned the corner. Breathing at once seemed less of a struggle. He tossed Brock's cap onto the seat of the rocking chair outside his door. As per his agreement with him, Wes was forbidden from even climbing the duplex stairs, never mind setting foot on his ex-lover's porch. He, instead, sent him a text.

Back inside, Wes showered, dressed, and disparaged himself. The mirror offered unfiltered truth. If he did a line, though, his prowess at self-deception would soar. Instead, he lay quietly atop his made bed. He lost track of the minutes. The stream of afternoon sunlight, filtered through the blinds, began to wane. Solitude and dismay—he refused to heed their refrains, groaned in tandem. He had a date with a man twenty years his junior, he had a stash of dope at the ready no matter what disquiet might descend, and, most importantly, he'd insisted Simon treat him like a man.

His phone chimed. *Your chariot awaits, sexy beast.* He'd been summoned. He didn't need Frederick to repeat the invitation. Locking the front door behind him, he paused, stunned at what he saw—or, more precisely, what he didn't see.

Brock's Cowboys cap was gone. The rocking chair creaked, a brisk springtime breeze the culprit. Wes had been inside only twenty minutes since sending his ex-lover that text. Did Brock await his messages with far more vigilance than Wes assumed?

A trio of short, sharp bleats snapped Wes from his speculations. A polished, powder-blue Camry idled at the curb. The driver remained hidden behind a tinted window, rolled down just far enough that a delicate, long-fingered hand could flick the ash from its cigarette. Another bleat from the car horn. No chariot, Wes knew, waited forever.

Before opening the passenger door, however, his phone chimed. He slipped it from his hip pocket. Surely, he thought, Frederick was no less preoccupied with smartphones than most homosexuals. After all, they met on Grindr.

Brock wrote, *You should've kept the hat.*

With a start, Wes jerked his gaze to the window beside Brock's front door. Those heavy lace curtains never parted—at least, not that he could recall. Had he glanced even a moment later, a moment later on that mild April evening, he might've missed them flutter.

"Our waiter? His ass makes me proud to be a Texan."

Wes recoiled. At least, he started, but he caught himself. The stacked bacon cheeseburger available on the plate before him, courtesy of the waiter his date brazenly desired, failed to rouse his appetite. To be polite, he turned his head and made no effort at discretion. The waiter, oblivious to both men's frank assessments, cleared plates and cups and utensils. They clattered their consent.

Frederick lifted his beer bottle to his lips. Instead of taking a sip, he grinned, let his gaze wander. His beer remained aloft.

"You ever seduce the help? Successfully, I mean."

"You mean a waiter?"

"Not just waiters. Bartenders, deejays…"

"Fishing for a dirty story?"

He kept the tone light and flirtatious, but inside, disappointment seized him. He planned to let Frederick fuck him. He'd made no statement, dropped no hint that might spark doubt. Yet still, the younger man didn't hesitate to engage in carnal competition. Wes didn't doubt, not for a moment, his trick's eagerness to start his own sordid story: hotter dude, hotter fuck.

"I cast my most expensive lure."

Wes conjured a smile. "Well, check this out. You have a nibble." The story, so much arousal for so untested a companion, started at a family pool, its shimmering swells and spray. No pool was complete without a pool boy—proudly shirtless, loudly shameless. Wes, at the time, was still a boy. Very tall, but very much a boy. If Frederick were truly that hellbent to trump his trick's stroke story, he'd erect a narrative so sleazy, Henry Miller himself would pause in admiration.

"You haven't mentioned his appearance." Frederick's beer refused to descend. Wes couldn't recall the last time he'd taken a sip.

"I didn't care what he looked like."

The beer bottle wagged from his hands, balled together beneath his chin.

Wes didn't grow up with a pool. At least, not a pool needing the attentions of some shirtless scoundrel. The story needn't be true to tantalize. Wes lied and lied, eager for the opportunity to study his trick's face.

The campus cad he'd expected from Grindr surely sent his regrets, hoping the wide-mouthed, impish frat daddy assigned to stave off Wes' disappointment would suffice. He couldn't stop grinning, Frederick, an outsized adolescent about to detonate a lewd punchline or welcome your next wisecrack. He was well over a half-foot shorter than Wes. Still, the tall man indulged vague fantasies of Frederick mounting him, allowing him to stick the dismount from his pool boy prattle.

Frederick insisted Wes offer proof of the oral deftness the pool boy who didn't exist couldn't bear to refuse. Before Wes could consult the evening's sophomoric script, Frederick began disclosing a long-ago sex romp.

Wes didn't listen. His trick made it plain when he expected reactions, and Wes had little doubt those desired reactions would appease. At some point, however, he noticed the dull white, bulbous burn perched atop the pad of Frederick's thumb.

Brock wrote, *What's the point of great sex if you can't remember?*

He added, *I haven't forgotten those nights.*

Gay men sporting that precise burn on that precise surface of that precise digit, it promised familiarity with a lingo largely unknown to men with blameless thumbs. Frederick smoked speed. Frederick had smoked speed recently. Amplified, he'd said days ago. He liked to amplify his sex.

Wes supposed his family, his friends—all those kind souls diminishing quickly in his rearview—would naturally assume a fierce feud raged within him. There was no feud, however, no disturbance within Wes Wink. He planned to smoke whatever tweak Frederick offered, the moment he offered. He hoped Brock would understand, believe despite the dwindling evidence, that he craved a future with his ex-lover so badly, no narcotic could compete.

"How come I haven't seen you online till just recently?"

Frederick finally took a gulp, a long one, from his hijacked brew. The query seemed to tax him, dimming his kilowatt grin. Wes couldn't help wondering how this plump, precocious man had remained below Grindr's radar: surely, not by choice.

He had an aunt, Frederick explained. Up north, some tiny, trifling state whose name no one spelled correctly on the first try. She needed assistance and the great thing about family was they rarely charged professional rates. She finally passed away, he said, last month. He'd returned to Amarillo to "regroup." That had been Wes' intention as well—after The Journey Home cut him loose. He wanted to warn Frederick about getting too comfortable, but Wes, himself, was not *comfortable*. Not even Annalise, his sister-in-law and occasional ally, possessed the prim pragmatism necessary to endorse that line of shit.

"Let's hear your sob story." Frederick was grinning again. Wes felt obliged to reciprocate. "No fag is complete without a tragic past."

That moment, the waiter they'd earlier ogled returned to the floor. He paused at a table, recently vacated, lifting each plate and cup. Disappointment ruined his winsome features: no tip, no remorse. Wes and Frederick both watched him recollect himself and start clearing the dishes, watched his high and tight rear end twitch as he moved. Wes' tragic past had eluded the spotlight, no less admirably than if by design.

He was touching Wes now, our friendly Frederick, as they ventured toward the parking lot. His hand drifted down the small of Wes' back.

Whenever another man showed him tenderness in public, Wes admired his courage—and rued his own meager stockpile of the trait.

*You should've kept the hat.* Those curtains, behind the window overlooking his balcony, they had fluttered. He was certain, he was confident. But it might've been a breeze. He hadn't truly slept, for a respectable length of time, until just two days ago. *You should've kept the hat.* He debated sneaking a text before he and Frederick got naked and joined the circus. He, not Frederick, would be so disappointed. His dismay, however, could be endured. His silence could not. Solitude and dismay. *You should've kept the hat.*

Rompers and Stompers was the last legitimate business on northbound Highway 87, the fast-food hovels and grimy gas stations relinquishing command of the dry and dusty county. It had been erected with an eclectic variety of splintering planks, nailed and slathered in purple paint. Uneasily angled neon pipettes spelled out its attractions: *videos, books, magazines, toys, pleasure*. Wes was taken aback at Frederick's heedless stride. Cutting past Wes, he swore he'd never stepped inside. Thought only douches and dumb fucks dared enter, he said. Wes switched tracts, insisted his knowledge of the bookstore came strictly secondhand.

Frederick lived with his widowed mother. Wes never let a first-time trick inside his home.

The lonely cashier didn't hide his elation at new customers. He rattled through all the perks awaiting those who applied for one-year memberships. Who were these craven men, Wes wondered, the ones reckless enough to allow their legal names on a fuck-farm's VIP roster? He fervently hoped the cashier didn't recognize him from the two visits he'd made last month.

"Hey there, Gatekeeper." Frederick was still grinning. "You showed these rooms the hose, right? I don't want any sex souvenirs sticking to me except maybe my own."

The cashier assured the men that cleanliness was the watchword at Rompers and Stompers.

Romper Room Four was the size of a junior-college classroom, empty spare for two sofas, facing one another from opposite walls, whose cracked vinyl offered no invitation. Also, a simple wooden chair, straight-backed, stood in the middle of the room. Finally, a bathroom scale cowered in a corner. Did Simon view his spartan décor with the same distaste he viewed this sadly sinister room known only by its numeral? He needed more furniture, Wes did. Chairs and end tables, however, might invite dismay.

"Fuck the alibis." Frederick whipped out his pipe. "Time to amplify."

A flat-screen hanging flush against the wall aired agreeable gay porn with unshaven models who had matters more pressing than the gym. The two men settled on the cracked vinyl and passed the pipe. Frederick's hand found Wes' crotch before the taller man found his. Wes took his trick's haste as a compliment. Bitterly, he bet the dead-end slaughterhouse job their fuck would require that pissant straight-backed chair.

"Pretend you're my big brother." Frederick's lips brushed his ear. "I wanna fuck like a man."

One might have assumed Wes' memory, if one knew the horrific scenes it concealed, had been concealing for almost forty years, would at that instant rip the psychic mesh and overwhelm his perceptions, no matter how vivid and dire. This broken man's mind, however, had erected countless compartments, eager to help bury his aberrant desires and debauchery. After all, if he could not maintain some semblance of worth in Brock's eyes, what was the point?

"Tell me how you like it," Frederick continued. Spit showered upon Wes' ear. "We're family now. We can do anything."

Wes smiled ruefully. "Do what you came here to do, filthy pervert."

"Hope Mom and Dad don't catch us."

Smiling, the effort needed, left him exhausted. Still, he felt confident their "parents" would not interfere. Because they had none. Because Wes refused to surrender to Frederick's fantasy. Sodomites, he reminded himself, didn't need a storyline.

Just as he'd speculated, Frederick had insisted he bend over and brace himself against the straight-backed chair. He'd had to drop to his knees to accommodate their height difference. Frederick's Morse code of invasions and retreats, Wes noted with bland admiration, never quite fell into a predictable rhythm. His trick was *present*. Wes couldn't have noted this unless he, himself, were present. Assured, however, that Frederick wasn't paying him undue attention, his thoughts drifted. These thoughts, they neared a destination both dreaded and destined. He'd been there so many times. Still, not even Brock knew its treacherous landscape.

Wes guided his LEGO firemen's boat along the surface of his bathwater. No specific narrative drove his play. Even at the underripe age of eight, he'd noticed that other boys enjoyed more boisterous schoolyard adventures than he did. He was content to steer his boat until the bathwater reached an exact tepidness, his signal to unplug the drain and snatch his favorite towel. He'd almost forgotten about the bubbles, slowly dissipating, slowly *dying*, except as unnamed obstacles for his tiny toy firefighters.

When his older brother, Simon, barged into the bathroom, Wes stirred but not with alarm. Despite the seven years between them, the two boys had long lived like sardines glad to be snug and secure inside their tin. He could depend on his big brother—his presence, his protection, his vigilance. Simon unzipped. The commode stood next to the tub. The surging splash commenced. If Wes wanted a look, now was the time. He *wanted* to look, too, and damn the dying bubbles.

The younger boy craned his neck, tilting his torso toward the tub's rear. He endeavored not to disturb the bathwater, knowing, of course, that Simon would pay as little mind to a ripple as he would an undertow. Not even their recent relocation from Arizona had slowed his stride.

His brother's penis was long, its hairless shaft flopped out over the bowl from a nest of flaxen pubic hairs mostly obscured from the boy's view. Its head reminded Wes of a certain type of mushroom, one his Scoutmaster forbade his troop from even touching, let alone tasting. Wes glanced beneath the water's surface, the bubbles having receded from the spot he wished to examine, and pondered his own penis. It was smaller, hairless like the rest of him, flaccid—a useless thing, a toy firemen's boat summoned to an actual blaze.

Still, he wanted a better look. He needed to know the exact specifications of his brother's superior appendage. His curiosity, needless to say, was in no way carnal, more a heedless grab for self-worth. He and his classmates knew just enough about sex to fear how much, indeed, remained unknown.

"You're lucky, good man. When I was your age, I had no idea what to think about my dick."

Caught! But this was his brother, and the boy was no less safe than in their very father's arms.

Wes lifted his head. "Why is yours so much bigger?" Simon was ready to meet his gaze, head twisted over his shoulder. His stream of piss had waned to a final splatter. He zipped himself.

"Because I'm becoming a man. Men have bigger bodies than boys."

"I can't wait to become a man!" Wes splashed among the feeble suds.

Simon knelt beside the tub, resting his forearms upon the rim. He was a handsome boy, yet it was beauty likely to ripen too soon, maybe abandon him during his middle years. His smile, though, reminded Wes that he was loved, and unlike a grown-up's love, his brother's affection didn't have to be *earned* through good behavior and achievement.

"You've still got a-ways to go, good man."

"No, sir! My penis will be even bigger than yours!"

Simon laughed. His cupped hand dove beneath the water's surface, the belt of water striking Wes in his ear. He didn't mind. He was happy. His big brother loved him. The LEGO boat wandered wearily toward the faucet, forgotten.

"My brother, you tell lies." His breath left him as a shudder. "Show me your proof."

"It's right here, silly." Indignant, Wes stabbed his finger into the water.

Simon's hand had yet to leave the bathwater. Recalling this encounter, and Wes often did recall it, like a locker combination or a deathbed promise, his memory blurred as to when he first felt imperiled. One moment, he and his big brother were joking about their dicks. The next, his childhood had ended. There was no impartial witness, no fanfare. The bubbles kept dying and the LEGO boat kept drifting.

"Good man," Simon breathed, "you've impressed me in an elemental way."

Annalise insisted on cloth diapers. Wes could recite her sales pitch almost by heart, having first heard it with Lance, then two years later with Lionel, and now, just this year, she extolled for him the virtues of sparing her newborn son, Leonard, the "ambiguous materials" favored by Huggies and Pampers and the other diaper dealers she deemed forever suspect. She was swift and she was studious, changing her youngest son's nappies. A fold here, a puncture there, a tug or two elsewhere—she was the quintessential young Amarillo mother. Indeed, very much younger than Simon. Wes, even after a decade, still hadn't decided whether her insistence on treating him like a fellow fishwife was subtle praise or thoughtless condescension.

"Quick," she said, surely realizing her stage whisper unnecessary, "tell me all the dirty, degrading details about young Mr. Frederick."

Wes lit a cigarette. He smoked only at Simon and Annalise's place. They expected it from him.

"Hurry, Wesley. Before my big, boring husband comes back."

"Go out and have your own hot, nasty sex."

"I'd love to, but I'm married."

Simon returned from inside onto the immense, scrupulously sanded deck abutting the rear of the house. He returned to his ministry of pork chops sizzling on the grill. Lance and Lionel, both of them grade-school athletic fixtures, endured a listless game of softball on a homemade diamond close enough for Simon to supervise, but distant enough for Annalise to ignore.

Wes let the smoke simply drift from between his parted lips. He was still coming down from the tweak Frederick had shared with him. He'd thought about texting Brock, refrained until—he promised himself!—he was truly sober, meaning at least ten hours of sleep the moment his mind reclaimed itself. He spied Simon marching toward the softball diamond. His big brother fancied himself a coach. Not once, in all his brother's weekends here, had Simon ever burned the chops, or the hamburgers, or the sirloins.

Annalise shifted the newborn to her shoulder, began patting its back. "Simon told me about that slaughterhouse position." Her mouth drew tight, the lewd sparkle in her eyes now departed.

Grindr's iconic notification alert sounded, an aggressive digital belch. Wes chided himself for neglecting to disengage that app's feature before Simon had chauffeured him to his place. He flipped his iPhone facedown on the armrest of his deck chair. He wasn't sure he wanted to see Frederick again, but if that ignored message had been his, Wes felt entitled to bask in triumph.

"The Mexicans handle the actual slaughter," he said. "Simon promised."

"Dominique's husband worked there two years. You need to hear this."

He didn't know a Dominique nor why she warranted attention.

"They're not at all hospitable to men like you," she continued. *Faggot* and *cocksucker* written on lockers and windshields. All sorts of ugly questions, she assured him, too rude for even her taste. Simon either didn't know or naively assumed Wes would be spared this low-watt harassment. "He's a desperate man, Wesley. At least when it comes to you."

Annalise wasn't jealous of Simon's ceaseless fussing over his baby brother. In truth, she feared it. She'd never admit as much to Wes, he knew, but her eyes, if you watched her long enough during his visits, were those of vermin praying hard to any available deity that the wolf never escaped its cage. He pitied her. He hated her. Simon started his return from the makeshift diamond.

"I know you're waiting for this Rehab Romeo to sweep you off your feet." She rushed her words. Wes, startled, turned his head and watched her speak. "But you go to Dallas, to Houston, there's a Romeo on every corner." The newborn began to fuss. She jiggled it, the baby's head bobbing upon her shoulder. "I know you want your own life. I want that, too. You won't find it here, Wesley." The newborn whimpered. The strain in her voice belied her thirty-one years. "Not in Amarillo. My husband won't hear of it."

Those three months ago, Brock had embraced him one last time and fatefully trekked upstairs to his duplex, his stipulations clear and his heartbreak, he insisted, no less punishing than the one besieging Wes. Annalise was the only person from his "actual" world with whom he shared secrets, and she'd known this secret even before Wes returned from The Journey Home. She would affirm, at any needed time, that his ex-lover was very much real and convinced he might finally tame his addiction, providing Wes with the fortitude to traverse his dreary, dope-hazed days.

Brock wrote, *There are 50 states in the union and 52 weeks in a year.*

He added, *In nine months, I'll be out of states to stitch. We've discussed what that means.*

Lance and Lionel ditched their half-hearted game when Simon called them for supper. The Wink family ate in silence. Simon and Wes had been taught, since the eldest boy could first speak, dinnertime was about food, not chatter. Annalise dared make goofy faces meant for Wes alone. She didn't tease her children. She didn't acknowledge them. When Lance and Lionel asked to be excused, it was Simon who granted permission.

"You two tigers get ready for your bath!" Soon, he promised, he'd join them.

Shortly after Simon had followed his eldest sons indoors, Annalise fell into a funk. On previous Sundays, several such Sundays, Wes had asked her why boys that old weren't allowed to bathe themselves. Tonight, however, he demurred. It did not matter what Annalise knew—it mattered what she could ignore. She gazed out upon the makeshift diamond where a few boys tossed and pitched. She asked Wes for a smoke. He didn't inquire whether the baby bouncing on her shoulder might object. They both knew these weren't his cigarettes.

Wes attempted sleep moments after Simon returned him to his duplex. He'd been doing speed enough years to reliably gauge if slumber was in the cards on a given night. The last thing he did before curling up on his side, like a baby beneath his Cowboys blanket, was investigate his earlier message. It wasn't Frederick. Indeed, an app member Wes recently dubbed the Ghost of Grindr Future sought a reply—and quickly! *I heard you and Frederick Pound went out last Friday,* his first message read. Wes was spooked, enduring a few moments of gooseflesh. No other queer had known about Frederick except Brock. *There's something you must know,* Grindr Future added. No third message. Wes rolled his eyes and tossed the device on his nightstand.

Wes was still sound asleep when his phone rang shortly after ten that morning. It was the boss man himself, at the slaughterhouse. They were damn impressed, he declared. How did next Monday sound? Wes relied on ancient etiquette to bluff his way through the call. Annalise's warning echoed through his mind. Still, he needed the job. He refused to leave Amarillo without Brock, and he had to get sober before lighting that lamp. He felt excited and flattered, he promised the boss man, the old buzzard doubting his enthusiasm. One thing, though, Wes blurted out. He wouldn't actually kill the animals, right? They'd discuss his duties in more detail next Monday, the old crone assured him.

Those fuckers would insist he help murder the animals. Wes was certain. Then they'd turn their heads as his hayseed coworkers swapped fag jokes, deciding which would rattle Wes the most when "overheard." If he could stay sober, however, Brock would gladly take his hand as the two zipped across the nation, just like they imagined doing at The Journey Home.

Brock, Mondays—how could he have not remembered until now?

The front door, left open as he stepped onto the porch, creaked as it crept backward. Wes used only his fingertips to lift his ex-lover's latest needlepoint from the same spot he'd been retrieving them these entire three months. Arizona. He'd wondered when Brock would lose patience and make a direct appeal to his heart. In their bedroom at the rehab, Wes had rhapsodized to his bunkmate about the miles of spun-sugar sand, the Technicolor mountains and a heat so dry and airless, one had no choice but to let it invade the skin. He'd spent his grade-school years there and been scheming to return ever since.

That moment, he swore to himself he was done tweaking. Brock, Arizona, freedom from Simon and Annalise—a craven urge was no match for a life's dream.

Wes gazed into the neighborhood, still rooted to his porch, the doorway yawning behind him. The polished, powder-blue Camry almost failed to blip his radar. Like he observed three days ago, a delicate, long-fingered hand flicked ash from his cigarette, the tinted window cracked just enough to accommodate its movements. He hadn't invited Frederick to return. Indeed, they hadn't traded a single text or message through Grindr since Frederick had delivered him home late Friday night. Wes, in that moment, regretted blowing off Grindr Future's implied warning. He crossed his yard, calling Frederick's name.

"Since when do you collect needlepoint?"

"It was a gift. What are you doing here, Frederick? Don't you have a job?"

The sky swarmed with churning dark clouds, each fat with rain—or maybe flakes of snow. It was April, but it was frigid. An arctic air mass had slammed the city shortly before dawn. Wes wondered how Frederick had stayed warm during his interminable wait.

Frederick hadn't rolled down his window any further. He implored Wes to allow him inside. He wasn't looking for sex and he wanted Wes to hear the truth. They'd had fun Friday night, hadn't they? Hadn't they?

"You're still tweaked, aren't you?" Wes felt relieved having occasion to scold another.

"I took a few hits waiting to see if you were home. Or, you know, awake."

"Come on inside. One bad idea deserves another."

They crossed the yard, Wes grim and resolute, Frederick jittering even mid-stride. Outside his visitor's sightline, Wes chuckled, the crisp morning breeze snatching the sound from his mouth. He recalled the vow he'd made just moments before—his sincerity had left him bedazzled by stupid, stupid hope. He harbored no doubt Frederick planned to produce a pipe once they settled.

Frederick paused in the middle of the living room, hands on hips, twisting this way and that to behold the entire vista. He looked mildly baffled, as if served the wrong meal in his favorite diner. Whatever the disappointment, Wes suspected, it would reap this series of bland expressions.

"What happens when you have more than one guest?" Frederick joined Wes on the sofa. His only option was a recliner, Simon's typical throne, wedged into the room's far corner. His guest shifted positions. He patted his jacket's breast pocket. Wes steeled himself for the coming moral dilemma, but Frederick's hands returned to his lap.

Moments passed, silent each and every one.

It was treacherous terrain, former tricks attempting to converse, to observe, to connect—all of it with neither booze nor speed to grease the gears. He and Brock had found a way, Wes reminded himself. Indeed, he had yet to encounter Brock bedeviled by any illicit substance.

"If you need to take a hit," Wes said, with more irritation than intended, "don't let me stop you."

"I hate getting tweaked alone. It makes me feel like a junkie."

"You got high in your car."

Frederick smiled sadly. His lips parted, but he did not speak. They parted again. "It's no trouble if one night was all you wanted. I just needed to make sure that AARP asshole wasn't tipping the scales."

"Smoke your shit already." Wes rose from the sofa and entered the kitchen. By his return, energy drink in hand, Frederick was already sucking from the stem. "Tell me why I should be leery of you," Wes said and perched on the sofa's edge.

"Love is a lie," he announced brightly. "Time to amplify."

"Frederick, that wasn't cute the first time."

The needlepoint of Arizona lay on the coffee table. Wes needed more furniture. Chairs and end tables, however, might invite dismay.

"I don't have an aunt. At least, not one on her deathbed."

Wes sipped his drink. He expected men to lie about their pasts. He did likewise, bitterly convinced every man was a volatile, self-serving ream of fiction. If Frederick sought validation before he elaborated, Wes thought, he'd need to refill his bowl before being indulged.

"I did time in the pen. Huntsville. My parole finally came through. That old fuck must actually visit the state website..."

"You mean Grindr?"

Brock wrote, *We're only as sick as our secrets.*

Moments later, *No drug can win you freedom.*

"He caught me jacking off. He started asking questions. I had no idea I was being seduced." He held out the pipe for Wes, who declined with a quick wave. "I've banged at least a half-dozen fags with the same story. Now I have to live with Mom until she dies and leaves me the house while his twink ass gets plowed at Texas Tech."

"What did you *do*, Frederick?" Wes was not an oblivious man, not a dim one. It was one of Simon's gifts to him: vigilance. He'd measured his words with precision—their arrangement, their volume, their context. A part of him didn't need his uninvited guest to supply the punchline, but the part that craved true intimacy, not the mamby-pamby contrivance of sexual role play, would not be denied.

"My brother, Franklin. He was fifteen." Another bank of dense, bright smoke. It cleared, Wes noticed, with an uncharacteristic swiftness. Wes had no choice but to behold the pervert. So *that* was the website in question—the Texas sex offender registry, a hotbed of mugshots and lascivious details, including addresses. Frederick took another hit.

Those convenient, ever-accumulating compartments, the bottom from every last one dropped out like the hinged plank beneath the condemned, noose slung around his neck. All the shames and pains tumbled into Wes' lap. Really, he thought, Frederick should leave so he might drown in solitude, not to mention dismay. But Frederick was describing his first "consensual" encounter with his young brother. He didn't sound sorry. He was sucking from the stem when Wes clubbed his jaw, fist firm and fast. Wes didn't notice the distinct, guttural crunch of glass shattering inside Frederick's mouth. It wasn't until blood, bright red and eager, streamed down his chin that Wes realized it was the consequence of violence—his fist, his rage.

For a moment, the older man forgot about the lifetime of sour sorrows suddenly clamoring for redress. He instead watched Frederick stagger to his feet, open hand pressed against his clenched jaw as if a toothache pulsed. He spit out the grounds and tiny shards of glass. Finally, he gazed back at Wes, not with fright as Wes expected, but honest befuddlement. It became clear to his host that Frederick had trusted him—quickly and foolishly, to be sure, but trusted him all the same. His knees gave, and the outsized young man tumbled to the carpet.

Wes slowly rose from the sofa. His expression had relaxed. His eyes, they held no clue, no precursor to his next response. Indeed, he seemed devoid of panic or anxiety or rancor. He circled the coffee table to where Frederick bled and babbled beneath his breath.

His first kick launched squarely into Frederick's gut. The series of kicks that followed were less precise but still made contact—the thighs, the kidneys, the chest, the head. Wes was not, by nature, a violent soul. His aversion to slaughtering cattle extended to his fellow man. But he refused to regard Frederick as a man. He would keep assaulting him until his conscious mind resumed command, but repressing rage for four decades only for the dam to burst so abruptly—?

He stopped kicking. Exhaustion dropped upon him. He began to sob.

Frederick's clumsy defense, his one free arm slung over his head, fell by slow degrees. He gaped upward, with the naked wonder of a child beholding a skyscraper, as Wes sobbed into his cupped hands, shoulders shaking. So consuming was the pain, it dominated his thoughts, his movements, his perceptions. When Frederick risked a one-armed embrace, however, Wes froze—the sobs suddenly ceased.

"It's okay, buddy." Frederick hardly managed a whisper. "Whatever's wrong, it can't stay wrong forever." The blood had slowed to a trickle, but he spoke with a slur, his tongue lacerated. "You need to sit down?"

"You really must leave now." Wes gasped. "I think I might try to kill you."

"What...? Wes, I can hardly—" Frederick kept his arm tight around his host's shoulders.

"I will try to kill you. I think I might succeed." The two men locked eyes. "Now, little brother."

Frederick, lifting his arm, slowly backed away. That his steps took him closer to the front door was no coincidence. He promised, in a tone betraying a deep and baffled terror, that he'd never speak of this morning to anyone. Wes could feel free to block his Grindr profile, he added. He'd never mention Wes' name. He wasn't angry, he promised, hand seizing the doorknob.

"I'm not a bad dude." He stood framed in the doorway. Behind him, a flurry of flakes struggled to make landfall. "Try to remember that, okay?"

Wes gazed, uncomprehending, at the door after Frederick shut it behind him. He'd threatened the man. He'd assaulted him for reasons he could not articulate even if compelled. As the agreeable, affable man made his verbose departure, one word echoed through Wes' mind: *stay*.

Solitude and dismay. Here they were. They'd never left. Such rude houseguests, no concept of *welcome* or whether theirs had lapsed.

The uninvited guest had left his dope, alongside the broken-stemmed pipe, its jagged end smeared with blood, unclaimed on the coffee table. There remained, Wes recalled with miraculous clarity, roughly half a gram secured behind the needlepoint of Montana. He rarely snorted but knew this situation called for a manner of ingestion most likely to invite oblivion.

The dope was gone within moments of being crushed and tamed upon the table. Wes flopped back onto his sofa, his limbs spread wide. His thoughts zipped and zapped, urgent yet weightless, neither memories nor anxieties able to achieve foothold. He was experienced enough with tweak to feel confident he'd brokered at least two solid days of sheer white-noise wonder.

The hours passed. The sun went down. Wes made no move to banish the invading darkness.

He didn't notice the click of a key maneuvering the lock at the front door.

Wes, of course, recognized his voice at once. Simon, his brother and benefactor, his slow-drip destroyer. Why hadn't he been answering his phone? Simon had been calling from work. Even Annalise had tried to summon him. Wes gurgled, the words bunching and tripping over one another as they left his mouth. Simon flicked on the overhead light. The harsh brightness refused to be ignored, and Wes was once again, so often these last three months, reminded how little comprised his daily existence.

Simon brushed snowflakes from his shoulders. You called me, Wes finally managed, voice breaking as it rose. Yes, his brother spat, looming over the sofa, glaring down at Wes' extended form. The truth was obvious. His brother wouldn't stop ranting: how could he keep a job fucked up on this shit, what about Simon's promise to their father, what about his nephews, those blameless boys who admired him so? A phone rang. Wes jolted, determined not to let *this* call elude him, but no—it was Simon's phone, no doubt Annalise. He hustled into Wes' bedroom, already apologizing to his wife, apologizing again and again. The door swung shut behind him.

Wes was left alone on the sofa in his drab living room. He glimpsed his phone lying on the coffee table. Someone had texted him. No, he'd sent a text. Dear God, not Frederick! The fear seized him like a starved animal fed a carcass. Afraid to touch the device, he leaned over to read what he'd written.

The one and only message: *I just need a man to hold me like I'm worthy of love.*

His breath left him. He flopped back onto the sofa. His bedroom door creaked open. Wes grabbed the phone and flicked it back to its home screen. Simon may have had the key to his apartment, but Wes had refused to grant him *total* access.

Simon sat beside him on the sofa. Wes didn't know how he should respond.

"Did the slaughterhouse call today? Did you notice?"

He nodded. "I got the job. I start next Monday."

His brother whooped with joy and wrapped his strong, tanned arms around Wes. He babbled nonsensical nothings of praise and hope. Their sincerity didn't make them any more bearable. But wasn't this what Wes wanted—a man to hold him like he was worthy of love?

Outside, the snowfall intensified. Wes still hadn't fathomed the day's wintry agenda, and how the inevitable evening had fostered more flakes, falling faster.

Simon insisted he should stay until the worst of the high had passed. Wes hoped Brock wouldn't respond. Wes hoped Brock responded right away. The two dueling desires had embarked on a game of chicken behind his eyes, between his ears. Wes failed to appreciate how his brother granted him no moment to express gratitude. He simply spun inside himself, spinning, spinning, within Simon's desperate embrace.

The darts were smuggled from the rehab's rec room. They'd seen happier times; their shafts had started to splinter and their feathered ends had turned raggedy. Still, they flew, and with Wes Wink at the helm, they hit their targets with ease. His last throw had landed precisely where he wished: Arizona. If his recall of its municipal matrix could be trusted, the point penetrated near Flagstaff.

"That's your favorite spot in America?" Brock asked, incredulous. "No exceptions?"

"The sand is so fine, your toes sink. You forget all about the damn heat."

The Journey Home's administrators decided long ago to tack oversized maps of America upon the walls in each bedroom. It was meant to provoke wonder, a sense of possibility. Addicts, more than most, needed hope for places they hadn't seen and peace about the places they hoped never again to trespass. Not long after Brock had arrived and been assigned Wes, already two months into his stay, as a roommate, he'd insisted that Wes demonstrate his skill with darts. Don't tell me where you want to go, he always said. Land there with the force of destiny.

"I've lived in San Antonio over thirty years. Heat never lets you forget."

"Let's go there together. Arizona, I mean." Wes gazed up at the slats of the upper bunk. So many of his most intimate conversations with Brock transpired with the two men stacked like flapjacks, each a mere voice, close but never close enough. "After I rack up my month of good time."

"Your optimism doesn't go unnoticed, good man."

The first time Brock had uttered that endearment, they'd been both half-naked in a supply closet at an obscene hour. Wes never entreated his new lover to refrain from that phrase. There would be questions, and questions had an irksome habit of attracting answers. It was a fluke, Wes always assured himself, one prank out of millions played by a pitiless God.

In better news, Wes had been jittering with excitement the whole evening. During his weekly call home, Annalise had informed him of a cheap, respectable duplex on the outskirts of town. Plenty of room, she promised, for this boyfriend who refused to share a bed, or a toilet, or even a front door. It had been easy drafting his sister-in-law into action; the moment he floated the fib that Simon had insisted he stay with them after rehab, Annalise launched her offensive. She and Wes agreed that the identity of his neighbor should remain a mystery to Simon, a riddle referenced only when it must. Brock had promised, more than once, emphatically each time asked, that he would share a duplex with his rehab lover.

The stringent conditions he'd imposed on Wes seemed oddly reasonable, if just a month's sobriety would nullify them. He had almost a year to make good on his vow. Fifty states, fifty-two weeks on the calendar.

"It sounds like a great place," Brock said mildly. "You've thought of everything."

"Plus, we can rent out the bottom floor when I make my month."

Brock grunted, made Wes think of failed laughter. He needed to know Brock had faith in him—he, at the moment, had only the shakiest of faith in himself. He didn't particularly want to stay sober. That LEGO boat was still drifting atop the bathwater, those bubbles still withering like a wallflower's dream of a kiss on the dancefloor.

*Good man, you've impressed me in an elemental way.*

"I'm not gonna let you down, baby." Wes wished he could gaze into his eyes. "No one's ever believed in me like you do. No one."

Brock's bunk shuddered as he settled in for sleep. Wes never learned whether he'd heard his last confession. The darts had all converged in Arizona. Surely, Wes thought, his precision was not only thanks to a minor form of athleticism. Destiny—and desire, too—had honed his aim.

Simon had insisted on lying beside his brother while he navigated his monster tweak trip. Simon, though, soon fell asleep, arm slung over his wide-awake dependent. Wes needed a distraction that welcomed hourlong stares. His search again illuminated one simple fact: he needed more furniture. Chairs and end tables, however, might invite dismay.

His brother slept heavily, so it took little effort for Wes to squirm from underneath his sentry, rolling off his bed and onto his feet. Before he could orient himself, a light and rapid knock surprised his front door.

Wes crossed the living room, eager to intercept this visitor before he knocked again, likely louder, and woke his brother. The single glittering star, navy blue, upon a nest of ornate, fussy font didn't register with him. The image floated at head-level, seen through the sheer curtains obscuring the front door's peekaboo window. Wes threw open the door. He'd never formulated any fears about his visitor's intent.

"You, good man, are very much indeed worth loving."

Brock slipped off his Cowboys cap and playfully slapped it over Wes' wayward hair. His crazed clutter of dark-chestnut curls took full advantage of their new freedom.

He wrapped his bony arms around Wes. Unlike him, Brock had donned a padded winter coat. Wes allowed the younger, shorter man to embrace him as hard as he pleased. Brock was thin, gangly despite lacking the height associated with that trait, but the clench left Wes breathless upon the threshold to his bare and woebegone home. If I let him go, Wes thought, he'll vanish for good. This was what he'd wanted, after all—a man to hold him like he was worthy of love.

"Brock, wait, I'm not—I'm so glad you're here, but I'm…" Now separated, he returned himself to Brock's spooky, seismic gaze. "It hasn't been a month," he whispered. "It hasn't even been a day."

"If I needlepoint one more goddamn state, I'll burn this duplex to the ground."

Those eyes, Wes noticed, are so dark, the pupils are difficult to distinguish from the irises, but he stared long enough and their dilation became apparent. Wes stumbled backward a few steps. This "contract" between them offered so few guarantees, perhaps Wes could be forgiven for making assumptions—namely, this: Brock would never relapse. He'd sunk his feet into Arizona sand to find it cold and curdled.

"Come upstairs and see where I live." Brock grinned, his eyeballs twittering. He glimpsed around Wes' shoulder. "When were you planning to buy furniture?"

Wes drank in Brock Merriweather in his entirety, his totality. He summoned the focus to inform Brock that he must scratch out a note to his brother before finally, after three long months, ascending that staircase. Brock laughed, and Wes at last fathomed how much self-control Brock had needed to hide his intoxication even briefly. He watched his ex-lover trot up the stairs. His door remained unlocked, he called.

The moment the door clicked shut, Wes staggered out into the swirling snowfall as if dazed. He tore off the Cowboys cap, and the cascading white swallowed it.

An escapade in Arizona—nothing stopping them. No goddamn snowstorms in goddamn April. Wes and Brock, high and harmonized, their love so apparent, so ordained not even Simon could temper its sheen. Simon, who offered safety and certainty, a dull job to complement a dull life—bills paid, however. Wes couldn't recall Brock ever mentioning a job or source of income. The porch lights from both stories of the duplex blended, blinding him.

He ran. He ran deep into the snowstorm. He wore only jeans and a hoodie. By the time he reached the curb, the frigid night had tamed his existential panic.

He sat on the curb, the snow slowly soaking his jeans. He cradled his head. A decision faced him, one impossible to delay, both options requiring he accept circumstances sure to ruin him—maybe not till

Arizona, maybe not till the hundredth bolt he drove through a blameless bovine's skull. Ruin adhered to its own schedule. The snow fell. Night offered no respite.

Solitude and dismay—they asked so little, ultimately, of the souls they sought.

A man's hand clamped down on his shoulder. He jerked, head snapping around, tilted upward to see who wished to claim him. Wes wasn't surprised. Wes was relieved he hadn't taken longer. He offered his hand to the savior standing above. This courtesy, it was the least Wes owed him.

"Come with me, good man." He spoke to Wes not unkindly. His grip was strong, and Wes surrendered. "It's cold and dark. I need you back home. We'll discuss the matter like men."

Wes followed. He lost himself in the colorless light spilling out from the duplex.

By morning, a foot of fresh snow welcomed his neighbors. The Cowboys cap, forgotten beneath the snowfall, days later resurfaced—but no one emerged eager to claim it.

# About the Author

Thomas Kearnes graduated from the University of Texas at Austin with an MA in film writing. His fiction has appeared in *Gulf Coast, Foglifter, Berkeley Fiction Review, Timber, Hobart, Gertrude, A cappella Zoo, Split Lip Magazine, Cutthroat, Litro, PANK, BULL: Men's Fiction, Gulf Stream Magazine, Wraparound South, Night Train, 3:AM Magazine, Word Riot, Storyglossia, Driftwood Press, Adroit Journal, The Matador Review, Pseudopod, Underbelly Magazine, Black Dandy, the Best Gay Stories series, Mary: A Journal of New Writing, wigleaf, SmokeLong Quarterly, Pidgeonholes, Sundog Lit, The Citron Review,* Dark Ink's psychological fiction anthology *Shadowy Natures,* and elsewhere. He is a three-time Pushcart Prize nominee and three-time Best of the Net nominee. Originally from East Texas, he now lives near Houston and works as an English tutor at a local community college.

His debut collection of short fiction, *Texas Crude,* was a finalist for the Lambda Literary Prize in 2020 and is available at Lethe Press, Amazon, and Barnes & Noble.

# Open Up and Let Me In
## Laura DeHaan

Dana's wife stares at her from the mantelpiece.

It was a clear summer sunset on St. John's Signal Hill, a warm wash of pinkish light softening the old crevices of Cabot Tower. The wind blew strongly up on the hill and she'd warned Misao to hold onto the broad straw hat she favored on sunny days. She'd tried to pose beside the tower and gave it up for the sake of modesty, one hand at the collar of her light jacket, one hand clutching her hat, her knees pinched together to capture the hem of her dress. Seconds before Dana snapped the picture, the wind snatched Misao's hat from her long black hair.

Now Misao stares at her from the mantelpiece, her dress dancing around her thighs. Her straw hat is already a yard away, a fragile UFO skimming towards the ocean. The faltering light caresses her face goodbye. Taken fourteen years earlier on their honeymoon, it's still Dana's favorite photo of Misao.

Except it's not the same photo at all.

In the photo she saw yesterday, Misao's back was turned and she was reaching out to grab her hat. The photo she saw yesterday, she'd seen for fourteen years.

Now Misao stares at her.

"I'm sorry," Dana tells her, as she tells her every day, every hour. "I couldn't stop it."

All Misao does is stare, as her hat makes its escape.

Dana's rented bungalow is small and came furnished. All she brought with her when she moved were her clothes, her electronics, and the photos and paintings she and Misao had taken and bought together. It was an even easier move than usual, at least in that respect. They'd moved around so much for her work that they hardly had anything permanent.

Her workplace had been supportive, as much as it could have been. After the trial, she'd tried to go back to the world of memos and meetings and weekly quotas, but selling communication devices was hard when your wife was dead. When Acquisitions from the Little Itty Book Nook had asked what the battery life was on some handheld version, she'd answered, "Longer than my wife's." She stopped going into work and, by unspoken mutual agreement, she stopped getting paychecks. A week later she'd moved to Sudbury, leaving the troubles of Kelowna behind.

"I'm sorry," she tells the photo again. "I couldn't stop it."

The man who'd killed her wife is now in a psychiatric hospital. The knife he'd used had not been kind to any of them: Misao dead by it, Dana herself with fresh red scars on the hairless parts of her forearms, the man with a badly sliced lip and a tongue shortened by an inch. Dana had watched the man stab her wife, stab her and stab her in the neck, and it wasn't until the man had turned the knife on Dana that she had acted. Violently and crazed, but at the trial proven no more crazed than the killer himself, a well-known homeless man in the area with a history of schizophrenia. A psychiatric hospital was best, and kindest, and no less than the man deserved.

"Do you hate me?" she asks the photo, who stares at her with her hair in disarray. "Do you want me to die, too? I didn't even try," she says. "I couldn't stop it."

Still Misao stares. Surely, she didn't always stare. Nobody in Sudbury knows her well enough to give a second opinion. She calls her best friend in Halifax.

"Tom-tom?"

"Dana! Christ, I'm glad you called. How are you holding up?"

"You remember that photo I kept on the, the, side table? Misao, at sunset, beside the tower?"

"That photo? Uh, maybe? It's been a few years since I've visited. It was from your honeymoon, right? In St. John's?"

"That one, that one. Which way was she facing?"

"Facing? Geez, Dannio, I don't remember. Something about a hat? Her hat had blown off, right?"

"That one, that one. But which way was she facing? Was she looking at me?"

"Uh...geez, I don't remember. Did you lose the photo? That's terrible, I know you loved that photo."

"No, I have it here. But she's looking at me now, Tom-tom. She was grabbing for her hat when I took the picture, and now she's looking at me."

There is silence on the line.

"She's looking at me."

"Dana. Have you had, you know, counseling for what happened? Been to see someone?"

"She's bleeding, Tom-tom."

"Dana! Dana. It's been hard, I know. I wish to Christ I could have been there for you, but I think you should talk to someone. A professional."

"They're all opening up on her!"

"Dana! Calm down! You gotta go outside, you gotta get someone to take you to a hospital. You hear me, Dannio? Keep it together just a little longer. Stay on the phone."

"She's still looking! Stab! Stab! All on her neck!"

"Dana!"

Dana can't hear him anymore, just the squishy thunk-thunk of a blade driving into flesh. The next sound she's aware of is a stern recording telling her she has to hang up.

Misao stares at her from the mantelpiece.

There's an email from Tommy.

> From: Tommy Youngblood
> To: Dana Sacks
> Are you okay? I hung up and called 911. Did they show up? They gave me a pretty hard time, calling from Halifax about someone in Kelowna. Hope you're okay. Give me a shout. – Tom-tom

Tommy doesn't know she's moved. 911 would be doubly upset. There's an email from Sophia.

> From: Sophia Perera
> To: Dana Sacks
> Haven't heard from you in a while. Let me know if there's anything I can do for you. xo – Sophia

She's turned the photo around so she doesn't see her wife being stabbed. It doesn't matter. There's another photo, on the wall, she and Misao riding an elephant at a zoo. Before, Misao was snuggled against her back, both of them laughing, Dana grabbing tight to the seat's railing with one hand and reaching back to touch Misao's thigh with the other. Now, she touches nothing, laughs with no one. Misao stands in front of the elephant and stares at her while a cut opens up on her neck.

Stab. Stab. Stab.

She staggers to the wall and yanks the picture down. Still she sees it: inch-wide punctures biting into her neck, the blood that spurts out like the flailing death throes of an insect with impossibly long red legs. She crawls to her laptop and aims for the keys.

> From: Dana Sacks
> To: Sophia Perera
> she won;'t stop bleeeding i think iu'm going crasyz what dio ui do

It takes a few tries before she can hit the send button. When she can see again, there's a new message from Sophia.

> From: Sophia Perera
> To: Dana Sacks
> Do you need me to come over? I've got some vacation time coming up. I can be on a plane tomorrow. Are you still in Winnipeg?

Winnipeg was before Kelowna. She sends a one-word response: **No.**

She stares at her inbox, at the name Sophia Perera. No is a safe answer. No is the best answer. No should be her default answer.

In the laptop screen, she sees her face, just an outline with a fringe of short hair.

Then it starts to grow.

The outline changes, the cheeks stretching, the chin rising. Dark slashes spread open in her neck and spray redness across the inside of the screen.

The time on the laptop says 8:28 PM. It's an hour later than she remembers.

Shakily, she jabs at the keys again.

> From: Dana Sacks
> To: Sophia Perera
> Shge was in my cdomputerr. I don;t kjnow what she wants.

She gets a response minutes later. Sophia must have been waiting for her to reach out again.

> From: Sophia Perera
> To: Dana Sacks
> Dana, get help. You need to see someone about this, whatever it is.
> I'm here for you.

She stares at the keyboard, at the spacebar, just barely unable to see the screen. Clumsily, with only her peripheral vision, she navigates a return message to Sophia, a one-word response: Yes.

She's lucky the psychotherapist can see her on such short notice. Indira Rasmussen is a large blossom of roses and oranges, her hair tinted with henna and a careful smile on her lips.

"Why don't you tell me where to start," she says.

Dana's mouth hangs slightly open, still pretending sleep in the hopes it will come for real. A patch of dry skin sits unnoticed in the dip of one nostril: an easy fix if one saw it in the mirror, but mirrors have become terrifying. Her eyes, bloodshot, focus on a spot somewhere near Indira's left elbow.

"My wife is dead and I couldn't stop it," she says.

Indira casually stretches her hand to the cassette recorder and makes a minute adjustment to the microphone. "Go on."

Client: She's haunting me now.

Therapist: Your wife is?

C: Photos. Mirrors. Anything with a reflective surface. I think she's in one of the paintings, too. I only saw a shadow.

T: And how does she look, when you see her?

C: Blood. There's blood. She stares at me and then her neck starts bleeding and then I...I think I black out for a while.

T: And when you regain yourself, is she still there?

C: No. Not bleeding I mean, for a little while. Until I look at a photo or a reflection again for too long.

T: So this has been happening—

C: All the time. Everywhere.

T: Now? In here?

C: (There is silence for several seconds as the client scans the room before dropping her gaze to the floor.) No. Not yet. But I didn't look very hard.

T: It must be very upsetting.

C: I couldn't stop it. I still can't.

T: How did it happen? If I may ask.

C: A madman...no, a schizo, schizophrenic, he's not...right in the head. He came into our house...broke into our house...he stabbed her, right there in the kitchen in front of me, and I couldn't stop him.

T: Were you attacked as well?

C: Yes. It wasn't until he came at me that I could act.

T: Where is this man now?

C: At a psychiatric hospital. On the West Coast.

T: How do you feel about that?

C: It's fair. It's fair. He needs help.

T: What would your wife think?

C: (shouting) I could have stopped it!

(brief silence)

T: You feel your wife has more anger towards you than her attacker?

C: She should. I let it happen.

T: And now you feel she's haunting you. Why do you think she's doing this?

C: I told you, she's angry with me.

T: To what end is she haunting you? What does she wish to gain?

C: I...I don't know. I don't know.

T: But you feel you deserve it, whatever she plans?

C: It was all me. I could have stopped it, and I didn't. I wish I knew what she wanted. She can have it.

(silence for two minutes)

T: I'd like to try something next session. I'll need you to bring in a photo of your wife. Can you do that for me?

C: A photo?

T: Please.

C: What are you going to do?

T: There's a process called memory reconsolidation. Memories are not infallible. Nor are they static. When you see the image of your wife, it becomes the strongest memory you have of her: in this case, one where she is angry, vengeful perhaps. I believe we can find a way to interrupt that memory, change it to something more benign, but to do so, we first need to call upon this memory. You cannot erase a drawing without first laying down the paper. (short silence) Can you do this for me?

C: I'm frightened.

T: I'll be right here with you. If it gets to be too much, we can take a break. Do you want to give this a try?

C: No.

T: Because it frightens you?

C: If I bring a photo and I see it happen but you don't see it happen, then I'm crazy. I'd be crazier than...

T: (short pause)Than whom?

C: Than the person who murdered my wife.

T: Whatever you see is valid. Okay? No matter what it is. (pause) Will you bring me a photo?

C: All right.

(Session ends.)

At home, she apologizes to her wife. She's sorry they had to move so often. She's sorry they never stayed in one place long enough for her to make friends. She's sorry they couldn't get a dog. She's sorry she wasn't a good lover. She's sorry she left ketchup crust on the bottle. She's sorry she didn't stop it. She's sorry. She's sorry. She's sorry.

Under the photos turned towards the wall and placed face-down on the mantel, through the cracks along the sides of her laptop screen, catching in the brush marks of an original oil painting they bought together in Winnipeg: blood, running and running. In a sweet little memory box, their wedding album floats in its own iron puddle.

From: Sophia Perera
To: Dana Sacks

Let me know how you're doing. Please, Dana, don't shut me out. I want to see you. Won't you let me visit you? xoxo – Sophia

She wants to reply, but there's too much blood on the screen.

Therapist: How has your week been?
Client: Terrible. Worse.
T: I'm sorry to hear that.
C: She's getting everywhere. In the grain of the table. In the folds of the bedsheet.
T: It must be very upsetting.
C: She's always at me.
T: The anger hasn't changed?
C: Look, damn it. Look at her. (The client produces a photograph depicting a young Japanese woman standing in front of a tower on a hilltop overlooking the ocean. The woman is quite close to the camera. Behind her, a straw hat is flying away.)
T: It's a very powerful photo.
C: Look, I said. Here. (The client comes to stand next to the seated therapist. She holds the photo in front of them both.)
T: And how long does it take for the image to change—
C: Shut up. Watch.
(Silence, one minute.)
C: See that?
T: I...I'm not sure.
C: You saw her blink.
T: I saw...something.
(Silence, twenty seconds. The therapist gasps. There is a heavy sound as the client drops to her knees.)

T: (Inarticulate gurgling sounds.) Dana! (Sounds of the therapist lifting the client's body onto a couch.) Client's eyes are open but aren't tracking me. Mouth is moving but no sound. Limbs are unresponsive. Pulse is fast and strong. (Fingers snap.) Dana. Dana. (Silence, thirty seconds.)

C: Uhhh.

T: Can you hear me?

C: Uhhh. Yes. You saw?

T: ...Yes.

C: What did you see? (Silence, twenty seconds.) What did you see?

T: Wounds opened up on her neck. There was...they bled a great deal.

C: Yes.

T: All right. All right. I understand...this must have been a very difficult week.

C: You understand.

T: Yes. No. May I tell you what else I saw?

C: What else is there?

T: She wasn't angry. (Silence.) She wasn't angry, Dana. I did not see anger in her expression.

C: What?

T: Let's look again. Do you think you can look again?

C: Again?

T: We'll only look for a few seconds. Do you think you can do that?

C: I...can try.

T: All right. (Brief silence.) What do you see?

C: My wife. She—

T: Yes?

C: Put it away. (Brief pause.) I saw my wife.

T: How did she look?

C: I didn't really...she was staring.

T: Yes?

C: At me.

T: Anything else?

C: Let me look again. (Brief silence.) Okay.

T: Did you see anything new?

C: Hurt. I think she looked hurt.

T: But not angry?

C: No.

T: Want to look again?

C: Yes. (A slightly longer silence.) She doesn't understand.

T: What doesn't she understand?

C: Why I would do it.

T: Do what?

C: Why it happened in the first place.

T: Yes?

C: There's no reason...let me look again. (A slightly longer silence.) Uh.

T: Yes?

C: I didn't...

T: What are you remembering right now?

C: I'm sorry. (Sounds of getting up.) I have to go. I can't...I'm done for today.

T: All right. All right.

C: I'm sorry. I didn't—I'm sorry.

(Session ends.)

Sophia sends her at least five emails a day, all begging. To write. To call. To visit. Is she okay? She needs Dana. Dana needs her. Please.

When she gets back from therapy, yet another email awaits.

> From: Misao Sacks
>
> To: Dana Sacks
>
> I know I can't take her place, but please, let me visit you. xoxoxo – Misao

In the long scroll of her inbox:

From: Misao Sacks
To: Dana Sacks
Let me know how you're doing. Please, Dana, don't
shut me out...

From: Misao Sacks
To: Dana Sacks
Dana, get help. I'm here for you.

From: Misao Sacks
To: Dana Sacks
Haven't heard from you in a while. Let me know if
there's anything I can do for you. xo – Misao

In the screen, Misao's face. Not angry.

She turns the photos to face the room. Opens the blinds. Takes the
oil painting out of the closet. Flips open the wedding album. Misao's
staring at her, hurt. She's hurt her so much, by not stopping it.

Back at the laptop, her fingers move swiftly over the keys. She tells
her where she's living. How to get there from the airport. Which are the
best side streets to take. She tells her about Indira the therapist, and the
photograph therapy, and how it's helped her. It's really helped her.

She tells her: **Please, hurry.**

A response: **I'm coming.**

The doorbell rings. Dana slouches over to answer it. Through the
screen door she sees Sophia, scraping her boot against the steps.

"It's muddy, isn't it, out here in the boondocks," she says, and then
she flings herself into Dana's arms and they stagger together as the screen
door bounces against her heels. "Oh Dana, I was so sorry to hear about
Misao." Dana swings her inside and shuts and bolts the front door. "I
didn't want it to be that way. I was happy, truly, really I was. But then it

happened and I didn't hear from you and you never wrote or called and it was just...it was terrible, wondering. How are you? Really, how are you?"

"Better," Dana says. Sophia leaves her coat and her boots by the door and Dana brings her to the living room. "The therapy's helped a lot."

"It hasn't even been that long, has it? Oh, that's wonderful. What were you doing again?"

Dana goes to the kitchen and places the cutting board and a loaf of sourdough on the counter. "Memory reconsolidation. The idea is that you have to retrieve the memory and let it hurt you before you can retrieve the memory and then change something a little so it doesn't hurt you."

Sophia laughs. "That sounds tricky."

Dana takes a kitchen knife from the drawer and slices into the bread. "Misao knew about us."

Sophia is very quiet.

She considers the bread, then leaves it in the kitchen, bringing only the knife with her into the living room. "I did it for you," she says and sits down next to her. Sophia is very quiet and very still and very, very pale. "Misao was a wonderful wife. She was. But she said...horrible things about you, and I thought, she's so jealous, she wants herself to be the only stable thing in my life. That all we can have is each other. I loved you too, Sophia, I loved you both. I couldn't stop seeing you just like that. It wouldn't be fair. I told Misao I had to see you again, to say goodbye."

Sophia can't stop staring at the knife. From their honeymoon on the mantelpiece, Misao stares at Dana.

Dana taps the knife on the back on the couch, a nervous tic. "We said some things. Both of us. I'd been making dinner, and I had the knife, and I just started stabbing. Once I got started, I couldn't...I couldn't stop. That poor man, he must have heard us, he broke in through the window. He was only trying to help." Tears gather in the corners of her eyes. "I really think I could've killed him. He didn't deserve what I did. That poor man. I hope they're treating him kindly. He shouldn't be punished for what I've done."

Sophia is trying to slide away, but the couch is old and squeaks an alarm under her weight. Dana flexes her wrist and the knife jumps to Sophia's throat.

"I'm not going to hurt you," she says. "That's part of the memory reconsolidation. I have to bring you here, like this, and not hurt you, like this, and that's breaking the cycle, you see? This is just therapy. If I can have you here," she brushes Sophia's neck with the flat of the blade, "like this, looking scared, like this, and bring back all those horrible memories and still not hurt you, then I'm cured. Aren't I? She'll stop staring at me from everywhere. I won't see those stab wounds in her neck."

Sophia says, "These stab wounds?"

And from out, out of her body flows red and red and red.

Dana leaps from the couch, a short sharp squeak. "No!"

"If you wanted to leave me, you could have just left me," says Sophia, whose voice is not her own. "I wouldn't die from divorce. Instead, your answer is to kill me?" She rolls her eyes. "Idiot. You think your life is better off without me in it? Then why don't you prove it?" She thumps her chest. "Go ahead! Such a brave heroine, what she does is for love!"

She can't stop herself. She jabs upwards with the knife, right under her sternum. It catches against something, a vertebra or some cartilage, and Dana has to plant her foot on her chest to yank it out.

The punctures on her neck close up, but the extra mouth in her breast keeps flapping its red wet tongues. Sophia slumps on the couch, her face shocked and only her own.

"Sophia?" Dana's voice, as uncertain as a chick's first flight. The knife drops, breadcrumbs sponging up the blood.

Sophia's fingers twitch.

"Misao," Dana whispers. "This was what you wanted?" She looks at her photos for her answer.

Misao's not there.

In Newfoundland, a straw hat has no owner. At the zoo, Dana is alone. As Sophia's breath rattles out of her chest, Dana grabs the wedding album from its carved memory box and flips through it.

Altar. Reception. Limo. Alone. Alone. Alone.

She brings her hands towards her face, one bloodied, one clean, both shaking as she starts to sob.

Before she can hide her face, her limbs stiffen and freeze, cold as death.

"I could be in you, too," says Misao with Dana's mouth. "But what kind of life would I have?"

And she's gone, the deadness inside Dana lifting, leaving her full of runny fluids and shame. She looks at Sophia, slouching lower and lower, gravity taking the place of her will. She looks at the photos, empty, and at the knife, red. Nonsense syllables burst from her throat as her stained hand fumbles for the handle.

Sophia's limp body melds with the couch, whose prolonged box spring screech harmonizes with her own last exhalations. Dana's cries are an ugly thing, an obvious, out-of-place thing. Someone might hear. Someone might come. She gulps air and looks at the clean white ceiling until her hands stop shaking.

It's so quiet now in the little rented bungalow. Dana promises herself she will be quiet, too. No one is going to break a window and stop her this time. She sets the knife edge against her throat.

The dead woman says, "I'll be waiting for you."

The sudden noise is startling and her hand twitches, the knife dropping with a clatter onto the floor, missing anything vital as it falls. She'd been ready, she'd been ready, how would she be ready again, that voice in her memory, hurting her, hurting?

Change your memory, she thinks. Take it out, let it hurt you, put it back; take it out, change it, just a little, change it, put it back; repeat, it gets better, it will heal.

Dana picks up the knife and lies on her back on the floor, out of sight of the windows, out of her mind. She holds the knife point-down, high above herself, and winces, and lets it fall.

Again.

Again.

Again.

# About the Author

Laura DeHaan (she/her is fine) is a nonbinary author and healthcare worker in Toronto, Canada. Her novelette, *Becoming Beast*, a queer genderbent retelling of "Beauty and the Beast" where the godmothers are dead and true love will not save you, is available through Grace & Victory (GraceandVictory.ca). For updates (sporadic), announcements (frequently late) and a full listing (this part is true) of her publications, visit her website, iaminyoureyebrain.com. You can also follow her on Twitter @WritInRooster, as long as you keep your expectations low and your amusement at Pagliacci jokes high.

# The Red Candle

Louis Stephenson

"I guess witches don't live forever after all." Mama shrugged painfully as she wheezed into her nebulizer. The little blue contraption buzzed and bubbled away like a miniature electric cauldron as it sat next to her on the bed.

The ailing woman lay propped up against four large pillows. Her long, wavy white hair clung to her pale, old face as it reached down past the shoulders of her bobbly, over-washed synthetic nightgown.

Her grandson Craig lit a match and held it up to the untouched wick of a thick, red candle. She raised the boy, now barely 13 years of age, as her own since the morning the devil that was cancer took her daughter to an early grave. To everyone else she was Helena, but he had always known her only as Mama.

"You're no witch, Mama," Craig said as he carefully placed the red candle inside the hollowed-out pumpkin on his grandmother's bedside cabinet. "That's just simple village talk. They'd eat the grass under their feet if you told 'em it was made a' sugar."

"Do you have my makeup, darlin'?" Mama brushed away the hair from her sweat-covered cheeks. "Gotta make myself look all nice and pretty for the coroner now, don't I?"

"Right here, Mama." Craig sat down on the bed next to her, clutching the makeup bag as he held back tears.

"Don'tcha cry now, honey." Mama patted him on the arm. "We both knew this day was gon' come."

"But I'm not ready," Craig whispered.

"Nonsense, of course you are." Mama crossed her arms. "You're a strong soul. Always have been. Now lipstick first, if you please."

Craig sighed as he swallowed back his sadness. He unzipped the makeup bag. "What color, Mama?"

There was no reply.

"Mama…?"

Her face looked frozen, as if time had stopped in its tracks. But as Craig could feel the breath burning inside his chest, he knew that this was not the case. Mama was gone.

"Oh, Mama…"

The boy slowly bowed his head. He felt the soul within him shrinking, like watching burning paper turn black and crumple up before it all fell to ashes.

Several moments passed before he could muster the strength to move again.

Instead of reaching for her hand, instead of surrendering to the need to make physical contact with her one last time, Craig carried the open makeup bag across the bedroom to Mama's vanity mirror. And there, with tears rolling down his trembling face, the boy began to apply his own lipstick.

When he finished, he looked himself over from all different angles. It was a perfect job.

"Hope you didn't keep that candle burnin' too long, darlin'," a voice said. "I left a little somethin' in there for ya."

Craig stumbled over to his Mama's bedside. But she lay there exactly as he had left her. There was nothing he could think to do but obey her last words, wherever they had come from.

Pulling the carved lid from atop the pumpkin, he reached inside and yanked out the red candle, the force of which extinguished the flame. Examining it, Craig carried it back over to the vanity mirror. Taking a breath, he slammed the candle off the edge of the dressing table. It split into two halves, revealing a folded piece of paper inside.

Unfolding the paper, Craig began to read.

The next morning before class, Craig dragged his best friend Stacey into the girls' bathroom.

"What the heck is with you?!" she yelled at him, beating away his grip. "Explain yourself, Craig Anderson!"

Stacey dropped her book bag to the tiled floor as it was tugging at the askew shoulder strap of her denim dungarees. She readjusted her dirty blonde hair with a hot pink hairband.

"You're still a virgin, right?" Craig asked intensely. "You haven't done it with Bobby yet, have you?"

"That is none of your damn business." Stacey scowled at him in her annoyance. "I thought you only liked boys, anyways."

"I do," Craig assured her, "and yes, it is my goddamn business. You're my best friend."

His words on their friendship calmed her a little. "Well, not that it matters, but yes, I am still a virgin. What's it to you?"

"Okay, I got a favor I need to ask of ya." Craig held her by the shoulders. "I'll give ya twenty bucks if you'll bite me as hard as you can."

"You serious? Twenty bucks?"

"Twenty bucks." Craig nodded as he let go of her and produced a twisted-up twenty-dollar bill.

"Sounds good to me." Stacey shrugged as she snatched the twenty and stuffed it into her bra. A belated pause. "Wait—why?"

"Because there is somethin' that I need to do." Craig popped open the top half of his flannel shirt, bearing his chest. "And in order to do that some*thing* I need some*one* to bite me." He pointed at the space where his heart would be. "Right here. Hard as you can."

"You are nuttier than a squirrel's nestin' hole."

"Just do it, tramp."

Offended, Stacey marched in, teeth bared.

As Craig had suspected, the bite barely broke the skin. He pushed her off. "Aw, come on! What was that?! I could get a nastier hickey from a ten-dollar whore!"

"Don't be such a butt-hole." Stacey growled. "I'm the only person in this whole damn world that'll talk to you, besides your own grand-mama, and you can't tell me you don't know that!"

Craig bowed his head, an apology ready to escape his sullen lips.

"You want a bite? I'll give you a bite." She damn near tackled him this time.

But it still wasn't good enough. Not even close. So he grabbed a chunk of that frizzy hair of hers and mashed her face into his chest.

She screamed into his flesh for him to let go but that only made him pull harder. He could hear her hair ripping out at the roots.

A hot, nasty wave of searing pain bloomed over his heart as Stacey administered the bite he had paid her for. And she bit deep.

"Gah! Shit! Fuck!" he yelped, stomping his foot.

Gasping, she stumbled away from him, uttering a thousand gargled curses as he released her, blood smeared across her nose and mouth.

Craig ignored her as he made his way over to one of the girls' mirrors. He produced a small plastic baggy and poured out what appeared to be some kind of ground-up plant. He began stuffing it into the gory bite mark on his chest, filling it up and smoothing it over.

"What the hell are you doin'?" Stacey managed to choke as she wiped away the blood on her face.

"Just a little somethin' my Mama done taught me." Craig replied, transfixed on the mirror as he held up the piece of paper found inside that red candle. "She gave it to me after she died. It's some kinda spell. I know it. It's gonna give me everything I always wanted."

Stacey picked up her book bag as she backed her way towards the door. "You're not right. You're not right. You've gone crazy. I don't think we can be friends anymore."

"That's okay, hun," Craig said as he continued to pat the mixture into the wound, "cuz I figure this'll be the last time you ever see me, anyways."

The girls' bathroom door squealed open as Stacey burst into tears and ran to class.

Craig arranged to meet his seventeen-year-old lover, Boyd, at the lookout point that night. It was situated up in the woods behind their tiny village, a popular spot for those who liked to get hot and heavy in secret. Except on that night, Halloween night, the place was deserted. Thanks to decades of cheesy slasher movies, it had seeped into the collective psyche that such settings are to be avoided at that particular time of the year.

The two boys sat side by side on the hood of Boyd's car as they lay back against the windshield. Together they gazed up at the stars.

"My God, it's so big tonight." Boyd marvelled.

"Tell me somethin' I don't know." Craig quipped as he reached for the belt on Boyd's jeans.

"Boy, get your mind outta the gutter!" Boyd swiped Craig's hand away. "I'm talkin' about that moon. I've never seen it like that before."

"Yeah, it sure is mighty pretty." Craig was looking at Boyd instead. He looked at him like it was the last time.

Boyd smirked confidently as he met Craig's gaze. Leaning in for a kiss, he stopped as he noticed something under the pale glow of the moonlight.

"Are you wearin' lipstick?"

Craig covered his puckered lips immediately.

"Craig, now I told you I'm not into that kinda thing." Boyd sat up straight on the hood. "I don't mind if other people do it. That's their choice. But I like my men to be men. How many times have I gotta tell you that?"

The car rocked as Craig rolled off the side of the hood onto his feet. The gravel of the small parking area crunched under his boots as he walked to the barrier edge.

Boyd slid down off the hood as he could hear his lover crying.

"Oh, Mama," Craig sobbed. "Why did you have to go and die? You were the only one that understood what was going on with me."

"The funeral's tomorrow, ain't it?" Boyd already knew the answer. He just didn't know what else to say.

"I can't face all those people. I can't." Craig sniffed loudly. "I know what they all think of me."

"There'll be people that loved your Mama. And you."

"They don't love me!" Craig yelled. "They just want a front row seat to my sorry little shit-show. I hate 'em. I hate 'em all. I probably hate 'em…even more than I hate myself."

Boyd reached out his arms. "Come here, baby."

Craig's shoulders shook as he wept his way back over to the car and into Boyd's loving embrace.

"I'm sorry." Boyd said comfortingly. "I don't mind a little lipstick now and again."

Craig laughed through his tears.

"At least as you kept your hair short," Boyd joked as he ran his fingers through Craig's spikey, red hair.

Boyd drew in a sharp breath as Craig's head snapped around in the direction of the bushes.

"Did you hear that?"

"You scared me." Boyd hit him lightly across the chest.

"Ah!" Craig winced in pain as he stepped away, still staring into the thick shadows of the woods that surrounded them. "I'm serious. Didn't you hear that?"

"No."

"Well, I heard somethin'."

"Oh, you didn't hear a thing. So just—" Boyd stopped as he squinted at the mark on Craig's shirt. "Baby, are you bleedin'?"

"I ain't bleedin'."

"Yes, you are. What have you been doin' to yourself?"

"It ain't nothin'." Craig muttered as he marched around the side of Boyd's car and stuck his arm in through the open window.

"Now what are you doin'?" Boyd stood behind him with crossed arms.

"I'm goin' to have a look in the woods," Craig replied as he retrieved a torch from Boyd's glove compartment. He flicked it on and off to check if it was in working order before marching towards the treeline. "My Mama just died, so I am not in the mood for any crap tonight!"

"Baby, come back here and sit on the car with me," Boyd pleaded as he patted the hood.

"Don't you worry yourself," Craig called back as he entered the shadows. "This won't take long."

Sighing, Boyd lay against the windshield on the hood of his car alone as he watched the night sky in silence. It had only been a few minutes since Craig had disappeared into the woods in search of his phantom noise, but Boyd had already given up waiting.

And then, clear as a bell, he heard the crunching of gravel underfoot as someone returned to the parking area of the lookout point.

"You know I nearly called the damn Sheriff on you," Boyd said without turning his head. "Runnin' off in them woods like the dumbass that you are."

There was no response, only more footsteps. They were getting closer.

"The full moon won't be with us much longer," Boyd carried on. "It's movin' slow, but I reckon that cloud there is gonna cover it up real soon."

"Then I guess we better get started."

Craig suddenly appeared by Boyd's side, covered in dirt and clutching a spade.

Boyd turned to him just as he brought the spade down hard. The car shook a little as Boyd's head bounced off the windshield before he fell quiet. He was out cold.

The moments of fractured consciousness that followed flashed through Boyd's mind like a waking nightmare. He lay sprawled across the roof of his car. Each limb was bound to one of the vehicle's four doors by leather straps.

His head swam as a naked Craig kneeled over him, cutting away.

"Craig…?" Boyd managed a whisper.

Craig paused.

"Not for much longer," he said breathily as he rallied his strength.

Splashes of blood speckled his face as he gritted his teeth in a glaring red grin. He continued sawing harder and harder, faster and faster as he spoke. "I been prayin' for this ever since I was a lil' 'un. You see, I was different from all the other boys. I knew it. And Mama knew it, too."

Boyd felt his pelvis buck as something below the waist finally tore away.

"All she ever wanted in this life was to see me happy."

Darkness followed.

The car rocked, awakening Boyd again as Craig leapt off the hood onto the gravel floor. Somehow, he managed the strength to prop himself high enough off the car to watch his lover as he stood as bare as the day he was born under the moonlight.

Craig raised his arms high, a bloodied dagger in one hand and a drooping, dripping roll of meat in the other. Holding Boyd's severed penis over his head, he squeezed it with all his might. Thick, slimy dollops of blood rained down on his face and trickled down his neck.

*"My heart's one true desire..."* he whispered to the moon as he tossed the blade aside and touched the bite mark on his chest.

The mark began to sizzle and glow.

With a deafening pounding inside his head, Craig shrieked into the night sky as every cell on his body began to burn. Dropping his boyfriend's crushed cock to the gravel, he clutched at his throat as his screams' pitch rose to ear-splitting heights. The outward jut of his Adam's apple sank soundly into his neck like a whale disappearing below the water's surface, back down to the crushing dark of oceans deep.

His knees shook violently, their caps rattling like dice as they braced against the agony of stretching bones and contracting muscles. Hips expanding. Shoulders narrowing. Sweat running and nerves searing.

He bucked forward with a sickening squelch as two bubbles of flesh bulged out of his chest like a pair of living cysts. They quivered and wavered like lava lamps as each one sprouted a bloodied nipple.

Last of all, his own manhood withered like a dying branch. As it broke free, a string of translucent gunk lowered it to the ground where it began to rot and decay until it was nothing more than a putrid puddle of sludge and melted skin.

By this point, Boyd had lost too much blood to comprehend what was happening before him. But just before he drifted away, he was almost certain that he saw the hair on Craig's head grow down past his shoulders into long, beautiful fiery locks.

In Boyd's last moments of life, he watched from beneath a crushing mound of dirt as a naked woman drenched in blood buried him alive.

Before the earth began to fill his sockets, Boyd finally saw his former lover as the beautiful being she truly was and always had been. And if he'd had the strength during his dying breath, he would have smiled.

# About the Author

Louis Stephenson resides in the North-West of England, and he came out as gay to his friends and family when he was sixteen years old. He is a dedicated lover of horror films: the first queer horror movie he ever saw was *Hellbent*. This anthology also marks his first venture into writing queer horror. Louis has worked with Dark Ink previously as a writer for 2018's *Ghosts, Goblins, Murder, & Madness* and last year's *Shadowy Natures*. With any luck, he hopes to have a small family one day. Until then, he has a beautiful bunch of three nieces and two nephews to keep him overjoyed.

# Razor, Knife

Elin Olausson

She calls me Twiggy, and I call her Bell. We're cousins, but everyone thinks we're twins. We share a birthday, but her mom's in jail and mine's dead. That's all you need to know about us.

Bell's thoughts are toxic green, they twist around mine like phantom limbs. My thoughts, she says, are violet. Like stormy skies or a bruised wrist. We sit on the porch as the moving van drives by, neither of us speaking. We don't have to. Rex scuttles between us and the gate, tail beating. He's Aunt Gin's favorite, the one dog allowed inside the house. Big and dumb, but I let him into my bed sometimes. After Bell has gone to sleep and won't notice.

"Shut up that damn dog!" Aunt Gin calls from the backyard. She's burning trash, there's that nauseating smell in the air of charred plastic. Bell picks up a pebble and aims it at Rex, but the lawn swallows it.

"Be quiet, stupid." Her voice is flat, she hardly ever uses it in school. I've heard people call her the Mute.

"He's not ours," I say. "Let her deal with him herself." We lean our chins in our bloodless hands, hair like sand and ashes falling into our eyes. Bell is as flat-chested as I am, I'm short like her. If it weren't for our clothes, no one would guess one of us was a girl and the other a boy. Another car drives past, a white sedan, three people in it. Aunt Gin has told us that the priest moving into the vicarage is married, but we haven't heard anything about children. Bell's eyes sting my face and I bury my violet thoughts out of her sight. We don't care about other people. We don't need them.

Still, we sneak to the vicarage that evening and crouch in our old hiding place by the hedge. The moving van has left but there are boxes piled up on the porch. All the windows are open, there's classical music coming from inside. We know Wagner, because Aunt Gin likes him. We don't know these silky piano whispers.

*I bet he's a freak*, Bell thinks. *Priests are always freaks.*

I pinch her bony little hand, and she pinches back. Her nails are scissor-sharp.

*We should do a pagan ritual in their garden. Sacrifice something tiny.*

Sometimes I don't know if the words coursing through my mind are hers or mine. Sometimes I know all too well.

"Let's go to the altar," I hiss. "This is boring."

A boy comes out of the house. He's in shorts and a tank top, barefoot, tan. He scans the garden before grabbing two boxes. They hide his chest, neck, face, but not his hands. They're veiny like a man's. I glance down at my child-fingers, then look away.

"Jock," Bell says once the boy has gone inside. "I smell it from a mile away." Me and Bell, we don't approve of jocks. They're high up on our list.

I force his hands from my brain. "Come on, let's go."

Bell stands, brushing grass and imaginary beetles from her skirt. The cotton has been washed so many times that there's barely any pattern left, but I remember when it was strewn with lilies. Most of our clothes are like that. Tattered and torn, with memories attached.

The altar is our home. It's where we come to be ourselves. No one walks as far into the woods as we do—most places around here are uninhabited, and all the neighbors are Aunt Gin's age or older. They stagger to the mailbox and then back inside. They don't see the paths we make at the back of their gardens. They don't notice the sparkles we leave behind.

We built the altar out of stones, in a clearing halfway up the hill behind the cow field. The deer skull came later—we found the deer close by the clearing, long dead, and we went home to get the wood-axe and Aunt Gin's hunting knife. Flies swarmed up when we sawed the head off, crawling around our ears and nostrils. Bell yelped when the head rolled away and maggots spilled out on the moss. She'd never admit it, but she did.

The skull is beautiful now, clean and raw with no flesh clinging to it. The antlers spread out like the wings of an eagle. In a way, I'd like it if someone came by and discovered this place. I'd like them to fear us and wonder. But then they might discover the list, and we can't have that. The list is for me and Bell only.

It's hidden under a stone in front of the altar, wrapped in a plastic bag. We hold our breaths as we lift the stone and seize it.

THE DEATH LIST

Blood on lined notepad paper. I've got a Swiss army knife in my pocket, Bell has a pink razor. It gets messy, every time we add someone to the list, but we don't mind a mess.

PONYTAILS

Ponytails are the popular girls in school. Most of them are called Jessica, but our name is better. I don't hate them like Bell does. I just don't care whether they live or not.

JOCKS

Some things don't need an explanation. My thoughts brush against tan skin, veiny hands, and I slice through them until they're dripping.

MRS. LINDEN

The English teacher with her cow eyes and tilted head, her too many questions. Once, she asked me whether I wanted to "talk to someone."

~~REX~~

Bell's written it, I've scratched it out. That's the difference between me and her. I believe death lists are for people.

MOMS

Because they left us. Because if Mom hadn't died, I'd still be living with her in the city, and I'd be a different person.

"We should put him on there," Bell says. She stands so close that I can smell her—that familiar blend of dog stink and cheap fabric softener. "The boy in the vicarage."

"We don't even know his name." People like him could be called anything. Anything would suit them.

"We'll find out." Bell fidgets with something in her skirt pocket. The razor. "And then we'll write it down right here." She taps the paper twice.

"Right here," I echo, only to camouflage the violet stirrings in my head.

*Can he die and still be my friend?*

We return to the house with the night chill and the shadows. Aunt Gin doesn't care what time we get home, as long as we do our chores. Rex knows she'll be mad if he barks, so he trots into the hall and whimpers quietly.

"Whatever you want, you're not getting it," Bell mutters. She slinks up the stairs, her long legs white as milk. They remind me of a pair of blindworms we saw once in the woods, thin and lightning-fast. Bell is always quicker than I am.

"Tommy, you remember the door?" Aunt Gin shouts over the TV noise.

"Yeah," I call as I reach out to lock it. This is how our conversations go—she tells us to do something, and we do it. The only reason Aunt Gin isn't on the death list is because she's better than foster care. For now.

Bell has shut her door when I come upstairs. Whenever she's alone, she writes in her diary, a book I've never seen and have no idea where she keeps. *Some things are just for me*, she said that one time when she told me about it. *And if you peek, I won't like you anymore.*

I don't want to read her scribbles. I know Bell inside and out, her green wires. I've seen her dig the razor into her skin, and the look on her face when she does it.

There are other things I want to know. His name, his age. If he's going to stay, and what his hands would feel like on top of my own. I used to be the only boy in the world, but now there's two of us, one broken and one brand new. I have no book to put my wishes in, no hiding place safe enough. Only a short while at the end of the day, when my thoughts are all mine.

We have no tombs to visit at the graveyard, but we go there anyway. It's our favorite place besides the altar. Bell balances on the stone wall, arms spread out like birdwings. I hum funeral psalm fragments as I scan the inscriptions. Most of them are boring, old couples who lived forever and died in peace. We want the young. The deaths wrapped in velvet, laced with heartbreak. The ones with tragedy and crushed dreams mixed into the soil.

"*Her golden curls turned to hay,*" Bell chants in her graveyard voice, like a girl-priest in a faded sundress. "*Her blue eyes dead, hollows gaping in their place.*" She curses as an old woman walks through the gates carrying a bunch of roses. "Don't people have anything better to do?"

"She should leave soon." Our eyes follow the woman as she grabs a vase, fills it with water and finds her grave. We watch her arrange the flowers and clean away some withered lilies. She knows we're there, the knowledge is in her jerky movements and downcast eyes. Our stares don't leave her until she's gone back to her little car and driven away.

Bell jumps off the wall, cat-smooth and quiet. Her barrette has slid to the side, and she pushes it in place. It's plastic, bright red, cheap like everything we own. She's worn it since we were six. Her thoughts swirl like December snow, I can barely catch them. They are dead girls with grinning skulls and green ribbons in their hair, but I don't know what they're saying.

"To the new ones," she says, skipping along the path, waving for me to follow. There's a corner of the graveyard that's only been in use for five years, with plenty of space left between the rows of stones. We like the graves there because the stories require no digging. A thirty-year-old, dead two years ago—we can find out what he looked like and what he was like and what he died of. I think the old graves are more romantic, but Bell craves family photos and Facebook profiles. I once saw her print a photo of a dead boy from one of the school computers.

We've almost reached the wall separating the old cemetery from the new one, when she stops with a hiss. I notice him a moment after she does. The new vicar's son. He's perched up on the wall, shadowed by the oak-trees on the other side. Crouching at an awkward angle, face turned upwards, which makes no sense until I spot the camera in his hand.

*Come,* Bell shoots at me. The command drives through my mind like a syringe. *We don't want to go near him.*

"Hey!" He's noticed us. He hangs the camera over his shoulder, then jumps to the ground. Bell was a cat but he is a tiger, all power and flexing muscles. "Do you live around here?"

*Don't answer.* He's everything we don't like. His grin tells stories of Mom's apple pie and soccer games with Dad. His sneakers are stark white, they lap up the sunlight. And he's in clothes that fit him, not outdated hand-me-downs left by his dead mother.

He's so beautiful that my black heart twitches.

"You do, right?" A crease appears between his eyebrows. I'd like to smoothen it with my thumb. "I saw you come through the gate before. Figured you live close by."

Bell takes a step toward me. Her fingertips brush my forearm, cool and damp. Bell, the Mute.

"What if we do?" I say. "We've got as much right to be here as you do."

"Yeah, of course!" He fidgets with his camera, strokes the controls and shiny buttons. It looks new and complicated, just like him. "I just meant that, you know, it's nice to see some people my own age. Hadn't expected that when we moved here."

I wonder where he's come from. Where he's been up until now.

"I'm Martin," he says, holding his hand out. I'm a moth, glued to those long fingers. I want to reach out, clasp, touch, but there's Bell and Bell's eyes and her toxic warnings in my head.

"Tommy." Technically, I'm not telling him it's my name. Bell is mad at me, I feel her wrath like wasp stings under my skin. "She's Bell."

"Nice to meet you." He drops his hand. There's a pause in which anything might happen but doesn't. "Um, I... I couldn't get a picture of the two of you? Sorry if it's a weird question, it's just that it would make such a cool photo. Twins in the graveyard. You guys are twins, right?"

"Sure." I smile at him for the first time. My skin stretches awkwardly around chapped lips. I want to tell him that I wasn't always like this. If only Mom hadn't died, I would have lived in the city and I wouldn't have been stuck with Bell.

"So, can I snap a photo? Just one?" He grabs the camera, removing the lens cap. The lens is like a huge all-seeing eye, eager to expose our secrets.

"No," I say, staring at myself through that hungry eyeball, seeing nothing. Nothing anyone like him could want. "We have to get home."

"Oh, okay. Some other time, then."

Bell starts walking before I do, her red ballerinas hitting the ground. I don't catch up with her until we're at the edge of the cemetery.

"What an idiot," I say, making my voice light as air. "Right?"

Her shoulders are drawn up, sharp-angled and tense. The green oozes out of her. She doesn't speak until we're past the hill and Aunt Gin's house closes in on us.

"Now we know his name," Bell says, her whisper-voice like dripping icicles. "Now he goes on the list."

Altar, razor, knife. Martin's name bleeds onto the paper, finger-thick letters crossing the lines. Bell hums something, I don't know what. I have no music in me.

"Because we don't like him," Bell says once the list has gone back in its hiding place. "Because he thinks we're freaks." She drags her fingertip across the deer skull, blood streaming toward the eye sockets. War paint. "No one can think that. No one but us."

I recall the first time I met her, by Mom's hospital bed. Bell came with Aunt Gin and a social worker. *Here's your cousin Isabella. Won't it be nice to have someone to play with?* Bell said nothing. She was weird and tiny, and her milk teeth left angry red marks on my skin. I knew that Mom would die. And I'd have no one but Bell for the rest of my life.

Aunt Gin's booming voice comes to find us the next morning, while we're on cleaning duty in the kennel. The dogs tumble around us, all German shepherds, starving for attention and warmth and whatever dogs need. Bell hates their long hanging tongues and tells them as much. When Aunt Gin calls, the dogs stop moving, eyes fixed on the open backdoor, and Bell smothers her skirt with a grimace.

"Kids, come here! You've got a visitor."

It's Martin. He's on the porch, petting Rex, who skips this way and that with his tail wagging. Aunt Gin has gone back to the TV.

"Oh, hi." Martin grins, scratching Rex behind his ear. "Sorry to barge in like this, I hope you guys weren't busy?"

We shrug, my scrawny shoulders mimicking hers, Bell mirroring me.

"Just thought I'd come by, see if this was where you lived. Didn't know you had a dog. What's his name?"

*Bell writing Rex's name on the list. Me, cutting myself just to be able to undo it.*

"Rex," I say, knowing I'm breaking the rules one by one. Bell doesn't want Martin here, so I shouldn't want him here, but I do. His t-shirt clings to him in the way t-shirts are supposed to, not because he's outgrown it. The print on it says *BE PROUD* in violet letters.

"Invite him in, for God's sake," Aunt Gin shouts. "Show him your rooms or something."

We walk the stairs, Rex tagging along. Bell's door is closed and stays closed. I open mine and let Martin into my room, which is really just a closet with a slanted ceiling. Rex darts to the bed and lies down by my pillow, but Bell stays in the doorway. Her thoughts are too quiet for me to hear, or perhaps too loud.

"Very cozy," Martin says, and I know he's lying and I regret taking him here. The ceiling lamp is broken in my room and there's a sour smell seeping out of the walls. Martin probably has new furniture and an expensive computer and a phone that wasn't stolen. His brain isn't twisted like mine and he's got parents. I watch his symmetric face, all straight lines and glowing skin, and I want to stroke it and tear it to pieces.

"Tommy, right?" He looks at me, his scissors coming for the stitches that hold me together. "Your name?"

Before I answer, Bell steps into the room, shaking her head. "He's called Twiggy. *A little boy with twigs for legs, and a girl with a bell around her neck.*" She laughs, and I hate her.

"Is that from a song or something?" Martin asks me, not Bell. Because he likes me? Because I'm the least freaky one?

"Oh, yeah," I lie. I want to be alone with him. I want to scratch his name off the list and carve it into my chest.

"Well, I should head back home. Promised Mom to help unpack a few more boxes." He makes a face. A face as pretty as the rest of them. "But we can hang out sometime, yeah? I don't know anything about this place. Would be great if you wanted to show me around."

As if there's anything to see except cows and dung and dirt roads. As if someone like him will want anything to do with us once school starts in September and he gets to know other people.

"Sure," Bell says. There's that laugh again, and I remember her smearing the deer skull with blood. "We want that very much. Let's be friends." Once he's left, she sneaks up behind me and forces her bony hand into mine.

*You don't need any other friends, little Twiggy. You have me.*

Martin with his suntan and chestnut hair, his two living parents. I've locked him in a drawer inside my head and I only take him out at night, when Bell is busy with her diary. We never spy outside the vicarage, we never do anything to seek him out. He comes looking for us, always with that camera over his shoulder, always smiling.

"What do you guys do in the summer?" he asks in the backyard, while the dogs push themselves against the kennel fence and howl at him. Rex is circling around us, licking Martin's hands whenever he gets close enough. Martin's fingers glisten and he laughs, and I exchange looks with Bell that I hope he doesn't notice.

"There's nothing to do here," I say, shooing Rex away. "Obviously."

"But there has to be a lake nearby, right? We could go swimming. Do you have bikes?"

Bell scoffs, but doesn't say anything. Her dress is too short, the scar high up on her thigh shows. Not that Bell cares about things showing.

"No. No." I tilt my head as if Martin is the pathetic one. "Swimming is for kids. But if you really want to do something with us..." I pause. My brain reaches out for Bell, but all it finds is anticipation buzzing in the air around her. She leaves this decision up to me. She wants to see what I will do.

"Let's meet up at the graveyard at midnight. If you've got what it takes, that is."

"Oh. Okay, sure. Might be able to get some good pictures." His voice is light, I don't know if he's scared or not. He's too shiny for me to read. "See you tonight, then."

The kennel racket doesn't die down until he's left the backyard. Rex slips into the house, dragging his tail behind him. If I were a dog, I'd do the same.

"What's going to happen to Martin at midnight?" Bell murmurs, toying with the razor in her pocket.

"Who knows?" I say, pushing my whole weight against that drawer. Turning the key.

We get there first, our four feet tiptoeing past the parking lot, through the open gate. Martin comes five minutes later, carrying a chunky flashlight that stings our eyes.

"So," he says, too chipper for midnight, too sensibly dressed in a hoodie and jeans. We're in the same clothes as always, bare-legged, cold. Neither of us has ever had a tan, and mosquitoes don't bite us. Mrs. Linden once told me I need to go out more and get some sun. It's one of many reasons she's on the list.

"So," Martin says again, lower now. There's a glint of something in his eyes. Something newborn and vulnerable. "What are we doing?"

Bell murmurs in my ear, but the only word I can make out is *him*.

"We spend some time with the dead." I can't look into his face so I watch the curve of his shoulder instead. It's big and broad and everything else that I'm not. "If you dare."

"Yeah. I'm not scared of ghosts." His smile underlines the words, shows he's not lying. "Are you?"

I shake my head. Bell's thoughts worm themselves into my head, uninvited but always there. *We're not scared of anything. We're scary.*

"Let's go." For a moment I'm in an alternate universe where it's just me and Martin in the middle of the night. But even in that universe, Bell is there, right outside the frame, watching. Waiting. She's quiet when he's around, none of the usual chanting. But I hear her sad-girl poetry in my head, eerie whispers about blood-specked handkerchiefs and hangings. Martin snaps pictures here, there. The flash perches on top of the camera like a gargoyle, spewing light. His day-world seeps into ours, brightening the gloom with flares and talking.

"This is really cool. Thanks for bringing me here." He talks about developing the photos; he'd been using the darkroom at his old school, but his dad is going to help him set one up in the basement. "It's a bit old-fashioned, I know, but I like it. You've got no idea what anything's going to look like until you're in the darkroom. You don't even know if you'll have any decent shots at all." He runs the flashlight over the graves we pass, murmuring the names to himself before crouching to snap a photo. Bell brings her arms out, swaying ahead of us like a tightrope walker. The shadows swallow her whenever the flashlight isn't pointed forward.

*I want to climb the tower*, she hisses without sound, and her hands reach into the star-heavy sky. *I want to be up there and look down at everyone.* The church tower reaches for the stars just like her, never-sleeping, lit up by spotlights in the dark hours. I imagine Bell up there, but I don't know if she's the locked-up princess, or the witch.

*Not now.* I glance at Martin, at his shifting light. My thoughts sink back into the fairytale and he's the prince pulling himself up, his hands running through golden hair. Gripping hard.

Bell spins around, a ghostly shape splitting the darkness, rearranging the pieces. Her head is crammed with singing and her fist slips into the razor pocket.

"Can't I get one of you two? You didn't let me that other time." Martin stops, flashlight hanging from his wrist, camera ready. "Please. It would make a really nice picture."

We don't want it. But Bell's eyes can't do much talking in the dark and I'm held back by fingers that aren't there, fingers grabbing my hair. I step forward and she flutters back and the flash blinds us.

"Perfect," Martin says. "Thanks."

I know it's not perfect, and nothing to be grateful for. That sliver of us locked in the camera, dark where we are supposed to be light, light where we are supposed to be dark. Two broken, twisted shadows leaning toward each other in an endless white night.

The storm comes in the dead hours, after Bell has put away her diary and I've slipped from Martin-thoughts to sticky Martin-dreams. Our sleep is shadowless and heavy, and we never see the monstrous clouds or hear their roaring. When we come down in the morning, the air is clear and thin as if something has died and been born again, and Aunt Gin barks from the TV room.

"Damn weather last night. Neighbor came by, said the church was struck by lightning."

Bell shows her teeth, laughs without sound. But her giggles fill my head, *hee-hee-hee*, sharp and sweet like rotting fruit. Her eyes pin mine down and when Rex trots into the kitchen, I don't reach out to pet him. Bell stirs her muddy tea, wormwood-bitter and scorching. Shameful secrets whirl and waltz in her stare.

"God is a poor little girl," she says, the spoon whining against the cup's brim. "God is a boy made out of sticks."

We slink away from our chores once Aunt Gin has dozed off, following the road up the hill and past the vicarage. The church parking lot is packed, cars blocking each other, old men grouped together like wrinkly children on the first day of school. Bell hisses a string of curses, sliding in behind a toolshed, squeezing herself past a hedge while I follow, dog-like. Her mind glows, flares.

*Fucking idiots. Just because this is the first exciting thing that's ever happened around here.*

We move like water, trickling, away from people. Our eyes seek the church, the gaping hole in the tower. A tear in bone-colored silk, a missing tooth in an angel's mouth.

*I want to get closer*, we think, green and violet, violet and green. *I want to see everything.*

"Hey, wait up!" Martin. He comes jogging after us, tousled hair, pet eyes. "I thought you might be here. Can you believe this happened? Dad is freaking out."

Something twirls in my chest so I have to strangle it and make my voice mean. "Why? 'Cause he thinks it's divine punishment?"

He laughs. Whatever it was that I just killed stirs to life again. "Yeah, right! He's starting to realize what the repairs will cost, more like."

Bell lurks behind me, anemic, writhing. Her anger scratches my neck like nails, like the blade of a razor.

"Listen," I tell Martin, gathering broken green wires, hoping to mend them. "You wouldn't happen to know where the tower key is, would you?"

"The church tower?" He watches me warily, tension sharpening the lines of his face. "Why?"

"*Two little boys went out to play,*" Bell sings, voice distorted by a childish lisp. "*Snip, snap, snow hid the corpses away.*"

"Don't you want to see what it's like up there?" *Grab my hair and pull.* "Come on, bring the key and meet us at the gate by midnight. You might get some good photos."

It's forever until he nods. His smile has faded. I'm not sure if I'm going to see it again. "Okay. As long as no one finds out."

*Oh, Martin. We'll be sure to leave no traces.*

He's at the gate when we get there. Camera in one hand, key in the other.

"Don't touch anything," he says once we're past the church porch and the entrance door. "You'd better not get me in trouble."

Bell's thoughts dance around mine, electric. Magnified.

The church air is stale and heavy, paper-dry. Martin has left the flashlight at home and none of us have brought our phones. Bell skips up the tower stairs first, weightless, humming. I go after her, and Martin last, shutting the whiny door. The darkness eats at us, swallowing our limbs and clothing until we're invisible. Step after step after creaking step, the walls brushing against us from both sides. Bell sings, but I can't make out the words over the wailing in my head.

The tower isn't fit for neither princesses nor witches. Murky walls, heaping dust, and nothing to see except for the bell. We press our backs to the walls to get past it, around it. Bell's giggles crawl under my skin like maggots. Martin stands by the lightning-hole, his breaths hard and shallow. I picture myself beside him and our hands touching, merging. I picture many things, violet-laced, pure.

*Not for you,* Bell whispers, teeth sinking into my hesitation. *Not for us, Twiggy.*

Would it make you feel better if I cried? If I didn't just walk up to him and tap his back?

"Martin. What's your favorite flower?"

He spins around. The world shifts, turns as sweet and minty as his toothpaste-breath. I know what's about to happen, and that's the only reason I dare to place my hands on his chest. He's warm, with a drumming heart and blood rushing in all directions under my fingertips.

"Flower?" The spotlights from outside wash over me, blinding, slicing through. I can't see him. Only a shadowed hole where his face used to be. "Carnations, but why are you—"

*Push.* Easy and not easy at all. His scream is a yelp, a distant cry. Bell stands by my side when he hits the asphalt. Her fingers curl around mine, cold, burning.

"And we leave," she says, her voice a songbird's. "We depart this world and become angels."

Outside the church he lies, skull crushed, a game of jack straws. His hand rests against his chest, still warm, veins rising. I swallow and swallow while Bell looks for the camera. It's landed by a nearby tomb, cracked apart just like Martin's head. Bell grabs the film roll with the picture of us, the one picture. When we reach our altar, we dig with our little hands, dig a tiny grave in front of the deer skull. The film roll slides into the ground and dies, and our inverted shadows die with it.

Bell forces her thoughts at me as we walk back home. *He sleeps. He would have left us but now he's ours forever.*

I lock my own thoughts away from her. *Carnations, but why are you—Push.*

There's a bus going to town once a day. Aunt Gin doesn't know about the money I take from her purse, and she doesn't see me leave. I come back in the evening with flowers wrapped in hissing paper. At midnight I head to the graveyard.

His grave is the newest, strewn with lights and flowers. No one thinks his death was anything but an accident. We've heard that his mom is in a home somewhere, his dad doesn't leave the house. But Martin is right here.

I lay the carnations down—I'm the only one who's brought him carnations, because I'm the only one who really knew him.

I lie down on the night soil, in a sea of flowers. My fingers dig down, bury, bury deeper. I reach my hand out for him, fist sinking into the ground, wrist, forearm.

*Grab me and pull.*

And he does.

# About the Author

Elin Olausson writes psychological horror and weird fiction. Her works have appeared in anthologies by Dark Ink Publishing, Belladonna Publishing, and others. When she's not writing, Elin works as a librarian. She lives in Sweden. Visit her website, ElinOlausson.com, and follow her on Twitter @elin_writes.

# The Procedure
Daniel M. Jaffe

"In my eye?" asks Harry through the gray cloth mask covering nose and mouth. "You want to stick a needle in my left eye?"

"I know it's scary," says Dr. Thelma as she adjusts her blue paper surgical mask. "But I'll put in numbing drops first." She rests a latex-gloved hand on his upper arm. "You won't feel a thing."

"No injections in my eye. Period."

"Not an injection. An extraction. Just a bit of fluid. Not enough to miss. If you'd prefer, I could sedate you, but I'd rather not. Further sedation while you're in recovery from coma is not advisable."

"I'm not risking my vision for anything."

"I assure you—there'd be no risk of adverse effect whatsoever on your vision. None." He folds his arms and glares.

"You're being rather petulant for a 35-year-old man."

He shakes his shaggy blond head.

Dr. Thelma slips clenched fists into the pockets of her white smock. "I'm trying to show respect here, Harry, requesting your consent and cooperation. But the bottom line is that you have no choice. We won't release you until we extract fluid from your eye."

"You've no right!"

"I've every right. The President has signed an Executive Order as part of the Covid-35 State of Emergency. And I don't mean a general Executive Order concerning all patients. I mean an order regarding you, in particular."

"The President signed an Executive Order about me?"

"I don't tell you this to exert pressure, just to emphasize your importance. I want you to *want* to help us, Harry. Let me step out of the room for a few minutes and give you time to think. Consider, Harry: after all we've done for you, don't you owe us? Just a few drops, for research. Think about that." She leaves his hospital room, shutting the white door behind.

Is she right? That he owes them? The truth is, they've been treating him for—what? three months now? Not that he can recall the first two months here. The last thing he remembers is falling ill in his studio apartment. A typical evening, kicking back naked on the gray sofa bed watching the floor-to-ceiling telescreen, participating in one of the UN's international online Zoom orgies. He'd entered a site he hadn't played in before, the Uzbek Bears Over Thirty orgy room. He was enjoying all the guys showing off their big brown hairy chests, tweaking their nips. Then he received an invitation to a private screen play session. Harry, pale and wiry without any chest hair at all, was flattered.

That thick-muscled mustachioed guy had the most gorgeous deep brown eyes Harry'd ever seen, the perfect contrast to Harry's baby blues. Harry couldn't get enough of those deep brown eyes. And boy, did that guy know it—winking, seductively batting his thick black lashes, widening his eyes, narrowing them. Harry felt himself practically falling into those gorgeous eyes. But then he started to feel dizzy, gradually began to swoon, his vision tunneling narrower and narrower. Something was wrong.

Wanting to get a glass of water from his kitchenette, he stood from the gray sofa bed. The room swirled. Just as he lost his balance, he cried out to the telescreen, "Call 911—I'm fainting. Unlock front door." He collapsed onto his carpeted floor.

The next thing he knew, two months later, he woke up in this white hospital room. A masked, gray-haired doctor was looking down at him, the wrinkles by her eyes and on her forehead crinkling in smile. Dr. Thelma.

A month of daily physical therapy ensued, and a constant web of intravenous drips. Endless counseling sessions. All for free from the National Covid Response Fund.

Shit, he thinks now. Shit.

Dr. Thelma steps back in. "Have you given the matter some thought, Harry?"

He nods, sullen. "Okay, so I owe you. But why the hell did the President get involved?"

She sighs. "I haven't wanted to cause you alarm, Harry. But maybe you'd feel better about the procedure if you knew: you're the only gay man in the U.S. to survive Covid-35."

Harry feels the color drain from his generally pale face. "What do you mean, I'm the only gay man to survive the virus? That's insane." What about his friends, his dozens of friends? "Are you telling me there are no more gay men in the U.S.? That I'm the only one left?"

"No no no, that's not what I'm saying. I'm so sorry. I didn't phrase my statement correctly. We're participating in both national and international systems of contact tracing, so we know who's tested positive and who hasn't, who's survived and who hasn't, although obtaining information from certain countries is much slower than one would like. Anyway, many gay men are still alive—those who have not yet contracted Covid-35. But every single gay man in this country who's actually contracted Covid-35—everyone except you—has died. Other countries are experiencing similar mortality patterns. Only you and a handful of other gay men around the globe have survived the virus. We're talking millions of gay male deaths so far, Harry, millions. That's why the President signed his Executive Order. That's why we need to study your eye fluid, in particular. You're the greatest hope for gay men in this country."

Harry shuts his eyes, tries to absorb all this. "So you're saying the newest Covid mutation is targeting gay men."

"I wouldn't say 'targeting.' 'Targeting' implies a consciousness absent from what is basically a strand of protein in a lipid envelope. For over fifteen years now, each Covid mutation has presented differently and affected certain groups more harshly than others—one year men, another year women, one year Anglos, another year Latinos, and so forth. This year's mutation seems to replicate with especial speed and to be particularly virulent in men carrying a long variation of the chromosomal marker tied to male homosexuality, the Xq28 marker. Your Xq28 marker is the longest we've encountered."

He gives a dark chuckle, restrains himself from making a bad joke about having the longest…something.

"Let me clarify further," continues Dr. Thelma. "Women seem unable to contract Covid-35, only men. But whereas one hundred percent of heterosexual men recover, and fifty percent of bisexual men recover, almost no gay men do."

"Why the hell is that?"

"I wish we knew. All we've been able to establish are correlations, not causes-and-effects. We don't even understand exactly how the virus spreads. We've no idea, for example, how you contracted it. According to surveillance footage both inside and outside your apartment, you were strictly sheltering in place for three years before you fell ill, correct? You never stepped out? No human being stepped in?"

He nods. Ever since the Covid-32 pandemic three years ago decimated a third of the U.S. population, Harry hadn't set foot out of his apartment until this hospitalization, nor had anyone other than government robotic drones entered.

Not that his self-quarantining was different than anyone else's. As each year since 2019 brought an increasingly severe strain of Covid, the Federal Emergency Management Administration developed systems to support human life during a possibly permanent state of shelter-in-place. The federal government nationalized all manufacturing, agriculture, and goods distribution. All functions became automated, managed over the Internet by computer from engineers' homes and implemented by a network of robotic drones. An underground anti-technology movement initially protested, of course, but was largely suppressed under necessary martial law measures. The new normal: permanent shelter-in-place alone until all Covid iterations were permanently eradicated or a lasting pan-Covid vaccine were found. Whenever that would be. If ever.

"We can only conclude," continues Dr. Thelma, "that somehow, a few droplets of Covid-35 survived on one of the drone food or clothing deliveries made to your apartment despite disinfectant procedures, as unlikely as that is. Or perhaps Covid-35 was actually present in your system before your complete shelter-in-place began three years ago."

"Is that possible?"

"Theoretically. The virus could have been lurking within you these past three years, much the way HIV was known to lurk for a decade before presenting. But that would be uncharacteristic of Covid. Theoretically possible, but unlikely."

So, this virus is attacking gay men left and right. Harry's one of the few who's survived. Of course they need to study his physiology. Of course he wants to help. "Of course you need virus samples from me. And I want to give them. But can't you just take my blood? Or my chromosomes if they've got something to do with it? Why do you need fluid from my eye, of all places?"

"That's the oddest part of the puzzle. Each time we extract blood and attempt to analyze, the virus decomposes under the microscope, right before our eyes. The only virus that remains intact is what we extract from the eye's aqueous humor. No matter how we try to eradicate the virus from a patient's system, even when patients generate antibodies and otherwise recover, the virus continues to thrive in aqueous humor. Seemingly permanently."

"But why?"

"Yet something else we don't understand. All the more reason we need to study." She stares directly into his eyes. "A few drops from your eye could potentially save millions. We're talking all gay men on the planet, Harry. On the entire planet."

He sighs deeply. "Okay, Doc, go for it."

As promised, the extraction from his left eye doesn't hurt at all. He spends one evening on painkillers, then the next morning is discharged. A drone drives him home, escorts Harry into his apartment, checks that housekeeping has properly stocked his kitchenette, and runs a microbial scan to confirm the apartment to be Covid-35 free. After signaling to the hospital switchboard "Mission Completed," the drone rolls out of Harry's apartment.

Harry plops onto his gray sofa bed. "Finally home," he mutters aloud. A message in red blinks across his floor-to-ceiling telescreen: "Telescreen Viewing History Has Been Downloaded Per Order of the Ministry of Contact Tracing."

"Message understood," he says to the screen. The blinking message dissolves. Harry already knew that: a few days ago, he asked Dr. Thelma whether any of his friends had checked in on him. She explained that all contacts listed on his telescreen memory had been notified of his hospitalization for Covid-35, "as part of contact tracing efforts. They probably assume you've died. We'll leave it to you to correct their misimpression. In your own time."

To the telescreen, he now says, "Display Friends List," planning to call one after another so they can FaceConnect and catch up. But…what if none of them answer? What if, in response to his calls, he receives a series of "Subscriber Deceased" messages? Or what if the first friend he calls turns out to be healthy, but details a litany of mutual friends who've died? Is Harry ready to cope with such overwhelming grief?

He abruptly instructs, "Cancel."

Eventually. He'll try contacting them eventually. But not today. Not this week. Maybe not even this month. First, he needs to clear his head and re-connect with home, routines, self.

He summons onto the telescreen his favorite meditation program, an ever-changing, 20th-century New York cityscape with honking taxis and bustling crowds rushing down one avenue and up the next. It's so soothing to see himself projected into a crowd, jostling and being jostled, walking through steam billowing from manhole covers, hearing this couple's argument, that lunatic's psychotic ravings, others' laughters and whines. He'll have to figure out how to program his avatar into a Bloomingdale's Labor Day sale—he can't remember what it felt like to be elbowed.

Emotionally centered now, he goes into his white bathroom, stands before the illuminated mirror. He braces himself to look at his eye. Despite Dr. Thelma's assurances, he wonders how injured it will appear after the extraction—bloody? cloudy? discolored? Slowly, he peels away the adhesive gray eye patch per Dr. Thelma's instructions. Normal, just as Dr. Thelma said. His left iris is as blue as his right, as clear and piercing as ever. He shuts one eye, looks, shuts the other eye, looks. Perfect vision, same as before. He breathes a sigh of relief.

His curly blond hair has grown over his ears these past months, and his typically neat beard is more than an inch too long. He slips his head into the RoboGroomer. "My usual," he instructs. A few moments of automated clipping, buzzing, blowing and brushing, then the machine switches itself off.

Harry withdraws his head, examines himself, notes his still-gaunt cheeks. Despite the hospital's intravenous nutrition, he hasn't fully regained all the weight lost during coma.

But he does feel a pleasing surge of energy.

As he was leaving the hospital this morning, he asked Dr. Thelma whether he needed to wait before "exerting myself in any way."

She gave a wry smile and wink at that, encouraged him "to do whatever you feel you can handle."

"Whew," he whistled with a light blush.

A quick shower, then he slips on his favorite leather vest. It hangs a little loose, reveals softened ripples of his former six-pack. Red leather thong, also a little loose.

He kicks back on the gray sofa bed, instructs the telescreen to bring up the UN's International Gay Zoom Orgy site. "Scroll Central Asian rooms." Harry wants to see if the Uzbek Bears Over Thirty orgy room is still online. He's hoping to find that hot stud he played with the night he fell ill. He remembers the bear's deep brown eyes. If the guy's there, maybe he'll agree to another private sex session so they can finish what they started?

Yes, the room's still listed. Harry states "Select" and "Enter," but the telescreen replies, "Entry blocked." He repeats the command, receives the same response.

That's weird. Harry's never encountered a blocked room before. Sure, the more popular rooms—Muscle Bears, Olympians, Super Shlongs—are frequently declared "Closed," meaning that they've reached optimum participation (two dozen men). But "Blocked"? This is new.

"List all blocked-entry rooms."

The telescreen lists the Los Angeles Porn Stars room, the Rio De Janeiro Carnival room, the Bangkok Trans Divas room.

What does this mean? A lot must have changed these last three months. He'll have to ask his next trick. If he wants conversation, he'd better choose an English-speaker for play.

He calls up an old standby, "Aussie Gingers." Yep, the room's still there and entry's allowed. Instead of the dozen or so Zoom screens he's accustomed to seeing in the room, only one screen pops up, that of a husky redhead with a furry chest. Yum. One hot man is all Harry needs.

Wearing only black boxer swim trunks, the Aussie salutes Harry, then stands up on his bed, dances clumsily around.

An exhibitionist. Okay, Harry can get into this. When the Aussie shimmies his shoulders, Harry applauds. The guy gives Harry a big grin, plops down onto his knees and brings his face close to the telescreen, so close that he practically presses his lips against it. Harry stands from his sofabed and does likewise. Then both men pull back. Harry gazes into the Aussie's green eyes, feels connected. How good it is to feel connected. It's been so long.

The Aussie returns Harry's huge smile, some spittle bubbling at the corners of his lips. The spittle turns to foam, and the Aussie starts to cough.

"You alright, guy?" asked Harry.

The cough turns into a hack, a series of near-suffocating whoops. Finally the Aussie gets his fit under control. "That's odd, mate. Never happened before." He stares into Harry's eyes. "Sorry for being so unsexy."

Just as Harry says, "No worries, pal," the Aussie sways gently forward and back. His face fills with alarm. "Please," he murmurs abruptly, "call—" His eyes roll into his head. He collapses onto his bed.

"Hello?" cries Harry. "Are you alright?"

No response.

Shit. Harry yells to his telescreen, "Call International 911." But instead of an emergency operator appearing onscreen, it's Dr. Thelma's face that appears.

"Dr. Thelma?"

"Harry, I'm so sorry."

"Dr. Thelma, what are you doing on my screen? Listen, there's an emergency. You've got to call International 911. It's an Australian man—"

"In Melbourne. Yes, I know."

"You know?"

"We're monitoring your interactions, Harry. I'm so terribly sorry."

"I don't care, I've nothing to hide. Quick, this guy just collapsed while we were Zoom sexing."

"I know, Harry. The Melbourne authorities have been alerted. They'll rush him to the hospital, not that he'll likely survive."

"You think it's Covid-35?"

"Almost certainly."

"Poor guy."

"Harry—the reason I'm here: the extraction from your eye. The tested fluid....Harry, the fluid shows the same viral variation as in the aqueous humor of that Uzbek man you Zoomed with three months ago. Identical viral variations. The same strain."

"That Uzbek? You extracted his eye fluid, too?"

"The Uzbek authorities did. The results of his test didn't reach us until this morning, after you'd already left the hospital. We just finished analyzing your eye fluid, comparing. Just now, this very minute. Sadly, not in time to save the poor Australian."

"I don't understand what you're saying."

"Three months ago, you contracted the virus from your Uzbek friend. And I'm quite sure you just passed it along to the Australian. I'm so sorry, Harry."

"That makes no sense. I never met the Uzbek in person. I never met the Australian in person. How could anything have passed from one of us to the other?"

"Harry, we're certain it did. The same viral variation in both the Uzbek and you, the same strain. Identical. Take a moment to consider the implications."

He shuts his eyes and shakes his head. "This makes no sense. None at all. How could it possibly have spread from the Uzbek to me, or from me to the Aussie? Our only contact was...was.... No, it can't be. Unless you're implying...but that can't be."

"Such a theory has been floating about recently, but was too horrific to accept. I dismissed the notion as anti-technology paranoia. But now...after today's test results.... And what I, myself, just witnessed happen to the Australian as he gazed into your eyes.... Actually, to give them credit, the Uzbek authorities figured it out before we did. They realized that every one of their gay citizens who played online with that particular bearish fellow came down with Covid-35. And died. It was their tracing of his contacts that led them to us, through you."

"You're saying that Covid-35 spreads *virtually*?"

"I know, Harry. It's horrific." She withdraws a tissue from the pocket of her white smock, wipes her nose. "I'm so sorry, Harry. Sorrier than you can imagine."

Harry takes a few moments to absorb the information. He caught the virus from that Uzbek bear's gorgeous eyes? "Dr. Thelma, did the virus kill the Uzbek?"

"Yes and no." She looks aside, then back at the screen. "I'm sorry to tell you this, Harry: he survived Covid-35, the way you did. But, the Uzbek authorities…admittedly, they panicked—understandable, but nevertheless regrettable. They were frightened, did what they deemed necessary in order to block the spread. And so that they could conduct an extensive autopsy."

"Autopsy? You mean—?"

"I'm so sorry, Harry. Different societies, different public health approaches."

"Holy shit! That poor guy."

"I know, Harry, I'm so very sorry. They were weighing alternatives. One life against many. Everyone wants to preserve the world's gay male population, an essential element of the world's ecosystem. It's a shared global priority."

"I get it. But still—to execute him."

"Listen, Harry. These developments. There's no way to cushion the blow. Look what just happened to the Australian."

"That sweet fella. And you're saying I did it. By looking into his eyes. I didn't know, Doc. I swear, I didn't know."

"Of course not. You couldn't possibly have known. Nobody's blaming you. But, we must accept the fact, Harry, that you're a carrier. A lethal transmitter, in fact. Unwitting, but nevertheless. We must address the situation as it is, not as we wish it were. We have to protect the world's gay men."

"Agreed, but…so that means…then the only way to protect other gay men from me is…. Are you saying I can't look other gay men in the eyes anymore?"

"That's exactly what I'm saying, Harry."

"Not in-person. And not online."

"That's right."

"But just for a while, right? Until you find a vaccine."

"We have yet to find a lasting Covid vaccine of any kind, Harry. One can't rule out the possibility, but there's certainly no immediate likelihood of discovering one."

"So…for the foreseeable future—maybe even forever—I can never look another gay man in the eyes?"

"I'm so sorry."

Harry's eyes burn. Tears well up. He swallows hard. "Then what the hell am I supposed to do from now on? Keep my eyes shut when Zoom orgying? That'd sort of defeat the purpose, don't you think? And what about when I FaceConnect with friends? Do you expect me to wear—I don't know—patches over my eyes?"

"You could still enjoy other men's voices. But, we couldn't trust you to keep your eyes closed, it would be too easy to steal a glance or blink. Even wearing patches over your eyes would be too risky, Harry. What if the patches' adhesive were to wear off, or if you were to forget to put the patches on in the first place?"

"There has to be some device you can give me for protection."

"Nothing foolproof. And we must protect our gay men."

"So, what do we do?"

"I've sent drones, Harry. To your apartment. I'm so sorry."

Harry squints in an effort to understand. "Don't tell me they're coming to remove my telescreen. To replace it with an audio-only connector?"

"I'm so sorry, Harry." She starts to weep. "You'll go down in history as a hero who sacrificed to save all gay men."

"What do you mean, 'sacrificed'? You're not sending the drones to kill me like they killed that Uzbek guy!"

"No, Harry, of course not. No one's going to kill you. We're not barbarians. But Harry, listen, I need to prepare you—"

There's a loud knocking on his apartment door.

"Dr. Thelma, they're here. What are the drones going to do? Why did you send them?"

"Dear Harry," she gasps. Then she squeezes her eyes shut tight, inhales deeply, mutters to herself, "Be professional." She takes a deep breath in, releases it slowly. In a matter-of-fact, steady voice, she declares, "Harry, they're surgical drones."

"Surgical drones? Why on earth would you send—?"

The knocking on his apartment door grows more insistent.

"Harry, they've come to surgically remove…" Her lips tremble as she visibly struggles to form the words. "To remove…"

"To remove what? Doctor, what are they here to…?" As a hint of understanding begins to form, Harry's eyes widen. "No," he whispers. "You can't be serious."

"I'm so sorry, Harry. Truly," says Dr. Thelma, nearly breathless. "But it's the only way to protect the public welfare with any degree of certainty."

"You can't mean…not my—" Harry reaches up to his face. He gently rolls fingertips over the firm bulges of his eyes.

The surgical drones break down his door.

"No," he whispers. "Oh my God, no."

# About the Author

Daniel M. Jaffe is a prize-winning fiction writer whose work has appeared in more than half a dozen countries in several languages. His newest short story collection is *Foreign Affairs: Male Tales of Lust & Love* from Rattling Good Yarns Press. Daniel lives in Santa Barbara, CA with his husband, Leo Cabranes-Grant, who one day tossed out a gem of an idea: can you imagine how awful it would be if Covid-19 could be transmitted virtually? Leo generously gave Daniel permission to take the idea and run with it. Only after writing "The Procedure" did Daniel recall a childhood stick-fighting accident that left one of Daniel's eyes mildly scarred. Inspiration—conscious and unconscious—comes from many sources. Read more about Daniel's work at www.DanielJaffe.com.

# Moi Aussi

Christina Delia

One of the things I miss the most about being alive is the feel of a cool May breeze on my arms and face. I'm talking about the kind of wind that blows through in a pleasant gust while you're sitting outdoors on a sunny day.

And lilacs! How I fondly (though only vaguely) recollect that certain perfume!

The way the wind moves through, you can almost hear it, like a Higher Power speaking in a foreign tongue. Now I know what that language is: the collective voices of all of the souls who have killed themselves. It's a lamentation.

In mourning—a warning.

If you saw my spirit, you would likely declare that I don't look my age. I took my own life in my prime, right around the time I realized that I'd never be famous.

You see, I was in the pictures.

And oh, how I *moved!*

Initially, I was a chorus girl. That's where I met Frenchie. Madeleine, just like Proust, but with a blonde bob of Louise Brooks-style hair.

With my black curls and rosy-but-porcelain complexion we were quite a pair!

The plum parts were few and far between, and I likened Frenchie and myself to two china dolls a little girl let slip under the bed and forgot *all* about.

We spent a lot of time in beds. Also on chaise lounges and couches. In this business, you've got to get to the top *any* way you can (and often that means letting some sneering man with a pencil-thin moustache and oil-slick salesman hair ride on top of you.)

They're called Producers.

And then you get pregnant.

Here's how I look at it: The Lord giveth (motion picture deals) and The Lord taketh away (abortions.) It's a common enough word now, but back then? Oh, honey! Frenchie and I were considered to be a certain type of female.

*Good for only one thing* is what the men thought.

*Better off dead* snarled these men's wives.

And then we were all used up. And then we *were* dead.

I can remember sitting by the phone, waiting for Buck Wheelcox to ring me—tell me, Buck, what am I supposed to *do*?

And he said, "Doll face, you grew up on a farm, didn't you? Out in the Midwest? Well, what did your daddy do with a hog that nobody wanted?"

I would have been a good mother.

In exchange for our "services," Frenchie and I were winning small roles in the silent pictures. Maybe you've seen some of them? I was Peggy in *Birds-A-Plenty*. Frenchie was Young Wife in *Please Be Mine*. I landed the role of Delighted Gal in *All the Live Long Day* and got to kiss Hugo Marvel.

Then afterwards, we did more than kiss. When he climbed off of me, I took a milk bath and cleaned my thighs.

Rinse, repeat.

At some point, the milk bath turns to sour water.

The French can seemingly justify these sinful indiscretions with a puff of cigarette smoke, but I was locked into my Midwestern Catholic guilt. I thought about all of the unborn babies in Purgatory that Jesus couldn't save. I thought of my grandmother playing the piano. How different Grandmother's piano sounded than the wild music at nightclubs! I wondered if there were nightclubs in Heaven or in Hell, wherever I was going.

Frenchie decided to come with. She was never too bold when it came to doing things without me: birds of a feather, peas in a pod.

When we got together with one of these important men? Well, the French called us a ménage a trois, and how much fun was it for these producers to do it with an *actual* French girl?

We were every man's fantasy—but what was *ours*? Frenchie and I never really had proper time to consider that, and then, we were gone.

First, however, we had been kept in a Spanish hacienda style house in the Hollywood Hills. There were nightly parties and raucous love making. Men who stumbled home at dawn in creased pants to demanding wives.

Frenchie and I uttered no demands. Who would have listened to us?

Buck Wheelcox paid the rent on our Hollywood house, and I sent some of the movie money I made home to North Dakota, so Grandmother could keep playing her piano with a roof overhead and think of me fondly.

Sometimes Buck Wheelcox got a little too handsy, like the time he ripped my dress and gave me a bloody lip *and* a chipped tooth. We were so drunk on champagne and pills, but I remember Frenchie screaming from the bedroom:

*"Non, Non, NON!"*

*"Like the men care what we have to say, Frenchie?"* I thought at the time. *"We're silent film actresses. We're lucky to be here. So be grateful, dammit, and open your saucy French legs for the man!"*

I used to call her Frenchie Frog Legs. I'd do anything to make her laugh. Maybe I loved her? Perhaps she loved me, too.

Grandmother often warned me of women who loved other women. *Deviants,* she'd utter like a curse, never knowing that I was one.

There's a word for ladies like us, and I know it now, though I couldn't have *possibly* understood it then: ABUSED.

Now I know better. What they did to us was wrong.

In the years since Frenchie and I swallowed those pills, that strawberry ice cream soda and champagne (to make death come on sweeter, I reasoned) I've seen *a lot* of abuse in this very house.

Rock stars abusing their groupies, producers making pornography with young ingénues, some as young as I once was when I started in show business. I thought there were laws about such things now? I don't know how I feel about pornography. On the one hand, the years (both my years being alive AND deceased) have granted me a more European sensibility when it comes to sexuality (and likely, Frenchie's influence!).

On the other hand, I've seen some of these young girls (and boys!) being forced to bite down hard on tear- and blood-stained pillows. *"Porn Star! Rock Star! You're gonna be a STAR!"* Only you're not. Next week there will be new fresh meat.

Growing up on the farm.

Rinse, repeat.

If I could impart upon these young people one piece of advice, it would be the guidance I wish some wise elder had given me when I was young, and alive:

*"You don't owe ANYONE any more than you owe YOURSELF."*

Back when I was alive, and I had an actual voice, and I didn't use it.

Frenchie and I, we had dreams, and they wouldn't come true.

Yes, we killed ourselves with studio-approved sleeping pills and the sweets it took to wash death down. We took our own lives, because the way we looked at it, they'd already been taken from us.

Hurting and humiliating us when we were young and impressionable made these already-powerful men feel like gods. I heard it in the way they crowed. Those triumphant faces of good ol' boys with Southern drawls come to Hollywood for a rendezvous.

I wanted to slit all of their throats: slowly enough to know that it hurt them, but quickly enough so that the expressions on their bloated faces would change dramatically.

Bloated faces make for excellent corpses.

I thought of my own father. I was never good enough for *him*, either.

Even in the post-life, I'd still see it: parents finding out that their children were not who they'd anticipated they'd be: daughters loving other girls, sons desiring to bed fellows. *Gays, flits, poofs* and that other word…the one the passive-aggressives coyly insult you with and then argue while smirking that they were referring to a European cigarette?

*"Oui, you mean fag,"* said Frenchie.

That's the one.

*Bull dyke, lesbo, rug muncher,* it went on. I tell you this NOT because I delight in it, but rather, because the walls of this once-lovely abode have absorbed a remarkably devastating amount of pain and abject cruelty throughout the years. You can't haunt a house without energy; the living will emanate it and the dead do, too. Often the worst representatives of the living give off the foulness that lies within them like a vile skunk stink.

Those slurs—all hideous words to confirm why parents would toss their children they were supposed to love unconditionally to the streets, the dogs, the jackals and wolves. All for other people's approval. And the absolute love and devotion to a God Almighty who might not exist or might not be exactly who they believe He is.

God Almighty might truly love each and every one of us unconditionally. If I ever meet him, I will let you know. He does not frequent our Spanish style house in the Hollywood Hills, but I have witnessed devils. I've seen the worst things civilized humans can carelessly do to one another. Human beings becoming bodies in covered-up crime scenes.

And it often starts with parents throwing their own children (the ones they raised until the point of disagreement) away.

I was one such body. Daddy and my stepmother knew I was different, so they sent me to live with Grandmother, threatening me to keep my "disgusting secret" to myself.

I lived like I was dead until I actually was.

And Frenchie and I tried in vain from our invisible perch on the walls and ceilings to save the little runaways and drug addicts, the pawns of prostitution rings and the victims of snuff films.

Until Frenchie came down with an idea, like a fever: What *IF* instead of trying to save the lost, frightened lambs, we instead slaughtered the Hollywood wolves? Those treacherous mongrels!

These hacienda style homes have beautiful bones *and* ghosts. So just like when we were alive, Frenchie and I found ourselves utilizing our best assets.

The day the newest tenant moved in, we vowed to destroy him.

Death practice.

"Such a young man to have a stroke," Frenchie said. "But he'll do."

And it worked. Lucky for us, Marlon Petrie was an overworked hotshot forty-something director. Cocaine and espresso and ciggies and champagne, with an occasional Cobb salad: the devil's diet. Uppers and downers and whatever the pills are that make you drive your car when you're asleep.

One night, when he was incapacitated after a bender, Frenchie and I seduced him. Frenchie hovered above him menacingly while I crept on top of him and then *inside* of him. And I don't mean the kind of *inside* that they used to do to me when *I* was alive. I mean inside as in I stared straight from his skull and out of his eyeballs into my beautiful Frenchie's dazzling, adoring face.

*"If only we were still alive, Frenchie,"* I thought bitterly. *"I'd kiss you hard on the mouth like I shouldn't have been afraid to do back then, unless we were drunk and a man with money commanded us to."*

I kissed my beloved's spirit, and the flesh puppet fool director tried to scream but was soon choking on his own tongue.

An overdose will do that to you.

A scare will do that to you.

In the end, we're just the worst kind of meat.

The chuck that no one wants.

The vittles, the mess.

End chow and entrails, meals for the maggots.

I love the dead. I love seeing the once alive become exactly as I am. This hotshot film director getting swallowed up into *our* house.

"Ghost got your tongue," I laughed, as his spirit tried to scream. Frenchie and I are getting better at comedy *and* killing. We are becoming positively vaudevillian, the way we possess these bad men and make them do awful things to themselves, for once, FINALLY.

Next Arnie Higgins came and arranged an orgy of drugged-out aspiring actors. It was miserable to watch what I'd not only lived through, but seen too many times since.

"Seizure this time?" asked Frenchie, but I had something *truly* special in mind for this dirt bag. I had become quite accomplished at materializing in my spirit form; so much so, that when I popped in to greet Mr. Arnie Higgins at 3:33 a.m. after his last "party guest" had lost consciousness, I gave him such a grand scare that he suffered an immediate heart attack.

When he was good and dead, and his rendered helpless ghost was peering at me, Frenchie and I used the mental focus we'd been working on, picked up his pudgy corpse *with our minds*, and made it dance.

I think the only thing scarier than learning that you're deceased is your newly carcass-free spirit witnessing two gleeful ghost gals choreograph your skin sack into a Lindy Hop, then take it down to a nice, slow, ominous waltz.

I love watching newly-dead men scream. Their faces contort in such a beautiful way—like silent film actors.

*Like me!*

Frenchie saw the newspaper headline. She floated in to tell me.

*HOLLYWOOD   DEATH   HOUSE!   RUMORED   TO   BE   HAUNTED!*

"Ooh la la, ma Cherie," I told her, laughing. I wished we could pour champagne down our throats again and hear our flutes clink together, that joyful tapping. I wished we could be free spirits instead of bogged down, used up, ghostly gal pals.

"We are *not* used up! We are brand new! Baptized in the blood of wicked men, and the fire in our own hearts!" Frenchie roared.

"Frenchie, we don't *have* hearts," I said sadly.

"Souls then," she sighed. "But we have more heart than most, ma Belle."

I don't long for yesterday. Nor do I dream of a future. Those would be exercises in futility. What I am is content to kill, to slay demons alongside the love of my life.

Now these men were as silent as we were.

I looked at Frenchie, her spirit hovering in the same light as the day I'd met her: blue-green eyes squinting, sun streaming in.

She doesn't have to squint anymore, but she does it anyway, remembering how cute I would say she looked.

My love is not conditional.

Our most recent "victim" was a nameless sex trafficker, because why should we bother to learn his name?

Instead, we amused ourselves with floating screen title cards written in his blood:

FIN

# About the Author

Christina Delia writes fiction and plays. Her play "The Mirror Had Other Ideas" was performed at The Secret Theatre in Long Island City, New York, and her play "The Robbery" was performed at The Burgdorff Center for the Performing Arts in Maplewood, New Jersey. Christina's story "Stuffie" was included in the horror anthology *What Monsters Do for Love: Volume Three* (Soteira Press). Her story "Like Abigail Winchell" can be read in the psychological horror anthology *Shadowy Natures* (Dark Ink Books). She lives in New Jersey with her daughter, Juliet, where she is currently at work on a novel. Find her on Instagram: @christinadelia_writer.

# The Other Boy
## Laramie Dean

"There's a boy who comes at night," I told my mother. "He comes up to my bedroom window and looks inside. He looks and looks." I was nine, almost ten; my mother pointed out to me that it wasn't possible for a boy, for anybody really, to look into my bedroom window at night or any other time. My bedroom window was on the third floor. But it didn't stop him, I insisted, that strange dark boy.

"Don't cry," my mother told me.

It seemed like both my parents were always telling me not to cry, my father especially.

In my first memory, my dad is throwing a football at me. And I can't catch it, or I don't, or I *won't*. He's this big, red-faced man, angry balloon over my head, filling the world, telling me, "Don't cry, it's not that big of a deal. Jeez, why do you always gotta *cry*?" But I do cry; all I do, I think, is cry.

In my memory, he's so mad, apocalyptically angry, but I like to think now that maybe, he was trying to control his temper. Later, as I got older, he was in more control, or he would try to be. I would watch him try to force his anger back down inside himself more than once, an animal that always, *always* tried to escape. But in that first memory, he's all I can see, and I don't want the football, and I'm crying, and I can't help it, and I try to tell him that I can't help it, that I'm not doing it to make him mad., but the words don't come out. And he gets madder and madder anyway.

So, it wasn't my father that I told about the boy but my mother. She smoked when I was very little, but I don't remember much about that; I remember her hands, and how the fingers were very squat. Did they tremble on that day, that sunny summer afternoon when I told her about the boy? Or was it raining? Did a giant thunderstorm roar across the sky? I can see her hands, and they are trembling, yes, because she wanted a cigarette and she wouldn't allow herself a cigarette; later, she would tell me that she saved all the money she would have spent on cigarettes and used it to take us to Disneyworld.

She told me there couldn't be a boy at my window: it was a nightmare, but I knew he was there because he came so many nights, and I did that thing where you pinch yourself to see if what's happening is real or if you're only dreaming. I pinched myself, but still, he remained. Filthy, oily hair, big eyes that never blinked. I saw him watching me at the park one day, just before he began to appear at my window. I was reading a book while my dad tried to teach my cousin Brucie how to pitch.

Brucie was a year younger than me and still teachable, I guess; Dad had given up on me by then. Brucie lived in western Montana, across the mountains, impossibly far away, and we were in the east, on the plains amidst the spreading grassy prairie. Mom and I sat on beach towels and wore our sunglasses and read our books, or maybe she had a magazine; the sky was that kind of flawless blue you always remember whether it was truly flawless or not, with no clouds, and it was summer, and maybe it could always be summer. I remember thinking that; I spent a lot of time trying to convince myself that summer would never end. Summer's end meant school, which I didn't mind, but it also meant resuming swimming in the tide with other kids, other boys, and I hated them. They hated me, too. I didn't like to think about it too much; *summer, summer,* I chanted to myself, *always summer.*

Mom had discovered an old Hardy Boys book at one of the junk shops she loved and gave it to me, and so I was giving the boys a try and tuning out the sound of Dad and Brucie, who was bigger than me and liked to punch me in the arm and the gut when he thought no one was looking. "You gotta really wind it *up,*" I could hear my father growling, "wind it *up,* Brucie," and Brucie grunted that he was *trying,* wasn't he, that all he could do was *try.*

I guess there were clouds after all, or maybe there was a wind or a breeze, because I was cold suddenly; the sun disappeared, and so I looked up. My mother's eyes remained on her book, but I looked up, and there he was, that other boy, just at the edge of this little copse of trees. Beyond the trees was the lake, but the summer had been too cold so far for the water to warm up enough to support our swimming, so we had all agreed to spend a few hours in the park instead. I could hear the sound of the water lapping at the shore, which was mostly rocks that would hurt my feet if I tried to walk on them. One time, my father had lifted me, laughing, and thrown me into the lake water. I don't remember if I asked him to do it; I don't remember if I laughed or cried. I remember that the water of the lake was cold. It was always cold. I could hear the sound of the water lapping at the rocks and the sound of swimmers braver than we, laughing and splashing in all that cold water.

Perhaps, I thought, that dark-haired boy was one of them.

He was watching us intently, and then he took a step toward us.

"Hey, Mom," I said, and pointed.

"Just some kid," she said. "Just some little boy. Not mine," she said and smiled and ruffled my hair.

"He's creepy," I said.

"Maybe he's lonely," she said, and turned the page. "Maybe his friends abandoned him."

"Maybe he doesn't have any friends."

"You should be nicer," she said, which stung. I let it sting.

The boy was backing away into the trees when next I looked at him; then, I watched him turn and clamber down the concrete steps built into the hillside that led down to the lake. I could hear his bare feet slapping against them as he went.

He appeared at my window that night, but he didn't come in. I told my mother, who didn't believe me and told me not to cry, though her hands were shaking. He came back the next night, and then the next, and I knew what he wanted. I thought about telling my father, but I couldn't for the world imagine how that conversation would possibly go; I tried anyway after dinner, when he took a can of beer into the room he called his office, but I couldn't catch him in time and the door closed and locked behind him. I stood there with my hands balled into tiny tight fists, but I didn't dare to bring them to the door. I didn't say another word, and the boy came into my room that night.

He slid through the window like he didn't have any bones and then crawled down the wall and across the floor. His eyes were fixed on me and they didn't blink. I think they were white with tiny little holes in the center. Or they were all dark, just empty holes. His mouth was firm and unsmiling; his hair hung over his face and was black, like scrawls of ink.

I sat up. I could hear him, his hands padding against the floor, his belly brushing against the carpet with a brusque hissing sound, but I lost sight of him.

I think I peed then. No, no, I didn't, but I wanted to. I wouldn't let myself: I remember that much.

He wasn't gone, and I wasn't asleep. "I'm not asleep," I said out loud, and I heard him laughing down there on the floor beside my bed. It sounded like someone crumpling up paper or scrunching up tinfoil.

"Go away," I said, or tried to say. "Go away, boy, go away, go away."

He clambered up onto my bed, or he pounced, like a big cat. His eyes stared into mine, unblinking. Unblinking. He glowed in the light from the window. After my father and the football, it is my most vivid memory of my childhood.

He licked his lips, then he moved forward and put his fingers into my mouth.

I tried to recoil, but he slid the fingers of his other hand around the back of my head and held me there. His fingers were cold and tasted like dirt. He wiggled them around, tracing circles against my tongue. I gagged, but nothing came up.

He took his fingers from my mouth and put them into his mouth. Then he put them back into mine.

I closed my eyes. I didn't cry. The tears wouldn't come.

He took his other hand from the back of my head and slid it inside my shirt, then down the front of my pajama pants. His fingers burned where they touched me. I tried to cry out, but his entire hand filled my mouth.

The tears were stubborn and wouldn't come.

"Stop," I said around his fingers.

He smiled at me, then took his hand out of my pajamas. I burned inside, but I burned cold.

He began to kiss my forehead and my cheeks, and his fingers still wiggled around in my mouth. They caressed my teeth, my molars. I felt my gorge threaten to rise again.

"Shhhh," he said through a mouth, a *throat* full of black, wet earth. "Shhh. Daddy loves you. Mommy loves you. We love you, we love you, we do."

I was trying to swallow, trying to swallow. He didn't blink, and neither did I. But he was smiling, and his teeth were black with mold or dirt or something worse.

He put his mouth onto my mouth, and we sat like that for a long time. I felt something pass from him to me, and back again, and back again, and back again.

Finally, we lay down together. I could hear my heart thundering in my ears, could feel the blood burning inside me, burning to go faster in my veins.

"Shhh," he said. "You are loved." And he giggled, a sick sound and a nasty one. "Love."

We lay like that for hours; suddenly, the sun was up and I was alone.

And there was something—mud, maybe—smeared all over my sheets and my blanket.

I grew into a sullen, secretive teenager. An absolute cliché. I refused to cut my hair. I bought weed at our high school from some senior I barely knew and was caught immediately, and my mother dragged me to the police station where they told me it was easier to not smoke or do drugs than it was to be arrested, to be locked up, to be separated from my family. I wanted to tell them that I was already locked up, but I knew the policeman wouldn't believe me. His eyes were hard like polished nickels, and his mouth never moved. My mother cried; I wanted to tell her, *No one likes a crybaby*, but I couldn't remember if she'd actually told me that when I was a child, or if I'd only told myself, so I didn't say it. I didn't like to hurt my mother's feelings.

I became very dramatic. I refused to wash my clothes. I took the football from the garage one night and stabbed it at least seven hundred times, then left it outside my father's office. He never said anything, but I knew that he knew. He was the football coach, of course: recruited from the other high school across town, offered an exorbitant sum to save our shitty team from extinction as he had saved that *other* shitty team. He taught U.S. History and Government, and I avoided him in the halls and would drop my head when he passed me; neither of us ever said hello to the other.

Sophomore year, while I was on an overnight choir trip, the father of the family hosting me and Zac Crawley (who was very ordinary but willing to let me do things to him), caught me in the act of administering Zac a blowjob. We were both sent home, expelled from the club; Zac had to change schools, but not me. No one was supposed to know. "Dude," one of the choir bros said to me later. "I heard you did Zac Crawley up the butt."

"I didn't do *that*," I said, batting my eyes and grinning.

My parents wanted to send me away; I heard them talking about it one night when they didn't know I could hear them. "Somewhere," my mother said, and she wasn't crying, but I could hear a tremble in her voice. I felt a stab of pleasure, and then shame, and then guilt, and then pleasure again.

"Somewhere," she said again, but I guess neither of them ever decided where that somewhere might be, because they didn't end up sending me anywhere, and I stayed at home. I didn't date anyone they might see, but I loved being the guy a classmate could turn to if he needed a handjob or a bj during lunch or between periods. I smoked more cigarettes; I wouldn't touch my father's beer but stole endless bottles of cheap red wine from the liquor store down the street from my high school.

No one knew what to say to me, so they said nothing. I thought, I'm happier this way.

One day, near the end of senior year, as I was passing all of my classes with As *and* staying out every night, late late late with my girlfriends—and their boyfriends, who loved me and thought I was hilarious, getting them booze and a good deal more whenever they wanted it—I came home from the library to find a stranger sitting at our kitchen table, drinking a glass of chocolate milk and blinking at me.

"Oh," I said, and stopped in my tracks. "Hi." What the *fuck?* I should have said, but I didn't. I was stunned; the words wouldn't come.

"Oh," he said. "Hi."

We stared at each other. He didn't move to lift the glass again, and I couldn't think of another word to say.

My mother called my name, then danced into the room with a plate of sandwiches, wheat bread because I hated white, and bologna and Miracle Whip, my favorite. She'd made six of them. "This is _____," she said, and I shook my head, because she hadn't said a name. A word had come from her mouth, or something like a word, or maybe a whine or the buzzing of a fly. I didn't understand, didn't know.

"What?" I said.

"_____," she said, with less patience now and a narrowing of the eyes. *Don't be an asshole,* those eyes said, though of course my mother would never say such a thing to me with her mouth.

"Hi," I said again.

"Hi," said the other boy.

"_____ is going to stay with us," my mother said, "for a while."

"Why?" I said.

"Don't be rude," she said, scowling at me, beaming at him. "This is good," she said and handed him the plate.

He took a sandwich and put half of it in his mouth. "This is good," he said through a mouth full of bologna. His teeth were stained yellow but darker, too, in places. I wondered if the stains were permanent.

"_____ is going to stay in the guest room," my mother said, still beaming. "For a while."

Later, when we were alone, "Listen," she said, "he's new at your school."

"I've never seen him before."

"Because he's *new.* Look, he's on the basketball team—" My father coached basketball now, as well; of course he did, of *course.* "And his mother is dead or maybe she's just not in the picture, and his father, well, his father, you know, he drinks. And he doesn't have a job. And he told poor _____ that he had to leave, that he couldn't live with him anymore."

"I can't understand his name," I said, "when you say it."

"Don't be *rude,*" she said, and her voice was almost a snarl. My mother had never almost-snarled at me, not once. "Your father felt bad. Very bad. So he invited him to stay with us until *his* father gets back on his feet."

The other boy had black hair that hung in his eyes and looked extremely unwashed; by this time, I could afford to be judgmental. I'd recently begun to wash my own hair with some regularity and saw to it that it was cut and groomed and that I shaved every morning before school. I changed my socks and underwear and tried very hard to look presentable. I wanted to go to college; I wanted a boyfriend; I wanted…I don't know, the kind of life the kids on TV I saw always had. Problems that you could deal with in under an hour. Even if they stretched across an entire season, they worked out in the end, and everyone learned and grew. I wanted to learn and grow. I tried to talk to my dad, but he wouldn't talk to me.

The other boy had black hair, oily and thick; his face was pasty and gaunt. He held his eyes very wide and they seldom if ever blinked. I knew almost instantly that he was the boy from my window, the one that I remembered from my childhood.

I tried to say his name: _____, but my tongue wouldn't work. I remembered his fingers in my mouth, I remembered the taste of dirt, I remembered how they had grabbed me and held on.

"You can't stay here," I told him that first night. He smiled at me wanly and said nothing but drifted down the hall to the guest bedroom, closed the door, and locked it.

I lay awake all night, waiting for him to glide into my bedroom, to rearrange his bones so he could slip under the door, but he never did.

I didn't go to school the next day, but he did.

I got up to piss sometime after school had ended; my father was waiting for me, sitting on my bed, when I returned. "Listen," he said, "you have to be kind."

"I don't know what that means."

"Don't be smart."

"I thought you wanted me to be smart."

He closed his eyes and heaved a deep sigh. That ugly alligator anger was struggling inside him, I knew: thrashing back and forth, hard to control. I wanted to see it come out; I wanted it to snap at my face, to sink its teeth into me. "_____ needs our help," he said and opened his eyes. "I shouldn't have to tell you this. I shouldn't have to tell you how to behave to a guest—"

"I don't understand why he's our guest."

"Because," my father spat at me, then looked down at his fists, which, clenched, held double handfuls of my quilt. He released them and instinctively wiped his hands on his slacks. "Because," he said, calmer now, "he isn't lucky like you are."

"I'm very lucky," I said.

He ignored this. "_____'s father abuses him," he said quietly. "I'm not sure how exactly beyond taking a belt to him. But I know at least *that* happens or happened a lot in the past."

I wanted to say, "I guess I'm lucky you never did that to me, huh," but the words stopped in my throat, as if big, ugly stones prevented them from forming. I remembered how the other boy's fingers felt as they stroked the teeth in the back of my mouth, and my stomach gurgled unsteadily.

"He's your age," my father said. "Which means that he's eighteen. He's going to graduate on time—what is that, a month? Only a month. A few weeks. Then we'll help him get back on his feet. Maybe go to Waxman, like you will." Waxman University was in Garden City, across the mountains in the western part of the state, where stupid Brucie still lived, though *his* parents had finally sent him to juvie after he robbed a convenience store at gunpoint at the tender age of fifteen. He shot the clerk in the arm. I wondered if he remembered my father teaching him how to pitch; I wondered if it was the same arm.

"Maybe," I said carefully, "maybe I don't want to go to Waxman anymore."

"Don't be such a goddamn baby," my father growled. He sounded very much like my mother had when she had snarled at me the day before. I was surprised at how unsurprised I felt. "We're going to help _____ get back on his feet—"

"Yeah, you said that already."

"And then...who knows?" He spread his hands out for me to see. Open, wide, blameless. Hands that had never slapped me or held me down or punched me. They held a football once upon a time, that was all. That was all. He was smiling at me. "That's not too much to ask, is it? You can share us for just a little while, can't you?"

"I'm an only child," I said, "we don't *share*," but I smiled back to show I was teasing.

He stood up and patted me heavily on the shoulder. "_____ needs a friend," he said. "So do you, I think." Then I saw his face change; perhaps he was remembering my other male friends; perhaps he knew more about how I utilized my lunch break and senior study halls than I thought he did.

"Doesn't it seem strange," I said, "that I can't understand his name? I can't even say it."

"Don't be such a goddamn baby," my father smiled at me and left me behind.

"I remember you," I said to the other boy that night. He was sitting on the couch in our basement den, which my parents had given to me as a kind of "thank you for not drinking and smoking anymore" present. It had a TV, a big one, and seven bookshelves that barely held all of my books. The boy was on the couch, thumbing through one of my *Batman* omnibuses, one of the really expensive ones.

"I remember you," he said back to me. He looked at me and grinned.

"No. Really." I tried to make my voice hard. "When I was a kid."

"When I was a kid?"

"I thought I dreamed you."

He shrugged.

"You can't stay here. You know you can't stay here."

Shrug, shrug.

I balled my hands up into fists. I thought about the sports my father loved; I thought about the violence, the real world games he liked to play. I wondered if I could hurt someone: really, actually hurt them. My head pounded for a moment. I wanted a drink; I wanted a joint; I wanted to get out, to just get the fuck out. "Why are you here? What are you going to do?" I snarled. "Kill me?"

"Kill me," he said.

"You think I won't?"

"I won't."

I stumbled backward. Something broke inside me and despair welled up like blood, and I was drowning, choking in it. The other boy only smiled. I tried to say his name and felt my tongue crawl with fire ants, the red kind, the kind that bite.

I ran out of the room, up the stairs to my bedroom, where I slammed the door like a petulant child in the midst of a tantrum. I won't cry, I told myself furiously. I won't, I *won't*, but of course I did, and the tears became sobs, long and drawn out, and I thought, I can't stop, why can't I stop? It was all coming out of me, tears and snot and sweat, pouring out. This is what *he* wants, I thought, trying to breathe, and I remembered how he put his hands on me and his mouth. I hated him, *hated* him. Was he even handsome? Yes, I think now, yes, I can admit that he was. I want to remember him as ghoulish, something white and slick having crawled out of a grave or from under a house: unwashed, unbathed, smelling of vinegar and piss and shit, but he didn't.

Perhaps that's only how I wanted to think of him at the time, when I hated everyone.

I watched him through my window, playing with my father in the backyard. Dad threw the ball and the other boy caught it. Routine. Normality. The kind of routine and normality I could never give my dad, certainly, but I wasn't bitter, or I tried not to be. I tried not to let that bitterness well up, replacing the blood, the *despair* with icy water. "Good!" Dad yelled. "Oh, that's good! Yes! Good work, _____!"

The other boy threw it back, then looked up at my window, found me easily, and grinned up at me with his stained, uneven teeth. His stink washed over me and I dropped the curtains and fell onto my bed and held myself and thought, *What am I going to do? What am I going to* do?

The dreams came whether I was awake or asleep. As soon as I closed my eyes, there he was, his hands on me, in me, touching me, holding me down and kissing me, whispering, "Love, love, good boy, love."

"Yes," I would say in those dreams, those wicked, wicked dreams, "yes, take me, I'm yours, I'm yours." I would think, *How do you kill a monster?* and remember of all of the movies I'd seen, all of my favorite horror films with their complicated and conflicting rules. My father hated those movies, preferred Westerns and war movies—violence, all is violence—but there was violence in my movies, too, wasn't there? It's all the same kind of different thing in the end, I guess.

Still, he wanted nothing to do with my superheroes, my comic books, my horror flicks. They embarrassed him. And I wanted nothing to do with the Westerns and the war: the stupid, straight, heterocentric, masculine bullshit, nonsense *bullshit*. All the same kind of different. Did the other boy stay up with him and watch *Bridge on the River Kwai* or something obscene and boring with John Wayne? He did; I knew he did; he *must have*. *They* must have. Together.

I thought, *Silver*. It was always silver in the movies, the stories. Silver *always* did the trick in the comic books and the movies.

Who had silver anymore?

*And why?*

Who knows; I didn't make the rules.

I thought, *Don't wait too long*, but I did.

It was the noise that woke me up a few nights later, not the dreams. The dreams kept me near the surface of sleep, just below, inches below, and the noise caused me to burst from the water and open my eyes.

*Someone in pain*, I thought.

I pulled on my shorts and a t-shirt and padded across my bedroom floor. My eyes flicked to the window, but there was no one there. Of course there was no one there. That would be impossible. Clearly.

*But I saw him there, I did. Once.*

My heart slammed in my chest; my blood screamed at me. My throat closed, and my testicles drew up.

*Someone, someone in pain.*

I slipped through my bedroom door and out into the hallway. The sound grew louder. I crept downstairs, to the basement den, my place that now belonged to the other boy. I slowly, tenderly opened the door to the basement.

Moaning.

Oh Christ. Oh Jesus.

I took a step down, and then another. Then another.

Until I saw.

My father was on top of him, the other boy, riding him. They were both naked, both slick with sweat. The other boy's body was whiter than I thought possible, and hard looking, like a statue in marble. He gleamed in the dimness of the room they'd rewarded me, and I remembered how white and gleaming he'd been that first night he came to me through my bedroom window. He came to *me*, I thought, and was numb.

My father's face, screwed up with the pleasure he received, was ugly. Was obscene, *obscene*.

My mother lay on the couch nearby, her face idle and dreaming. Occasionally, she would twitch or kick a little, like a dog does in its sleep. Her eyelashes fluttered gently; her smile was beatific.

The boy's eyes were silver, polished tin, and they found me easily. He grinned up at me like a hound. He put his mouth against the soft white curve of my father's shoulder, where shoulder becomes neck. My father's neck was thick but graceful, and that's the place where the other boy put his mouth. I could see how his teeth dented the white skin. My father groaned. The other boy's eyes didn't blink.

Then he bit down hard.

And my father made no other sound.

It was easy enough to do. I found him in the guest room day-dreaming, his eyes staring up at the ceiling, unblinking. His hands lay at his sides. He wore only a pair of black boxer briefs. The bulge inside them, I thought angrily, was considerable.

The sunlight from the world outside dappled the walls and made them golden. Outside was spring: renewal, life, and green, green, everything green.

The other boy's mouth was fixed in a slight smile.

His chest did not rise or fall.

It was easy, or it should have been, or I wish it had been.

Did he see me? I wonder that even now. I feel like he must have.

I put the butcher knife against the place where his throat met his chest, then I paused. A smell rose off him: vinegar, putridity, piss. It made my eyes water.

His mouth was moving, but no sound came out.

He was mouthing the same word over and over again.

My face screwed up with hatred and sorrow and jealousy and loss.

*Love*, he said, over and over, *love*.
I fell onto the knife.
*Then* it was easy.

I had remembered a short story I read a long time ago by Ray Bradbury. I loved Ray Bradbury. I always felt like Timmy, the little human boy in a series of stories Bradbury wrote about a monster family in Illinois. Timmy was the only "normal" one, like Marilyn in *The Munsters*, I guess. I felt Timmy's pain, his desire to be one of *them* and how lonely he felt that he never would, never *could* be one of *them*. But Timmy wasn't a character in the story I was thinking of when I decided what I had to do about the other boy.

*Silver*, I thought. Silver always does it.

And I was right. I knew I was right because of what happened when I took the jar of silver dollars my father had held onto since he was a kid, when he wanted to be the Lone Ranger or one of those other cowboys in the Westerns he loved. I took them from the bookcase in the bedroom he and my mother shared, took them and dumped them, *all* of them, into the chest cavity of the other boy, which, unlike the creature in the Bradbury story I remembered, was filled with perfectly recognizable anatomy: guts and blood and something twisted and white that I supposed must have been his heart, so maybe he wasn't so human after all.

I poured the silver dollars into the gaping wound I'd cut in the other boy and jumped back, because almost instantly, there was a reaction.

He didn't move; he didn't cry out; but steam or smoke or *something* white and filmy rose from the boy's body, and a baleful hissing sound filled the room.

The body didn't move on its own, but it began to curl up like paper does before a flame, writhing in the heat of an invisible fire. The hissing sound grew louder; an electrical smell, but sweet, so sweet, causing my mouth to water despite myself, issued from the body as it withered and shrank. The coins jangled and clinked against each other.

Then he was gone, and there were the coins all alone, unstained, un-scorched, atop the unstained and un-scorched bedding the other boy had never crawled beneath on the guest room bed.

I thought my breathing would increase. I thought I'd be gasping, or that I'd collapse onto the guest room floor in a faint. Or that I'd be angry or sad or jealous.

I wasn't anything.

I didn't feel anything.

Eventually, I went downstairs and fixed myself a sandwich.

I graduated, five years later, from Waxman University as I intended; my mother passed away during the spring of my freshman year. Breast cancer. Here today, gone tomorrow. We never spoke of the other boy ever again, none of us. They didn't even seem to notice that he wasn't there anymore. I returned the jar of silver dollars to my father's bookcase without issue.

I took a year off from school to help my dad and moved home, back into my old bedroom. We didn't really say much to each other, but that wasn't so unusual. I came downstairs to make him coffee one morning around the first Christmas after Mom's death and found him with his head in his arms, slumped over the kitchen table, his shoulders shaking, but his tears were silent. I froze, didn't know what to do. He wouldn't want me to see him like that, I knew it. So I crept back up the stairs and took a second shower. I remembered the last time I'd stumbled upon him by accident. He'd been so pale and so tired for months after I killed the other boy. I wanted to look for marks on him, but I couldn't think of a way to see him with his shirt off. He quit his job at my old high school and took a job instead at a store in the mall that sold sporting goods. I don't know if he was happy doing it or not. After I went back to college, we talked even less.

Today, I'm getting married. My father is coming to the wedding, as far as I know. He's booked at a hotel at the other end of town from the apartment I share with my fiancé. Dad's never met him. He has gently refused all of our invitations for holiday gatherings. Garden City is five hundred miles away, and Dad hates to drive—hates to leave the house, best I can figure.

But I hope he's there. He told me he would be.

I need him. I tell myself that I've never needed him before, but I do now.

I try to say my fiancé's name.

I'm trying to say it now.

My tongue crawls with little fire ants. They bite when it moves; they remember the icy feeling of that long ago boy when he put his fingers into my mouth and grabbed on.

*Why can't I say his name?*

Dad will know. He'll have to.

Will he be able to help?

Will he recognize him?

Did any of this really happen? Holiday parties for Dad to never attend; dating, getting engaged, planning for our wedding?

What does he look like? *Oh god, I can't see his face.*

I need to see his face.

Dad? Daddy? Are you there?

Help me. Please. I need you. I do. Because I'm afraid.

I'm so so afraid that it's _____ I'll be marrying today.

# About the Author

Laramie Dean is an author born and raised in Montana. He earned his doctoral degree in playwriting from Southern Illinois University Carbondale and has since then published four plays with Theatrefolk: *Frankenstein Among the Dead*, *Dracula*, *The Gorgon Sisters*, and *The Wonderful Wizard of Oz*. He has also published two stories with Qommunicate Publishing, "The Hunter" in the 2019 anthology *Hashtag Queer Volume 3* and "The Pink House" in the 2020 anthology *Geek Out II*. He is currently in the midst of the production of his first novel, *Black Forest*, from Inkshares. Laramie is the director of theatre at Hellgate High School in Missoula, Montana. You may find him on his website, bylaramiedean.com, or follow him at bylaramiedean on Instagram, Twitter, and Facebook.

# Cut Off Your Nose to Spite Your Race

J. Askew

"Did you hear, an enforcement dude got weed on board?"

"Where did he hide it? There's no room in there with that stick shoved up as well," Harper replied. The women laughed; the blue and whiteness of the clinical room seemed to resonate with their sniggers.

"It was only a seed. Can you get that under the foreskin?"

Harper cringed. "You're fucking vile." She smiled at the woman, Scarlett, across from her. Nothing about her was fierce like her name. She was a dreamer, more hopeful than Harper knew how to be. "Reckon we could get some?"

"Na. I don't know who I'd ask. But I've seen them smoking something in the air locks."

Harper loved Scarlett. She had never told her those words, but every night they snuck away from the breeding colony and fucked and laughed and made each other feel better. The only insecurity Harper had in her bones was Scarlett. Did she feel the same way? Or was she keeping herself amused during her stay at the colony? They had only been there a few weeks but the extensive testing on their bodies was soon to yield results. They were nervous. If their ovaries were viable, they'd be treated like queens. Not the kind that sat on golden thrones, but insect queens to birth a new generation of grubs, feeble and new.

"Do you think anyone knows about us?" Scarlett asked.

"Do you give a shit? Doesn't matter who we fuck. It matters how many kids we can squeeze out."

"I hope I can't. I hope I'm all messed up down there."

"Well, I know you're not. But it doesn't matter anyway. We're here and we're gonna have to have a stinking kid, but we'll make our kids fight each other when we're bored."

Scarlett laughed. Her dark skin acquired a shine as her cheekbones heightened. "How many do you think we'll have?"

"They make you stop at three."

"I think I'll have four, just to make a noise."

"I'll have five then, just to beat you."

Harper kissed her teeth at a passing male nurse. She wasn't interested in him, she just liked to make people feel awkward. The man avoided her glare like he did with most of the women in their wing. Harper never took to *domestication*, as she called it. She avoided anything mandatory, imposed by the fledgling government attempting to control the few planets humans had colonized.

She had visions of herself becoming a warrior. Not like an Enforcement officer, but integrating herself into the wilds of a new planet. Strutting through strange jungles scantily clad, sharpening sticks, creating a tribe, leading that tribe; this was the dream she had. Most people, used to living alongside modern technology, couldn't fathom a life like this, but Harper could. She wanted to live organically, free of technology, dirt under her nails, dreadlocks in her hair. She wondered if she could get pregnant on Mars, run away, take Scarlett with her, and they could give birth to their children together, in the jungles of Proxima Centauri B or even Gliese 667 Cc, if they ever learned if humans could breathe the atmosphere. It wasn't one of those dreams that would eventually come true if you read enough books or took enough tests; it was a wild dream, for a wild girl.

The mess room of the breeding colony was clinical but had a large window looking over the Sands of Mars. Harper knew Scarlett dreamt of being out there with the science teams, tapping at calculators, swimming in data, soil samples, but as a 17-year-old woman, she was rushing to complete her enlistment at the breeding colony so she could be free of mandatory duties. She wanted to get it out of the way and pursue her career. Needless to say, the job was easier for the men.

"You wanna quit staring out the window and look at me?" Harper asked.

"It's the special time, Harper. It's our 37 minutes." Scarlett didn't lift her eyes.

Harper smiled at the notion. There was a time in the day on Mars, the 37 minutes, that referred to the extra time it took the planet to orbit the Sun compared to Earth. It was still special to the two women, despite the fact they had both been born as children of the breeding colony and had never known a real Earth day.

"Exactly. We need to head back to our cabins. It's nearly midnight. I've been sharpening an old toothbrush, gotta finish it tonight."

"You're making a shank? We're not prisoners, Harps."

"You ever tried walking out of here?" Harper leaned back, spread her legs, and propped her head up with her hands. Scarlett was the kind of girl who followed the rules even when she didn't agree with them. She avoided conflict, avoided expressing her opinions. It wasn't her fault, it was the way she had been raised in the orbiting orphanage.

"No." Scarlett looked at her, sheepish, analyzing every word Harper said.

"I got as far as the dock. Armed guards gave me a gentle shove back inside." She leaned forward for effect. "Said I was the first one to even bother having a look around the docks. Isn't that weird?"

"Maybe you're the weird one, Harps." Scarlett piled three notepads up and bundled them into her arms. She had one pad for random musings, one for semi-formed ideas, and another for concrete theories she was teasing out.

"I think you're the weird one. Never questioning anything."

"I do. I just pick my battles, and I think it's far more important to question our understanding in science than the authority figures who feed us."

When they said goodbye that night, there was a shift, an awkwardness. The results of their fertility tests would begin to filter back to all the subjects on board the next day. It meant their fates would be decided. Some would receive them at sunrise, and others, the ones who were infertile, would hear late at night. They called it the Numbering, and both women secretly hoped to be barren. If they were fertile, it could take up to three years for them to meet the quota of three children.

Harper watched the liberal news daily. Protests were beginning to rise against the terms of the breeding colony. The campaigners understood the need for the colony, to ensure humans continued to exist where breeding was difficult. But they felt women should only need to birth a single child and be given a choice to either stay on Mars to take that child to term or be allowed to leave and not put their lives on pause for nine months and come back to give birth. Harper hoped, if she were fertile, the campaigners would get something done before she was due to birth her second. Oddly, the media never heard from the women who were barren, like they were blessed and never looked back.

"Sand, Harper," the officer read from his pad in the morning. His call echoed through the vast hall. It seemed to reach the tops of the ceiling and sprinkle down to the tables, chairs, and packs of cards that lay scattered around— a small distraction in a room of waiting women. Their faces sunk when Harper's name was called, like they thought Harper would never have been touched because she was so wild, untameable, strong perhaps. She knew the rest of the young women looked up to her, and the fact she was called in first made it feel like the officers were making an example of her.

Harper stood. She wasn't shocked to have passed the Numbering. She guessed she was pretty fertile. Her periods had been regular all her adult life, and she had had no issues gynecologically.

"I hope it has three heads at least," she muttered to the officer as she placed her palm on his scanner. It confirmed her identity and he led her away from the others, who were quietly giggling at her sarcasm. Scarlett's eyes started to shine as Harper turned to say goodbye, but seeing her clever, simple girl tear up made her gut hurt. Instead of the living goodbye she had planned, she simply held out her hands in horns like she was a rock-star.

"Do we get to pick our baby daddies?" Harper mocked the male officer as they marched down a hall of strip lighting. He had olive skin and a moustache that the 1920s were still looking for.

"We match your DNA with an appropriate male."

"Do you have any lesbian males?"

The officer laughed. Harper could always shatter the demure of authority. "No, Sand. You'll be paired with someone who heightens your natural attributes. You'll never meet them."

"Will it hurt?"

"No. Not at all."

"That's a shame," Harper replied.

The officer smirked again but his face straightened rapidly as a steel door rose before them and led them into a new wing of the colony. "Your room is B2. Settle in. When you have the procedure, you'll be asked to stay for the gestation of your child. Once the maternity and pediatric staff are happy with the birth and the child's development, you will have the procedure again. This process will repeat until you have birthed three surviving young or can no longer birth young. Then we thank you for your duty to humankind and you may continue your life, preferably with your children."

Harper rolled her eyes. She knew all this.

"Ms. Sand, may I suggest you get an education during your stay here? We have excellent courses that will set you and your children up for a fantastic future."

Harper rolled her eyes again.

When Harper Sand reached her room, she counted the doors leading to it. She hoped Scarlett wouldn't be placed too far. Inside, she rooted around erratically, searching for entertainment. Soon, she found the jackpot.

A mini-fridge rested in the small grey cabin. It was full of food and drinks. She laughed— there were pickles. A screen hung suspended from the ceiling and once Harper had discovered the remote, she chose the option for 1980.

*"Wouldn't you like to get away?"* the sitcom's theme tune sang.

"Fuck yeah I would," she replied, reaching for the replica cola chilled on the side. She shuffled the plastic shank she had finished the night before. It rested in her waist belt. Soon, her stomach would be too big to hide a shank in her pants.

Three episodes passed before Harper had consumed the contents of the mini-fridge. She enjoyed binging and hadn't been able to since she was with her mother. Although women were required to birth children, as soon as they had met their quota, they were able to pursue their careers and life. It was still preferable that the resulting children stay with their mothers, despite the fact they were never wanted in the first place, which is how Harper's story began with her own mother. When a child was unwanted, it was sent to one of the colony orphanages whose walls were now filled with the cries of abandoned children. Harper was lucky: her mother couldn't fight her maternal instinct.

An uninvited video erupted across the screen. A pale man and a dark woman appeared in lab coats looking official and ironic.

"Congratulations! You have passed the necessary requirements to fulfill the purpose of the breeding colony."

Harper cringed at the man's shrill voice and wondered if the woman was any shriller.

"Some time ago, humankind left the cradle and made it to the stars. We transported one percent of people from our planet, but unfortunately, a flu wiped out the remaining population." The woman had a surprisingly deep voice. Harper's interest piqued.

"We are now midway through a fifty-year program to breathe new life into our race, to support humankind, and to colonize the galaxy. We thank you for your service."

The room darkened and cast a strange purple light over the crumbs and litter radiating from Harper's binge. There was a strange hum. Harper searched the room for answers but accepted the happenings quickly. She thumbed at a necklace hanging at an odd angle around her neck. The pendant was a vintage bullet. Her mother told her it would make her invincible, but she thought she was already.

Her harsh face softened as the lights returned to normal. She felt relieved but quickly became annoyed at herself for worrying in the first place. She reached for the pad that powered the screen but before her black-painted fingernails could touch it, she was asleep.

"I told you it wouldn't hurt," Harper heard as she came to. The officer stood over her. Harper wore a medical gown, and her heart rate was being monitored.

"Just like that, eh? I was watching Netflix, then this?" Harper gurgled, her throat dry from the procedure.

"Hopefully. You're a high-risk case so we had to sedate. Your urine will be tested in a week."

"High-risk? Like something a bit off internally?"

"No, Sand. You misbehave."

Harper laughed but then gagged from the dryness of her mouth. The man passed her some water. An image of a tiny child rested in her mind.

She wanted to treat this with the same indifference she had felt her whole life, but something in her had started to crumble. She hated to think it, but there was a part of her that found a gentleness in the thought of having a child. It was a thing to call your own, a thing to be best friends with, a thing to be a warrior for. Harper imagined having a little version of herself, to swear with and teach the finer art of sarcasm. She wouldn't tell Scarlett of this softening within herself. No one would know that but her.

"Tell us your name then," she asked the officer through cracked lips.

"Officer Goodwin."

"Your proper name."

"Farol, but don't call me that in front of people."

Harper Sand laughed. "You'd be surprised how many of you officers break the rules."

"Don't tell me things like that."

"Can you do me a favor? When I get back to my room?"

Farol Goodwin nodded.

"There's a girl. She's one of the younger ones. She's only 17. Scarlett Alora. She's got dark skin. Real curly hair, black. Check on her for me, find out what her results were. I can't lie here thinking she's going through this, too. She's not as brave as me. She's one of the quiet ones, likes science and shit, not sharp sticks."

Farol handed Harper her clothes. Inside, the shank lay, ominous. He caught Harper's eye. He had seen it and was giving it back to her.

Harper bugged Farol Goodwin for days with no fear of consequences. He had kept his word and discovered Scarlett Alora was infertile. This made the life now growing inside Harper feel special, and she hated that. Scarlett was to be shipped back to her training academy so she could live her dream. Harper was pleased for her. She would be out on the sands of Mars in a few years with no burden, just her notebooks and her amazing mind with the horizon of the red planet ahead of her. Farol was due to deliver a message to the girl, a message from Harper. It was a farewell of sorts, and a question.

The day before Harper was due to have her urine tested for pregnancy confirmation, Farol came to her quarters. He didn't know it, but Harper had been stroking her own stomach, her mind chasing a child she had not yet had.

"Let's go," he ordered.

"Buddy, is this one of those official commands or is this a wink-wink situation?"

He winked at her in reply. She jumped from her bed where she had been lying, her shank resting innocently near litter and odd stains, and wiped food crumbs from her breasts.

"She's still here?"

"She's leaving tonight. I gave her your message. She wants to say goodbye in person."

"Can I get to her? She's going straight back to her academy, right?"

"Follow me," Farol said as he opened her cabin door and switched off the hall lights. "We need to keep it dark."

Harper counted twenty steps, then they took a right, then a left, but every corridor looked the same to her. When Farol raised his finger to his mouth, hushing her, her heart nearly sprang from its home. He pressed a code on a white door and the ship's hangar lay before them: the docks.

A line of women, fewer than before, boarded a ship, guided calmly by armed guards. Harper could not see Scarlett in the line, but Farol led her to the side of the large room where more women sat, heads down like they were ashamed. Some were tied up.

"Why are they tied up?" Harper asked him with volume. Whispering was a stranger to her lips.

"Keep it down. They're restrained, just in case."

"In case of what?"

"Look, shit is never perfect. We have a duty here but there are kinks, loopholes, budget issues. Some of these women now want to be in your position."

"Why the fuck would they want that?"

"Please, try to be quiet. Most came from the slums. Getting pregnant with us is the only way they can feed themselves, have a better life. Some of them study with us, gain many qualifications over the time they're here. But, some of the guards make contacts with less savory shippers out there. You've seen the news about the workers on early colonies?"

"Yeah—slave labor violations."

Farol just nodded.

Harper was puzzled, but it was clearing. Farol never told her things straight: every word was an insinuation. She gulped, the line of women ahead of her oozing with fear, with confusion. *They're the slaves,* she thought. She shuddered, felt ashamed for how lucky she had been. She had had a great life with her mother and siblings. Her mother didn't want children— that was clear—but what she found was something more. Harper's mother saw her offspring as friends, little versions of herself that she treated like she would want to be treated. Their relationship was informal. Harper's mother taught her all the swearwords she knew and taught her to be a warrior. She revelled in the joy she had shared with her mother. Her heart seemed to catch a second beat at this thought, like she had become two.

Harper's cat-like eyes flickered across the line of women, all of their hopes for a better life fading away. She saw Scarlett's hair halfway down the line and she bolted to her. Scarlett barely registered Harper as she sunk to her knees in front of her, grasping for eye contact from the girl.

"Hey, hey. Look at me. Scarlett, I'm here."

Scarlett looked up slowly. "Harper, it's not what I thought. They won't let me train for the science…" Her eyes darted towards the ceiling and glazed over.

"Hey, kiddo. Look at me. Please look at me. I need you to keep talking." Harper placed a gentle palm on Scarlett's knee. Farol was behind them, standing straight and trying not to look suspicious.

"There's a raffle," Scarlett whispered. "That's why they call it the Numbering. Not because we get pregnant, not because we multiply."

"And what happens if you get picked?"

"Companies buy the tickets, Harper. They buy tickets for workers. The breeding colony doesn't see us as people when we lose our value to them. Oh, Harper…" She began to sob. Harper's chest was a ball of agony, her eyes fed grief to her heart, the grief of seeing Scarlett cry.

"So, what then?" Harper rested her hands on either side of Scarlett's face.

"Then the raffle happens and they take away a new workforce, the companies. Most of the women who can't have kids go with it. I don't wanna go with it, not alone. Please, make it go away." Her eyes seemed to drift from this world to the next over and over again like she'd been drugged. "You didn't pass the Numbering, Harper: you weren't even in it."

"What happens to the others? The ones that don't get picked for work?"

"They let them go. Like we talked about. They let them live their lives and follow their careers like we all thought, but the breeding colony started making more money from these private companies selling workers, saying we all need to contribute. The odds are against us now, Harps. It's like a one in ten chance you won't get picked for a work force. The work they do, Harps, it's not me. It's not what I want to do. It's like the railroad work from Ancient Earth, like... like slavery."

"When are they drawing the tickets, Scarlett? You need to tell me." Harper's hands had begun to sweat against Scarlett's cheeks.

"They already have. I've been drawn. I told you, it's the odds."

Harper didn't react. Instead, her mind rolled over and over, searching every nook of possibility for a way out. She thumbed at the shank in her waistband, analyzed the armed guards.

"Don't, Sand," Farol warned from behind her. "You can't beat this. It's bigger than you, and you need to protect the life inside you." Harper was sure he was being genuine.

"Can we fight this?" she asked Farol.

He shook his head. "It's big."

Harper stood. She turned and took Farol by the collar of his white shirt. She drew him in, made his head rest on her shoulder.

"Where are these people being taken?"

"Titan," Farol muttered.

"It's fucking cold there. They gonna be building the domes? The little fucking greenhouses we need to invade that moon?"

"I don't know, Sand. Most likely."

"Scarlett, remember to pick your battles, don't question this, not now—trust me. Farol, take me back to my cabin." Harper looked down at

Scarlett as she let go of Farol. A few women looked at her but pretended not to.

As she left Scarlett behind, the air cascaded past her ears like she was flying at lightspeed. Everything around her was fast, as if she was enveloped in tar and could not move with the world around her. Her brow was permanently furrowed. Thoughts of running through an alien forest as Scarlett studied the flora and fauna flashed through her. She and Scarlett had different dreams, that was clear. Harper's vision of her future was selfish. She had always molded Scarlett to star in variations of it, but she was living in a time that was a colony gold rush. Rights didn't matter when land and money were available.

She thought of the life inside her. She felt like a mother, like she was the only person that child could depend on, like Scarlett had depended on her for the months they had been waiting on Mars. The child had no choice, and neither did Harper, neither did Scarlett. Maybe, when the kid was born, the rules would be better, the rights of space-born humans more important. Maybe, Harper's child wouldn't have to face the choice she now faced.

"Come back in ten minutes," Harper asked Farol as he led her back to her room. "Only ten. I won't need more."

When he left, Harper leaned against the wall. She thumbed at the shank, adjusted it over and over, and finally moved it into her bra, a place Farol wouldn't check. Maybe, just maybe, it would stay with her until she was able to make her next choice. Maybe that would take months, maybe years, but Harper knew there was nothing that could be done to calm a warrior soul, especially one that longed for the soul of another: a kind, smart, gentle being, Scarlett.

Harper Sand reached to her bed, took the comms pad meant for the television, and cracked it with her heel. It didn't break straight away but she went at it with all her twisted energy, digging and stamping her foot over and over. Soon it became two shards, wires and glass pooling from the device like a bad hair day. She lifted the biggest shard and let the glint catch her eye. Then she plunged it with all her force, all her strength, her character, her love, into her lower abdomen.

She howled. It took more pressure than she'd ever imagined to slice her own flesh with the fragile glass. She forced it deep, making sure it made the damage she so desperately needed. Fragments of it splintered into her flesh as the blood came, thin at first, but thickening as the fresh wound seeped. The tears filling her eyes trickled and joined the blood congealing in the seams of her clothes. She lay back on the bed, twisting in and out of consciousness with the rupturing pain that proceeded. She smiled and laughed at the lightness in her head, while the new gentleness in her heart vanished and the fight for Scarlett reared its head and enveloped her.

Farol rushed into Harper's cabin, hurried by her guttural cries. Harper turned to the man, her only kindness in a world where it paid to be tough. Her tears turned him into a mirage of warped slivers of images, and she let a sigh pass through her lips.

"Take me back to Scarlett. I won't be having babies anymore."

Saturn loomed in the yellow sky. Its rings looped around and around like an eternal train track. Harper Sand adjusted her breathing mask and heat suit and broke ground with the heated shovel she had become so used to operating. Scarlett lay a gentle hand on Harper's back and settled on the cold ground with her notepad, hidden from their guards by the ridge Harper had dug for Scarlett to study in. Her heart beat against the old plastic toothbrush shank, still hidden, still waiting.

# About the Author

Science fiction and horror writer J. Askew explores mental health issues, sexual identity, diversity, and disability through her fiction. She often shows weaknesses as strengths at the end of the world. She writes space operas, dystopian dramas, and weird fiction, all steeped in plot twists and stand-out characters. As an LGBTQIA+ activist, she aims to use her fiction to make the world a better place for the next generation to come out in. You can find her at JAskewAuthor.com.

# For The Gods
Robert P. Ottone

DeAndre stood in his new bedroom, staring in the full-length mirror his sister Amara gifted him before heading off to college. At twelve years old, DeAndre already felt something of a crisis about his scrawny frame. His arms were thin. His legs, too. He had hoped running track would somehow turn him into a muscle-bound speed demon.

"You're just a late-bloomer," his father told him, time and time again when he questioned himself for joining the team. Not the fastest or the slowest, he considered *middle of the pack* an apt descriptor. "You'll see, bud: you'll grow into yourself soon enough."

The added stress of moving to a smaller house in a new town worsened matters. His room was fine, and they had a pool, but in the end, he was without what few friends he had back in the Bronx and couldn't imagine how he'd go about making new ones during the summer. The town itself, Resting Hollow, was nice and all—*quaint* was the word that seemed to flicker through DeAndre's mind more than any other, probably because his last vocabulary test featured it and he misspelled it—but it wasn't the bustling metropolitan atmosphere DeAndre was used to. He'd have to get used to "quiet nights in the country," something his dad was all-too-excited to enjoy.

Wearing his Teenage Mutant Ninja Turtles bathing suit, DeAndre hoped a summer of swimming and working with his dad would help bulk him up. With school over, DeAndre was praying he'd be sent to summer camp with his friends from the old block, holding onto a distant hope that a summer together would help bridge the gap between his leaving the city and heading to the country. Maybe it would give him a chance to tell his friends how great his new house and pool were so they'd make the forty-five minute drive out to see him?

"Hey bud, dinner first, then pool time, okay?" he heard his dad say. "Look at you, you're getting ripped!"

DeAndre rolled his eyes. "Dad, come *on* …"

"Sorry, just bustin' chops. Five minutes, butt in seat outside," Dad said, smiling. "You excited to see Amara?

DeAndre shrugged. "I guess." He looked  around his room at the other items he inherited from his sister. Her record player. Her New Kids on the Block, Madonna, MC Hammer and other albums. Amara's Patrick Swayze and Brad Pitt posters secretly hung in DeAndre's closet, their intense looks greeting the boy each morning as he picked out what to wear.

Various items remained scattered around, most still waiting to be set up.

"You're too early for this 'moody teenager' shit, buddy-boy," Dad said, furrowing his brow.

"Dad, you cursed! Swear jar!"

"You're right, I did. Sometimes it's worth it, though," Dad said, pulling a quarter out of his pocket and turning towards the hallway.

As Dad turned, the closet door in DeAndre's room unlatched and opened ever so slightly with a creak. Dad walked over to it, looked at the latch, examined the hinges, and closed the closet.

"Another project for us, eh, bud?" With that, Dad turned and walked down the hallway, toward the kitchen.

DeAndre heard the satisfying clink of the quarter slipping into the former spaghetti sauce jar sitting on the counter of their new kitchen, one of the last of the renovation projects Dad had planned.

He hoped by the end of summer, the jar would be filled with enough quarters to buy the weight set he had his eyes on at Terry's Gym Supply in town.

DeAndre and his dad ate cheeseburgers fresh off the grill in their backyard. Lightning bugs danced in the sky, sparking, then fading in their usual summer choreography. The sky burned an intense orange-purple.

The pool sat nearby, stealing most of DeAndre's attention. The house needed updates and repairs, but the pool was perfect. It even had a heater. DeAndre, used to the square and rectangular pools in the city's various YMCAs and Boys' Clubs, found a kidney-shaped pool weird. But he realized that a pool was a pool, and at the end of the day, he'd be spending as much of the summer as possible swimming, floating and enjoying his own private slice of watery heaven.

"I saw that *Batman Returns* is coming out in a couple weeks," Dad said. "You wanna' go?"

DeAndre thought about when he saw the first *Batman* movie. His mom, still around then, hid her eyes during the fight scenes, which made DeAndre laugh. This was before she decided to head out for a pack of cigarettes and never return. DeAndre wondered late at night whether she *really* did head out for cigarettes and something awful just happened to her, or if it was just an excuse to slip away.

"Sure," DeAndre said. "That baseball movie's coming out, too, I thought that looked pretty funny."

"Baseball movie? *Major League*? Didn't that come out already?"

"No, I think this one's different," DeAndre said. "It's like, about women playing baseball."

Dad laughed. "That *is* funny. I'll look into it, kiddo."

Without warning, a backpack sailed over the fence to the side of the house, and with it, DeAndre's sister, Amara, bounding after it. Athletic, tall, hair that curled in perfect impossibility, the girl was a blend of their mom's beauty and Dad's natural athleticism. DeAndre's self-worth always took a hit when she was around, even though she never intended it.

"Something smells good!" Amara shouted, running over and hugging her little brother, giving him a big kiss on the cheek. He winced and tried to wipe his face. "You better leave that kiss on there, buddy-boy, otherwise I'll give you ten more."

DeAndre knew this wasn't an empty threat. He took another bite of his burger.

"How's my little girl?" Dad asked, hugging her and lifting her off the ground.

"Didn't you get my grades?" she asked, smiling.

"We got a letter, but we've been busy, and it's not addressed to me, so I didn't open it," Dad said.

"Dad, if it's from school, dive in, I don't give a shit," Amara said, grabbing a cheeseburger and pulling the bun off it. "No carbs for me, this summer, Dad. I need to cut weight for the fall."

"Swear jar!" DeAndre shouted.

"Swear jar?" Amara mumbled, her mouth full of burger.

Dad nodded. "Swear jar," and pointed toward the kitchen. He handed her a quarter and she slipped into the house.

That night, Amara and DeAndre sat by the pool, draped in towels, both of them drying off. The night air radiated warmth, and they kept their feet submerged.

"How was the end of the school year, kiddo?"

DeAndre shrugged. "Good, I guess. I got a C in woodshop."

"Woodshop? Making birdhouses and stuff?"

The boy nodded. "I forgot to drill the hole for the birds in mine when I submitted it."

Amara laughed. "Yeah, that'll do it."

"What's college like?"

She smiled. "Amazing. There's so many people. Everyone's different, and interesting, and there's so much creativity."

DeAndre smiled. "That sounds cool," he paused and looked at the water. Soft light lit the entire pool from within, casting an almost-radioactive glow to the area and bathing DeAndre and Amara in white-blue light. "Do you miss the city?"

"Nah," she said. "There are so many people at school; even though we're in a small town, there's so much to do. The city is a different animal, but like, at school, literally, every night is something new. It's so much fun." She looked at him. "Do *you* miss the city?"

He nodded. "Yeah."

She put her arm around him. "I'm sorry, Dee. I promise you'll get used to life here. You'll make new friends. You'll miss your old ones, sure, but you're young."

"You made new friends, right?"

She nodded. "A lot."

"Any...*boy*friends?" he asked, teasing, stretching *boy* out to obnoxious lengths.

She laughed. "You're such a dork."

"That's not an answer," DeAndre said, laughing.

"If you *must* know, yes, a few boys have taken me out," she said. She looked at him out of the corner of her eye. "Some girls, too."

"What?" he asked, looking at her. "Girls? What do you mean?"

"You know, like, I've gone out with guys, and some girls, too. Like, on dates and stuff."

DeAndre stared at his big sister. He was confused. DeAndre didn't know how to react. "Huh."

"That's it? Just 'huh'? Don't tell Dad, okay?"

"Sure, yeah, okay. So…you like girls, then? Does that mean you're gay?"

"First of all, how do you know what that means? Second of all, I don't know, that's kinda what college is all about. Figuring your shit out."

"Swear jar," DeAndre said.

"Damn it."

"Dad was watching *Roseanne*, and it was the one where Dan, the dad on the show, was upset because his son wanted to dress up as a witch for Halloween," DeAndre explained. "I asked why it was a big deal, and Dad told me that some people aren't accepting of people who are different."

"How did Dad sound when he told you that?" Amara asked.

A sudden splash in the water caught their attention. They looked into the pool, and seeing nothing, looked at each other.

"Maybe it was a rock?"

"It's late, who's out throwing rocks into random people's yards and pools?" Amara asked.

DeAndre slipped his goggles on, dipped into the water, and slowly treaded over to where the splash erupted. He slipped under the surface and looked around. The section of the pool where the splash happened, the eight-foot area, had been separated from the three-foot area by a plastic safety rope connected to white and red flotation devices.

Empty. DeAndre re-emerged, took his goggles off, and looked at Amara, standing nearby, wrapped in her towel. The wind picked up and she shivered. "Let's go inside, okay?"

She helped DeAndre out of the pool, and he placed his goggles down on the side, near the ladder out of the water, and wrapped himself in his towel. They walked through the sliding doors and into the living room where Dad was watching the news.

That night, DeAndre lay asleep in bed. His Ninja Turtle nightlight cast yellow-green illumination around the base of the floor between the door to his room and the door to his closet.

With a ferocity, the closet door swung open, slamming into the wall. DeAndre awoke with a start and looked around. His half-awake mind refocused and he glanced toward the closet. He thought he caught a wisp of breeze float through the room, pulling toward the closet. The boy shivered in the dark, and he tucked himself further into his blankets.

He watched as the closet door started closing slowly. Again, it slapped open. DeAndre rose and walked over to the closet, one hand on the door. He reached in slowly and grasped the chain hanging from the ceiling lamp. Clicking it on, he sighed at the piles of boxes still waiting to be unpacked, shelves stacked with various GI Joe figures, Amara's old Barbie and Ken dolls, a half-deflated basketball, pairs of sneakers, baseball caps, and a glove. His clothes hung on the left and right sides of the large space, which, if there weren't any boxes on the ground, would truly be the walk-in closet his dad promised him.

Looking around inside, he couldn't find any vents or openings. He still felt the wisp of cool air pulling him in, but he couldn't figure out from where it could possibly be coming.

He leaned into the closet more, trying to feel the air flowing around him. He moved his clothes around on the left rod. Just an empty wall. No space for a draft.

*Why would the air be flowing* into *the closet?* he wondered. A thick musk suddenly filled the space, and DeAndre breathed deep. It was heavy, but not unpleasant, almost minty in fragrance.

Turning to the clothes on the right, he heard a low *hiss* from within. Slowly, he began to part the clothes, expecting to find a snake, a Komodo dragon, or some other nocturnal hissing nightmare, and instead met a pair of glowing purple eyes: almond-shaped, piercing and beautiful.

DeAndre froze in place, his body betraying him, as every muscle tensed to burst from the closet. The light above flickered, and slowly, a hand emerged from the darkness behind the clothes. Thin. Bone-white. Fingernails sharpened to a point on each finger, more claws than anything else.

DeAndre shivered and felt a loss of bladder control. The hand caressed his cheek and wiped away a tear that suddenly fell. As quickly as it emerged, the hand slipped back into the darkness, the eyes closed, and the aroma and wind vanished from the room.

After his mind stopped firing in a thousand different directions, his legs fired in only one: directly out of the room and into Amara's, where she helped him get cleaned up. He slept uncomfortably through the night, his mind racing at what was lurking in his closet.

The next morning, DeAndre sat at the kitchen table, eating Pop Tarts with his father, who read the newspaper. He didn't know if he should tell Dad about what happened the night before, since he couldn't be sure if it *actually* happened or not. He knew that he peed himself, and it had been easy enough to change his clothes and wash himself before sleeping in Amara's room, but the entire ordeal felt more like a dream than reality.

Before breakfast, DeAndre checked his closet again and found nothing. No wind. No smell. No purple eyes hiding behind his Starter jackets. *Had to be a dream*, he thought, taking a hearty bite out of his second strawberry Pop Tart.

"Buddy-boy, today, we tackle the basement steps, then we work on that loose railing," Dad said. "If we get done early enough, maybe we grab some pizza in town?"

"Sounds good," DeAndre said.

Amara entered the room, scruffed her brother's hair, and grabbed the rest of the Pop Tart from his hands, scarfing it down quickly.

"What was going on in your room last night, bud? Why were you slamming the door?" Dad asked.

DeAndre looked up at Amara, trying to think of something. Dad had heard the door slamming. At the very least, the part about his closet door opening on its own had happened. "The wind, I guess. The door doesn't latch very well."

"Right, right, we can grab some stuff at the hardware store to fix that, bud," Dad said, placing the newspaper down. "Sweet girl, you wanna' join us for lunch later? We're gonna hit that pizza place in town."

"Barf, Dad. No carbs, remember?"

"They have salads, I'm sure," Dad said, rolling his eyes. "You about ready, Dee?"

DeAndre nodded. He and Dad rose from the table and started for the closet in the hallway. They grabbed the tools and headed for the basement door, which sat in the hallway, connecting to the stairs leading to the second floor.

DeAndre hadn't spent much time in the basement of the new house, so he didn't know exactly what to expect once he was able to explore the space. He imagined the Rat King or possibly Baxter Stockman doing experiments to finally figure out a way to defeat the turtles and Splinter.

Instead, he found some broken steps, a busted railing, and some broken lightbulbs. The rest of the space was empty, other than the crawlspace between the first floor and basement that started about five steps down.

The air near the crawlspace felt cold, and DeAndre noticed the faintest hint of mint coming from within. "Do you smell that?"

Dad sniffed the air. He shook his head. "Smells like a basement. Why?"

DeAndre shrugged. "Nothing, I guess."

"You know, buddy-boy, once we get all the repairs in the house totally done, we could maybe turn this basement into a cool den or something for me and you. Maybe hang some Yankee posters? Put up one of those huge televisions? Sound system? Hell, even a mini-movie theater!"

DeAndre couldn't take his eyes from the crawlspace. Inside, he heard the same hissing as he had heard in his closet. Then, softly, a sensual voice quietly whispered, *"DeAndre ..."*

DeAndre bit his lower lip, a shiver crawling up the back of his legs, the feeling becoming more of a tingle as it rose, the voice lingering in his mind, his body reacting as though tiny, sharp icicles were gliding their way up his spine. He exhaled slowly and thought, for a moment, that he saw his breath in the dim light of the basement.

Dad stared at the boy. "Dee? You okay, pal?"

DeAndre looked around. As quickly as it came, the sensation vanished. "Yeah, sorry: 'spaced out, I guess."

"I know. I even cursed and you didn't yell at me to put a quarter in the jar. Hand me that screwdriver, will ya'?"

That afternoon, DeAndre, Amara, and Dad headed into town. DeAndre was exhausted from a day of working on the house. After the basement, they tackled the railing, then did a quick assessment of the needed items for the closet door. Dad also wanted to get an idea of what he'd need to finish the basement once they were done with everything else, so he was in a deep conversation with the two clerks at the hardware store while DeAndre's mind remained focused on the feeling that had been coursing through his body in the basement.

At the store, even at the pizza shoppe, DeAndre couldn't shake the feeling from the basement. He couldn't get the voice out of his head. He couldn't escape those intense, purple, beautiful eyes. He remembered the cold feeling of the hand on his cheek.

When Dad got up to refill his soda, DeAndre kicked his sister under the table.

"Ow, you ding-dong!"

"Shh. I think our house is *haunted*."

She smiled. "What makes you say that? Because of last night?"

"A feeling I had in the basement," he said, his voice low.

"Why are you whispering?"

"I'm freaked out about it," DeAndre said, with a sigh.

Amara made a pouty face. "Little dude, there's no such thing as ghosts, I promise. It's a new house, in a new place. I swear, nothing can hurt you. It's just your excellent imagination running wild, okay?"

DeAndre nodded. Amara usually made him feel better about things right away, but this time, he still felt nervous about whatever happened in his bedroom and in the basement.

He felt almost as though he had kept some kind of dirty secret from his father, but instead of feeling guilt, DeAndre wanted *more*. He replayed the voice over and over in his mind, and each time, he felt the slightest hint of that familiar tingle in his legs, back, and arms. He recognized the element of teenage hormonal reaction—sure, he learned about that in health class—but it felt more like the excitement when one tries something new and *loves* it, or the feeling one gets while overcome with joy and happiness while dancing. Sprinkles of that level of love and joy, scintillated all through DeAndre's body, accompanied by an impossible heat in his chest that at first, the boy chalked up to being summer, but now, realized it had to be something *more*.

Pure, unfiltered *happiness*. And in that happiness, DeAndre felt remarkable *truth*. Whatever had been in his closet. Whatever hid in the crawl space. Whatever lurked in the *house*. DeAndre wanted *more*. More of that feeling. More of the excitement. Just thinking about it sparked tingling in his chest. He hadn't felt this way before.

And he *needed* more.

When they got home, DeAndre made a beeline for his bedroom. The closet door creaked open slowly. Dad followed him, and the two started repairing the latch on the door. It seemed like it took forever for DeAndre's dad to make the repair, and the anticipation of having his dad out of the room felt palpable.

"How much longer?"

"Almost done, kiddo," Dad said, tightening the screws. He stood up and closed the closet, listening for the catch of the new latch. He nodded and smiled once it clicked into place. He tugged hard on the knob, trying to get the door to open without turning the knob and found it wouldn't budge. "There we go, bud. Let's go watch the ballgame, huh? I'd say you've earned a bit of relaxing."

"Be there in a sec," DeAndre said, his eyes locked on the closet doorknob.

"Hey, did you want me to get rid of Amara's old posters? The guy from *Dirty Dancing*? That's more for girls, isn't it?"

"I like *Roadhouse*," DeAndre said, eyes darting to the floor nervously.

The old man smiled and shook his head, then left, and DeAndre's gaze remained fixed on the door. Slowly, the knob turned and the closet opened with a soft creak. The musky smell of mint wafted into the room, and DeAndre stepped closer to the closet, slipping inside and clicking on the light above him.

He felt the soft breeze through the light hairs on his arms and legs. He closed his eyes and let the air swirl around him. *Through* him. A tightness in his throat caused him to swallow hard, and the familiar intensity of heat swelled in his chest, then his stomach.

"*DeAndre…*"

He opened his eyes and saw two violet orbs staring back at him. More animal than human, the eyes had flecks of gold in them, with inky dark pupils that seemed dilated.

The eyes belonged to a figure: slender, almost emaciated, with skin a gray-white chalky color. DeAndre's eyes roamed the figure's form and he noted that its face looked human, but after staring at it for a while, he realized something was *off*. It was a perfect facsimile of a person's face, smooth in the right places, angular at others, symmetrical in a way that doesn't often occur in nature. It wasn't beautiful. It just *was*.

"Who are you?" DeAndre asked, his voice shaking.

"*I am whatever you want me to be*," the figure said softly. DeAndre felt the icy pinpricks run up his spine whenever the figure spoke.

"You know my name already…I should know yours."

The creature's eyes darted around the closet, glowing an intense amethyst, the way a cat moves while tracing a fly in the air. The figure pointed a slender finger to one of the posters on the inside of the closet door: a chiseled, long-haired man in torn overalls staring into the sunlit distance.

"Patrick Swayze?"

"*Sway-zee…*"

"That's what you want me to call you?"

The figure nodded slowly, eyes locked on DeAndre's. "*Swayyyyyyzzzz …*"

"I like that. Swayz.'"

Swayz nodded, smiling, his thin lips stretching in an unnatural way, almost too-wide. At first, DeAndre recoiled, but after a moment, he found it funny.

"What *are* you, Swayz?"

Swayz shook its head. It rose from its crouched position and stood about as tall as DeAndre, if slightly smaller. The creature appeared to have no gender, as it had nothing on its body to indicate male or female. DeAndre covered his eyes, embarrassed to see the "nude" creature before him.

"*Why cover?*"

"Not s'posed to see other people naked," DeAndre said quietly, hand still over his eyes.

Swayz reached over and placed an icy hand on the boy's wrist. With little force, he lowered DeAndre's hand, and the two stared into each other's eyes.

"*A face fit for the gods,*" Swayz whispered in the dim light.

When DeAndre exited the closet, something he would do thousands of times over the next three years, he always buzzed with happiness and excitement to face the rest of his day.

First thing in the morning, DeAndre would find himself slipping into the closet to greet Swayz, who, over the years, grew and matured as well, its lithe body changing, ignoring gender while also showing signs of both sexes. Swayz seemed unaffected by it. The being cared more about spending time with the boy than the gender-swapping that its body was soaring through every day. DeAndre found his eyes roaming over the creature's body more and more as they both grew older.

Over time, the house took shape, too, with DeAndre and his dad making renovations as they went slowly along. The basement turned into a man cave of sorts, decorated with Yankee memorabilia, neon beer signs, a bar, and other items. DeAndre's videogames were down there, so when DeAndre would slip downstairs after dinner, Dad just assumed he was playing videogames before bed.

Instead, DeAndre and Swayz were relaxing, listening to music while DeAndre did his homework. Sometimes he'd talk on the phone with Amara, who was going to law school, working hard, and partying even harder. She loved divulging the details of her nights out to her teenaged brother, and sometimes, during DeAndre and Swayz's basement dance parties, the boy would imagine himself in a Brooklyn nightclub, bathed in neon light, sweat glistening, music pulsing.

At bedtime, the two enjoyed each other's company, talking late into the night, Swayz on the floor between DeAndre's bed and the window, the creature's lavender-colored eyes beaming in the moonlight.

In those three years, DeAndre learned that Swayz didn't know his own history. He wasn't a ghost. Not a mythical creature from another dimension. Not *anything*. Swayz explained, the best that he could over time and with DeAndre's help, that he came into being that summer when DeAndre moved into the house. The world didn't exist for Swayz before then. He was tethered to the boy, and the boy, to him.

Borne from somewhere impermanent.

At track practice, DeAndre would sometimes spot Swayz hiding beneath the bleachers, watching him. He would wave to the huddled, nude figure hiding under the steel, and sometimes the creature would wave back, but mostly Swayz watched and waited for the boy to make his way home after school.

Dad had noticed how quickly DeAndre rushed through dinner to head down into the man cave. It was a nightly occurrence.

"Did you have a friend over last night?"

DeAndre looked up, nearly finished with his meatloaf. "No, why?"

"Because I thought I heard two voices. One of 'em was kinda weird-sounding."

DeAndre thought quickly. "Oh, I'm sorry, Pop. I've been practicing for the school play. I'm trying to get a part and thought it'd be cool to try a different voice."

Dad nodded. Part of him believed the boy. The other part of him knew better.

Eventually, DeAndre set up his record player in the basement and he and Swayz would listen to Amara's old tunes. One evening, on the last day of school while dancing around the space to Madonna, DeAndre heard his dad making his way down the steps. Swayz immediately rushed for the darkened space behind the bar and waited. It had become his usual hiding spot whenever DeAndre's father made his way down the steps.

"Hey, bud, I was in the garage and finally opened that random box of your mom's stuff, and I found a bunch of records I thought you'd maybe wanna add to the collection?"

"Oh, awesome," DeAndre said, lowering the volume on the stereo. He took the box from his dad and started flipping through the albums. He didn't recognize many of the artists, since they were from way before his time. Mr. Flagio, Fancy, Boney M. He did, however, recognize Abba, The Bee-Gees, A-Ha, The Pet Shop Boys, and a few others.

"Your mom loved her dance music," Dad mused, a hint of sadness in his voice. "We met at a disco, actually."

"You still have the leisure suit in your closet," DeAndre said, smiling.

"I do indeed," Dad said. "One day, that'll be yours, too."

"Oh goody," DeAndre said, laughing. "Thanks for these, Dad. I love them."

Dad hugged DeAndre. "You wearing cologne? You smell minty."

DeAndre looked toward the bar nervously and shrugged. "I'm trying a new deodorant?"

"That must be it," Dad said. "Can't believe how old you've gotten. Amara, too. 'Seems like yesterday we left the city. Time really flies, you know? Another summer in the boonies lies ahead of us."

DeAndre smiled and nodded. "I love it here, Dad. I don't miss the city much."

Swayz's eyes locked with DeAndre. They shared a secret smile.

After dinner, Swayz and DeAndre rode over to the park. DeAndre's dad thought his son had been joining friends for a night game of basketball, but instead, Swayz scaled the side of the house, hands gripping the siding like Spider-Man, effortlessly climbing down to the ground.

DeAndre handed Swayz an old wool coat, red with white trim, and the creature wrapped itself, smiling at the comfort. *This is beautiful,"* the creature whispered in the darkness.

"It was my mother's. Climb on," DeAndre said, gesturing to the seat of the bike.

Nervously, Swayz climbed onto the bike, and after settling in, the two rode off into the night, down the street, under cover of night, toward the park around the corner from the house.

Once there, they found a bench under a large dog tree, white blossoms spreading above them, nestled in a canopy of green. Swayz sat, looking tiny in the large, comfy coat, looking around the park. The creature could easily pass for human with the right clothing, even though this jacket wasn't doing any favors to Swayz. If anybody passed by, they might've thought DeAndre was sitting with his grandmother.

DeAndre placed his backpack gently on the table between them and smiled.

Slowly, the boy reached into his book bag and pulled out a small white pastry box tied with purple string. He held it out to Swayz.

"Happy birthday, Swayz," DeAndre said, nervously.

Swayz stared at the box, confused. *"What is a 'happy birthday'?"*

"You have to find out, silly. Open the box," the boy said, smiling.

*"I have never had a birthday before,"* Swayz whispered. *"I do not know what it means."*

"It's to celebrate the day you were born. Like when we have other holidays, presents, gifts, that kind of thing."

"*My…*birth-*day?*"

"We met three years ago today. Technically, it was a few days later, but, when we moved into the house, that's when you came to life, so, *that's* your birthday. The string even matches your eyes."

Swayz smiled. With bony fingers and sharp nails, the creature carefully untied the string, noting the color. "*Thank you, DeAndre.*"

Inside the box was a large cupcake: chocolate, with purple frosting. Three candles sat in the center, and DeAndre reached over with a Bic lighter and lit them. Swayz recoiled from the flames.

"It's okay. I won't let the fire hurt you," DeAndre said softly. "You have to think really hard, make a wish, and blow out the candles. Don't tell me the wish, because then it won't come true."

"*There are many rules to birthdays,*" Swayz said, staring at the lit candles. The creature thought for a moment, and a soft breeze blew through the area, blowing the candles out while its deep violet eyes remained closed and its thin lips remained tightly shut.

That night, in DeAndre's bedroom, the two sat in complete silence. It was Friday, late, and DeAndre couldn't sleep.

"*Did you mean what you said? About the city? With your father in the basement?*"

"Of course," DeAndre said in the dark, his voice soft. "If I didn't come here, I never would've met you. You're my best friend."

"*And you are mine.*"

DeAndre felt a swelling of tension in his chest. Whenever Swayz was around, he felt what he began to realize could only be described as "butterflies" in his stomach. An intense desire seemed to flutter, with flaming, acid-tinged wings, inside his belly and chest.

"Swayz?"

"*Yes, DeAndre?*"

DeAndre bit his lip and felt a swell of nerves lump in his throat. "Would you want to sleep in the bed with me tonight?"

Swayz sat up, cast in the silver glow of the moon outside the window. DeAndre sat up and looked at his friend. Slowly, DeAndre scooted over, the bed sheets rustling a bit.

Swayz, more animal than person, climbed into the bed. He felt the springy reflex of the mattress, and sat, cross-legged at the edge, confused, eyes looking around the room. The heavy, musky mint aroma was almost overwhelming.

DeAndre stared at Swayz. He gestured to the spot next to him. Slowly, the creature crawled up the bed toward the boy and rested its head on the pillow beside DeAndre.

"Isn't that better than the floor? More comfy?"

Swayz's eyes glowed in the darkness. "*My chest feels strange*," it whispered.

"Mine, too," DeAndre replied.

DeAndre and Swayz inched closer to each other, awkwardness growing between them. The tension they felt seemed to draw them nearer, until finally, they were nearly face to face. Cautiously, slowly, they kissed, and both felt an explosive rush of pure desire between the two of them.

Their lips touched merely for a second, but the imprint left on both of them felt impossible to shake. It was DeAndre's first kiss. And if Swayz had never existed until the boy entered the home, it certainly had been the creature's as well.

Swayz's slender fingers reached up to DeAndre's face and caressed his cheek in the dark.

DeAndre, his head still spinning from the sensation of Swayz's thin lips on his own, was racked with intense pangs of guilt and confusion. He had never felt anything for anyone at school before. At least, not in the way he was feeling for Swayz.

*But what does this mean? What is Swayz?* DeAndre slipped away from the pale, slender fingers and rested his head down. "Good night."

Confused, Swayz closed its eyes. "*Good night, DeAndre.*"

DeAndre floated lazily on his back in the pool. Dad and Amara were nearby, setting the table for dinner. The boy's eyes were on his bedroom window, where Swayz watched him, unable to join the family. DeAndre often wondered how his dad and sister would react to the weird creature that emerged from nowhere and had become such an integral part of his life. He wondered how they'd react if they knew that the night before, he had shared his first kiss with this being.

"Dee, almost time to dry off, bud," Dad said.

DeAndre didn't answer. He kept replaying the kiss over and over in his mind. He didn't know what his feelings were, the mixture of guilt and confusion and desire perpetually running through his mind the entire day: while helping to clean the house, taking a bike ride into town, and getting coffee with his sister.

It didn't help that Swayz had no clear gender. This added to DeAndre's confusion. Some days, Swayz resembled some of the girls DeAndre knew at school; others, he looked like the guys on the track team. No matter how Swayz appeared to DeAndre, the one thing the boy knew was that he loved and desired the creature that came from his closet more than any human in his life.

Being gay, or being bisexual: those concepts scared confused teenagers all over the world, but being *in love* with a creature from some impossible time and space?

That scared and confused DeAndre the most.

As DeAndre prepared for bed, Swayz rifled through things in the closet. He shifted some clothes around and took others off the racks.

"What're you doing?"

*"I thought you might prefer if I stayed in here tonight."*

DeAndre sat down on his bed. He looked out the window, the moon hanging high and bright. His Ninja Turtles nightlight cast a glow on the floor, a remnant from his childhood.

The boy shook his head and scooted into bed. "No, come here."

Cautiously, Swayz stepped closer to the bed, nervously looking around the room. All these years with DeAndre, and the animal fight-or-flight instinct in the creature remained ever-present. A light minty musk filled the room, and DeAndre realized Swayz must have been scared.

Swayz climbed into the bed and sat on its knees, the being looking as though it were in prayer. DeAndre looked over the creature, noting how distinctly feminine Swayz appeared in this moment, shoulders low, the smooth flesh of the creature's chest budding a bit where breasts might be on a female's body.

"Come here," DeAndre whispered in the dark. He took Swayz's wrist and pulled the creature closer, their lips locking together. Passion overwhelmed the two of them until their mouths were no longer two distinct concepts; instead, they simply became one.

There was no telling where DeAndre's ended and Swayz's began.

Swayz straddled the boy, its legs on either side of his body. They pressed hard, together, the heat between them sending them over the edge, their minds focused solely on the intensity of the moment, a first for both of them.

"I've been thinking about this all day," DeAndre whispered into Swayz's mouth.

"*As have I…*"

DeAndre's hands roamed all over Swayz's chest and back as the two continued kissing. Suddenly, the boy felt something hard pressing into his stomach. Confused, he broke the kiss and looked down and saw a bulge beginning to form between Swayz's legs.

The two locked eyes. DeAndre's lust shifted to confusion and he pushed Swayz off him, nearly throwing the creature to the floor. Though Swayz had the advantage of height over the boy, DeAndre remained the more powerful of the two.

Swayz scrambled off the bed, bracing itself like a cat on all fours on the ground near the closet door, hissing and confused; its glowing violet eyes flashing all over the room, searching for an unseen threat.

"I'm sorry, I just—" DeAndre began.

Quickly, Swayz opened the closet door and slipped inside.

DeAndre never saw such hurt or pain in another creature's eyes before.

DeAndre awoke the next morning after getting barely any sleep and felt awful about how he treated Swayz. The creature was his best friend, his first kiss, and deep down, the first person the boy ever *loved* outside of his family.

Slowly, he walked over to the closet and opened it, expecting to find Swayz huddled in a mass of clothing on the floor.

Inside, he found nothing.

He sniffed the air, hoping for the hint of mint that accompanied Swayz whenever he was around, but instead, found just the musty, woody smell of a closet in an old house.

Confused, DeAndre closed the door and went downstairs.

And so it went. For the next two years. Each morning, DeAndre would awaken, no matter the season, and check his closet for Swayz, but the creature had vanished. As time went on, DeAndre fell out of the habit of checking for the creature. They were simply gone.

Over time, the closet changed. DeAndre returned home from school to find Amara's posters missing, and when he saw them in the garbage behind the house, he knew his Dad had gotten rid of them. To fill the void left by Swayz's disappearance, DeAndre settled into a friend group of kids from the school's theater department and his teammates from track. He straddled both worlds.

The boy felt at home both on the stage and on the track. Knowing that eyes were on him as he performed, DeAndre felt incredible explosions of energy, nerves, and more, feelings he first felt with Swayz. The acid-winged butterflies in his chest and stomach only returned when he was under the lights of the stage or pushing himself further on the field.

In those moments, for DeAndre, it felt as if Swayz had never left.

When DeAndre had the house to himself, he would listen to his mom's records and dance. He imagined himself performing for crowds of people. From disco to 80's synth to modern pop, the boy worked out a variety of routines that he carefully executed when his dad wasn't around.

These songs remained in his mind as he dashed across the finish line. Over time, he found himself gravitating more toward theater and dancing and further away from track. Once senior year started, he had all but abandoned athletic pursuits in favor of artistic ones, much to his father's disappointment.

DeAndre had grown more muscular, and his body had finally begun to take shape the way he hoped. Dad was right, he was a late bloomer. The boy had gone from middle of the pack to being the second-fastest on the team, and while state records were attainable, none of it felt right to DeAndre. He simply didn't care.

From time to time, DeAndre thought he saw a pair of indigo-colored eyes watching from beneath the stands during his track meets, but when he investigated, there was nothing there, just a faint, familiar scent in the air.

"Kiddo, are you *sure* this is what you want to do? They give more scholarships for track than they do acting," Dad said one night at dinner.

"It just doesn't feel right anymore, Pop," DeAndre said.

Dad nodded. "I don't get it. But, if you want to throw away your talent and hard work, then so be it. You'll regret it later."

Little comments like that remained with DeAndre. *What didn't he get?* DeAndre would think, confused not to receive the support from his own father that he was getting from his former coach.

"Is it the theater-stuff? Is that what's making you do this?" Dad asked.

"What do you mean?"

"Dee, look at how you're dressing, I mean, you don't look—" Dad stopped. He sighed and lowered his head. "Dee, sometimes to *get along*, you've got to *go along*. It's rarely a good thing to stand out."

DeAndre fidgeted in his seat. He was wearing a neon-green hoodie, Madonna's face in black and white emblazoned on it. Black bike shorts hugged his thickening, muscular legs. "What's wrong with how I look?"

Dad just shook his head, got up slowly from the table, and walked into the living room. "Never mind, bud."

To Dad, these were signs.

To DeAndre, they were just who he *was*.

Prom rolled around. DeAndre asked a girl from the theater department who had become his closest friend since Swayz vanished. Dad took pictures and chatted with the other parents, happy to see his son with an actual *girl*.

At the dance, DeAndre and his date swirled and put on a show. DeAndre could really move, and so could his date. They hardly left the dance floor that night, and they certainly didn't mind: the night too perfect, too fun to settle down and relax.

Afterwards, DeAndre found himself in the backseat of the girl's car. They kissed, touched, and squeezed each other, but DeAndre barely felt anything for the girl beyond a friend. This had been especially noticeable when she looked him in the eyes and asked if he'd ever gotten a blowjob before, to which he nervously replied he had not.

When she started, he didn't find himself reacting in any way. He just laid back and remained nervous.

"What's wrong?" she asked in the dark.

"I'm sorry, I—umm…"

She sat up and sighed. "Why can't you get hard?"

"I don't know, I'm just, I guess I'm nervous."

"Don't you *like* me?"

"Of course I do," DeAndre said, unable to look her in the eye.

She ran her hands all over his body, and DeAndre began to feel a level of discomfort he had never experienced before in his entire life.

"Stop, I don't—"

"Don't be a fag. Let me do it," she said, her voice harsh, hanging in the air.

DeAndre started pushing her off him, but her entire weight on top of him pinned him down. "Please …"

Her hands squeezed moved lower and squeezed harder. The boy's groin tensed, and he buckled at the assault.

"I know you want this, even if you *are* a queer."

Tears began welling in DeAndre's eyes as she continued her assault on his genitals. She removed her underwear and mounted him, and through gritted teeth, continued an array of insults, his body never giving her the reaction she desired.

*Fag.*
*Queer.*
*Gay.*

DeAndre sat motionless in the hospital bed, waiting for his father to pick him up. He wondered if it was the cocktail of pain medications he was on, but either way, he felt destroyed, internally and externally.

The doctors examined his lower regions and noticed swelling and bruises, but nothing that would remain permanent. The entire examination left DeAndre feeling raw, embarrassed, and heartbroken.

Distinct tension hung in the air as DeAndre gathered his torn tuxedo and his father watched him.

"Not getting the deposit back on this," Dad said.

"I'm sorry, Dad," DeAndre said.

"Your sister's at the house, I don't wanna talk right now," Dad said, exiting the room, carrying his son's belongings.

At the house, DeAndre sat on the couch while Amara looked him over. She had started working in the city, had her own apartment and lived with her boyfriend. She wept when she saw her brother's injuries and held him almost too tightly, as if she were trying to heal him through her arms and chest, radiating love.

"What happened?" Amara whispered.

"You *know* what happened, Amara, don't get him started," Dad said, waving the question away as though it were a fly in the air.

"I want to hear it from *him*, Dad!"

"We were in the car, and I don't know what happened next, but she—"

"Bullshit!"

"*Dad*, stop!" Amara shouted.

"You know why this happened, Amara, just *stop*. I don't want to hear this. I *can't* hear this! How does a boy get *raped*? The *police* won't even hear it. They say he's lying!"

"This happened to *your* son, Dad," Amara said. "How could you not want to hear what happened?"

"Because he's not my son, okay? I've been living with him the past couple'a years and he's not my little boy anymore," Dad said, bubbling over with emotion. "The goddamn posters he was hiding in his room? The music? His *clothes*?"

Amara and DeAndre stared at him.

"You think I didn't notice? DeAndre, I clean your room at least once a week. You think I didn't notice Amara's old lipstick in your sock drawer? Christ, what I wouldn't give to find nudie mags. Instead, I find out my son is a cross-dresser!"

"Dad!" Amara said, standing up. "That's enough!"

"Growing his hair longer, quitting track, the clothes he wears," Dad rambled. "I can't take it anymore. I can't take what's happening to him."

"Nothing's happening to me," DeAndre said, softly. "I'm still your son, I'm still me."

Dad stared at him. "I don't want him here in the morning. I don't care where you go, but I don't want you here, Dee. I can't take you like this. Boys don't get raped. *Faggots* do."

DeAndre's eyes began welling up with tears. With what little energy he had, he stormed up to his bedroom.

He began packing a bag the best he could, hearing the muffled fighting of his sister and father downstairs.

He heard a creak of the closet door opening. Slowly, DeAndre turned, eyes tearing, his body wracked with pain. He desperately needed Swayz. Memories of their time together flooded his mind. He breathed deep, hoping to pick up the musky, pleasant smell of mint in the air.

He walked to the closet and looked inside.

Nothing.

"Don't try to lift anything, Dee, I got it," Amara said, taking DeAndre's luggage from him and helping him up the stairs at her and her boyfriend's apartment.

They had driven from Resting Hollow back to the city that very night, Amara agreeing immediately to take her brother in. Their dad gave her some money, and the two left quickly, emotions and adrenaline fueling the drive. They didn't speak.

Amara's boyfriend, Todd, came down to meet them on the street. DeAndre had met him only twice before, and he had always been sweet. He was a lawyer and was working his way up the ladder at the firm where he and Amara met.

"Hey Dee," Todd said, hugging the boy. "I'm sorry about everything. I set up the guest room for you, fresh sheets on the bed. It's not as big as your room back home, has barely any closet space, but we can maybe get you one of those portable rack things, if you like?"

"Thanks, Todd," DeAndre said, feigning a smile.

Once he was settled into the guest room, DeAndre found himself crying again. Todd brought him some hot chocolate and Amara sat with him, holding the boy close. He was holding a letter from his high school. He opened it. Inside was his diploma.

"I won't even get to graduate with my friends," DeAndre sobbed. "They took that from me. I hate them for that."

"I do, too, buddy-boy," Amara said, tears forming in her eyes, too. "Graduation is overrated anyway. They say your name, you walk across a stage, it's dumb. Who needs it?"

DeAndre smiled. Amara was doing her best to cheer him up.

Deep down, DeAndre cried for Swayz. Yes, he'd miss his friends at graduation, if they even *were* his friends any longer. After what happened to him got around town, he wasn't sure what to think, but he missed the love of his life, the one who accepted him no matter what. The mythical being sprung from the boy's own desires and heart.

DeAndre enrolled in Queens Community College and quickly joined the theater department. He didn't see or hear from his father once during that time and he didn't care to. Amara would exchange emails with her dad a bit, something that was foreign to the old man, but DeAndre couldn't be less interested in learning what his dad had going on back in Resting Hollow.

In class, DeAndre's skills were apparent, and he felt immediately accepted by his peers. Nights, he was out with new friends or his sister and her boyfriend, who saw DeAndre as his own brother. Days, he was studying or working part-time at a record store around the corner from their apartment so he could help pay the bills and eventually get his own place.

One night, DeAndre was tying his hair up. It had grown long, curling in the same way Amara's tended to. She watched him working with the curls and smiled.

In the mirror, DeAndre thought he caught a glimpse of a familiar face, smooth skin, thin lips—larger than he remembered—and eyes glaring with amethyst intensity, but when the boy spun around, it was gone.

The room had evolved over time from the empty space and bed of their guest room to a beautiful, warm space littered with costumes for shows DeAndre performed in, a large vanity mirror purchased and refurbished by Todd as a birthday present a year after DeAndre moved in. Makeup, wigs, and more littered the vanity, colorful and explosive, catching the eye immediately upon walking in.

Photos of DeAndre in various costumes from school performances hung on the walls with thumb tacks, others in frames. In some photos, he was in full drag attire, something he had become exceptionally good at. A few school recitals required him to explore this side of performance, and he relished it: so much so, he started attending drag shows at Queen Mab's, a Chinatown club that featured weekly performances by local drag queens.

"What's funny?" he asked, noticing Amara smiling in the mirror.

"You look like mom," Amara said. "You're beautiful like her. I wish I had your face."

"Stop it," he said, smiling.

"Hang on," Amara said, ducking from DeAndre's doorway. She returned a moment later with a shoebox and sat next to her brother. She opened it and inside, there were dozens of photos of their mom. She had dark skin, like DeAndre, and a bone structure that indicated much more of a resemblance than DeAndre ever imagined.

He held up one of the photos and looked in the mirror. "Amara, my god," he said softly.

"I *know*. I see it more every day."

"I always thought *you* looked like her," DeAndre said.

"When we were younger, sure. The hair. But I'm lighter than her. I'm more Dad's complexion. You've her in body and soul, I think." Amara played with some stray strands of DeAndre's curls.

"I miss her," he said, softly.

"I do, too," Amara said, hugging him. "I got an email from Dad. He wants us to come home for Thanksgiving. I told him I'd think about it."

"I don't wanna go," DeAndre said. "You can go, obviously. I don't want you to be swayed by me."

"I figured," Amara said. "You're my baby bro, we're ride or die. You should keep this one. She looks amazing here."

DeAndre looked at the photo. Their mother was wearing the red and white wool coat from Swayz's birthday. A flutter ran through the boy's chest as he looked at it. Amara rose and left the room.

He hung the picture on the vanity, tucked into the mirror and frame.

In the darkness of the stage, the opening string-plucks of a haunting Madonna track floated through the empty theater. DeAndre stood in the center of the stage and performed his routine, pushing his body and mind further than he ever had on the track in high school. Shirtless, beads of sweat forming on his muscular, toned body. Gym shorts allowed fluid movement.

It was the month of April, and DeAndre had been preparing for this final exam. The routine took a while to prepare, but he had nearly gotten it down. He knew every action, every fluid gesture, and he executed it to the best his design and body could allow.

He allowed a few moments for improvisational movement to accompany the song. As Madonna's perfect whisper echoed, DeAndre imagined his impossible love in the audience watching him. He wondered what Swayz looked like now.

As he finished his dance, DeAndre caught his breath, his mind still on the lust and love he felt for his long-lost friend. A sudden clapping in the back of the theater startled DeAndre, and he covered his eyes to block the little bit of light preventing him from seeing who it was.

"Bravo, Dee," the figure said, stepping into the light.

Dad.

"What're you doing here?"

"I wanted to see you, buddy-boy," Dad said, stepping closer to the stage.

"I don't want to see you," DeAndre replied, starting to walk away.

"Dee, please," Dad called. "I'm sorry, I didn't know what to think, it all just happened and I know—"

"You *don't* know, Dad. You pushed me away when I needed you the most," DeAndre said, his heart racing. He had imagined this confrontation a hundred times in his head and felt well-prepared for whatever nastiness his father had in store for him.

Dad nodded. "You're right."

DeAndre stared. "What?"

"I've been talking to a therapist. And getting updates about you from Amara. You're absolutely right. About all of it."

"Okay…"

"Not seeing you this past year. Learning how amazing you are, how hard you've been working, how you're becoming exactly who you were meant to be, on your own…you're amazing."

DeAndre held steady, even though hearing the emotion in his father's voice broke the boy's heart for the third time in his young life.

"Thank you," he said, softly.

"Dee, I love you, and I'm so, so sorry for how I treated you," Dad said, openly weeping. "I just want my family back. Losing you and Amara, talking to my doctor, I just can't bear to lose you two."

DeAndre stepped off the stage and walked toward his father. "You broke my heart, Dad."

Dad nodded. "I know I did. I'll spend the rest of *my* life making it up to you, if you'll have me back in *your* life."

The stage at Queen Mab's wasn't the biggest DeAndre had been on, but it would do for his debut as DeeAgio. He chose his on-stage persona based on the song he chose for his debut at the club: "Take a Chance" by Mr. Flagio, one of the records in his mom's collection that had quickly become his favorite.

The emcee stood on the stage, wearing a glittery top hat, monocle, and little else. The performances were about halfway done for the night, and in the back of the club, Todd and Amara leaned against their high-top, drinking cocktails that seemed to glow with electric fury in red and green.

The entire club was bathed in neon-blue light, pinks and gold accenting throughout. Many of the queens who had performed earlier littered the crowd, enjoying time with friends and family who came to see them perform.

Dad entered the club, waved to Amara, and walked over. They hugged. Dad shook Todd's hand. After a moment, Dad hugged Todd and thanked him for being so good to his daughter and son.

"Ladies and gentlemen, we have a virgin to Queen Mab's tonight!" the emcee cooed into the microphone.

The crowd erupted into cat calls and hollering. Amara smiled, and Dad looked around, more nervous for DeAndre than anything else. Todd catcalled, which cracked Dad up.

"Ladies and gentlemen, for the first time, may I present to you, a face for the gods…DeeAgio!"

Darkness engulfed the stage. A hush came over the crowd. Sharp, heavy footsteps plunked across the stage in the darkness, and everyone awaited the visage of the latest to take Queen Mab's stage.

As the 1983 Italo-Disco classic thumped with progressive abandon over the sound system in the club, purple light slowly lit up the stage. DeAndre, looking impeccable, stood in platform chunk Chuck Taylors, a red and white wool coat draped across his form, presenting an air of modesty.

His face, upturned to the lights, was that of an ancient goddess, painted and decorated perfectly, eyes glittering, lashes long, lips wet and supple. He looked otherworldly, a gift truly from whatever heavens saw fit to grace the assemblage in Queen Mab's that night.

As the infectious synth beat thumped forward, building to a pulse-pounding explosion of electro-tinged lyrics, DeAndre removed the coat, the light shifting, allowing his outfit to be revealed. A play on classic disco-chic, the entire ensemble was composed of purple pleather encrusted with sequins that seemed to radiate the reflective light on the stage. There was no need for a wig: DeAndre's hair was long and curly enough to stand on its own, the only addition that of sparkle-dust (a gift from Todd, who believed it would "tie the look together"). DeAndre's strong chest stuck out from the outfit, covered in body glitter.

He stood, beginning his performance, glowing like a moving disco ball on stage. In the crowd, the veteran performers and regular attendees stared in brilliance at the young man's moves and his impeccable look.

As DeAndre performed, he spotted his family in the crowd.

Suddenly, the smell of mint wafted into the room. DeAndre didn't react in motion, but he scanned the crowd more. In the corner, under the glowing red "EXIT" sign stood a figure, wearing a trench coat and baseball cap.

Purple eyes glowed from beneath the cap.

Butterflies on acid wings formed in the pit of his stomach and in his chest. Ever the professional, DeAndre continued dancing, intoxicated by the musky mint aroma of his love in the room.

DeAndre smiled and felt tears welling in his eyes.

# About the Author

Robert P. Ottone is an author, teacher, and cigar enthusiast from East Islip, NY. He delights in the creepy. He can be found online at SpookyHousePress.com, or on Instagram (@RobertOttone). His collections *Her Infernal Name & Other Nightmares* and *People: A Horror Anthology about Love, Loss, Life & Things That Go Bump in the Night* are available now wherever books are sold.

# Some Kind of Monster

Azzurra Nox

It was dark in the monster's belly.

That's how the nightmares always began.

I could never see the monster. I only knew that it was large because anytime I found myself in his viscid stomach, I was swallowed whole. Never chomped up in little pieces.

Last night, once again, I had the same nightmare. I was in the monster's belly, the acrid scent of his stomach acid making me gag as I floundered in it, blind. I couldn't ever see the inside of it because of how cavernous it was. All I could feel was the stifling sense of being wrapped in an unwanted hug.

The nightmare usually left me feeling unsettled. No amount of hot tea and buttered biscuits could comfort me back to normalcy. After one of those nightmares, I tended to spend the rest of the day jumpy and tense, my shoulders sore from my inability to relax. Another side-effect of this reoccurring nightmare was that whenever I woke up, drenched to the bone and shaking, I was so wound up that attempting to fall back to sleep was futile, even if I had three hours to spare before my alarm would sound off.

There I was, sitting in my cubicle, both in dire need of sleep and also very afraid of being met with the same feeling of dread and anguish that the nightmare always delivered. My eyelids felt heavy, like keeping them open was a task in itself, and one that I was certain I'd fall victim to if I didn't get my ass out of the chair and mainline some caffeine stat.

I hurried to the breakroom, not caring that I had already taken a break twenty minutes ago. My sanity depended on staying awake. I felt like those scream queens in *A Nightmare on Elm Street* where they conjured up inventive ways to keep themselves awake, lest they become savory kebabs for Freddy's expert razor claws.

"Another coffee? Tough morning, huh?" My co-worker Jack asked with an easy, shit-eating grin that made the other girls in the office swoon but that I despised. His Dockers were perfectly pressed and the button-down shirt impeccably ironed. He ran a hand through his sandy blond hair.

I knew I looked as much a disaster as I felt: my curls still tangled and pinned to the top of my head in a messy bun, yesterday's eyeliner smeared under my eyes, and a gel manicure outgrown its natural stay that my half-moons were visible. I just shrugged, not wanting to commit to an answer, hoping that maybe this would dissuade him from small talk.

"You look like you could use some sleep, Sharon."

No shit, Sherlock.

I plastered a fake smile and replied, "You're so very astute, Jack." I silently begged for him to leave the breakroom so that I could have a few moments to myself. But Jack lingered with his dopey grin.

"What's this?" He pointed to something on the side of my neck.

I hope it's not a hickey, although I haven't made out with anyone in weeks. I edged towards the mirror placed above the sink to inspect, and oddly enough, there on the side of my neck were three puncture holes. I carefully touched the wounds, not understanding where or how I could've gotten them.

"That's strange..." I murmured, more to myself.

But Jack sidled up next to me and chimed in, "Yeah, it looks like you made out with a Black Widow!" then laughed. I merely rolled my eyes and left the breakroom.

Somehow, a part of me knew deep down that the nightmares had something to do with the puncture wounds.

I just didn't know why.

The sky had darkened by the time I got out from work. I could easily feel the tug of sleep attempting to lure me in its embrace. But I defied it with another swig of Red Bull as I sped up my walk towards my dinged-up green Toyota that had seen better days in 2008. I absently touched my neck thinking about what could've caused the wounds. Suddenly, I was startled out of my thoughts by the loud caw of a crow. He looked at me directly and cawed once more, even louder than the last.

Something about his presence unsettled me until I remembered that childhood rhyme my mother would always repeat. *One crow sorrow.*

Shit, all I needed was more bad luck.

I got into the car, trying to outrun the speed of misfortune. And somehow all that running away brought me to my usual haunt, Poe's Pit. It was a quiet evening, and I sat in my usual booth nursing a dirty martini and trying to forget about the nightmares.

"Would you like some company?" A sultry voice interrupted my thoughts.

I looked up from my drink and turned to see a redhead with a top bun wearing a short black dress.

Under normal circumstances, I would've been more cautious in speaking with a stranger at a bar. But maybe because she was a petite young woman with a beautiful face, my natural instinct to be wary was undermined. After sharing three drinks with the redhead, who told me that her name was Ariel like *that* mermaid, I was even considering taking her home with me. Perhaps it was the way she laughed at my dumb jokes or the way her dimple surfaced every time she smiled, that I found myself feeling less cautious. It felt good to finally not worry about my nightmares, to just feel some semblance of normalcy, if even for a small moment.

"Do you always come here alone?" Ariel finally asked me. I'm sure it was something she had wanted to ask me earlier, but it would've come off as rude when we barely knew each other's names.

"Sometimes," I admitted, not wanting to let her know how crippling the loneliness could get for me, that sitting at a crowded bar was far better than sitting in a lonely apartment. Life hadn't been so easy ever since I had to relocate from a small town in New Mexico to Los Angeles. Making friends as an adult proved to be much harder than it had been in college or high school. Sure, Jack was always itching to be friendly, but his boastful macho manner had a tendency to aggravate me to no end.

"You look tired," she said, reaching out across the table to touch my arm.

I would've tried to lie if I actually hadn't been stifling yawns for the past half hour.

"I am. I haven't been sleeping well."

"Why?" Her green eyes widened with concern.

I looked down at my nails bitten down to stubs, a scab on the side of one finger from where I had yanked a hangnail off with my teeth. Maybe it was the alcohol speaking, but I soon found myself narrating the nightmares I had been having for the past few weeks. Ariel listened without interrupting. When I was done, she finally spoke.

"So, you're avoiding sleep because you're afraid of having the same nightmares?"

"Pretty much," I murmured, taking another swig from a new martini, wincing at the burning sensation as the alcohol made its way down my throat.

She bit on her pale lower lip, fidgeting with her fingers. I couldn't understand why she was nervous. I was the one with the nightmares, not her.

"I hope this isn't too forward but..." she hesitated a moment. "I was thinking...I could drive you back home. You could sleep, and if you seem like you're in any sign of distress, I could wake you up?"

"Why would you do that for me? You barely know me." My usual suspicion sneaked its way up behind the optimism of booze.

Ariel gave me a bashful smile, then replied, "I guess I like you. And I would like to be of help."

Something inside of me kept inching to decline the offer, but the martini in me relented my dubious nature.

"Okay," I said.

Outside, I could hear the far away caw of a crow, and the childhood rhyme came back to me. *One crow sorrow.*

I fought sleep as I tried to stay awake long enough to give Ariel directions to my home. Once we arrived at the tiny West Hollywood apartment building, the dizziness set in. All of my movements felt slow, almost out of body. I yearned for my bed, but it seemed like Ariel had other things in mind as she crushed her lips to mine. We drunkenly tangoed our way down the hall, leaving discarded garments along the way. It wasn't until we reached the bedroom that time seemed to speed up. Ariel kept the lights turned off as her lips burned kisses down the inside of my thighs. Her grip on me was strong for being so petite.

A streetlight cast shadows in the room and partially illuminated Ariel's face.

I looked down at her with lust in my eyes.

"You're so beautiful," I whispered, voice thick with arousal.

She smiled, and I watched as her teeth gleamed with a strange glow. I was certain that the alcohol was playing tricks with me, because I could've sworn that her limbs looked different. Her skin was no longer milky white but looked gray and prickly.

I felt a tiny prick. A grin spread on my lips, of course she'd be *that* kind of girl. The sort of girl to become overcome with passion that she'd get carried away. Take a little nibble, leave marks the following morning.

I tried to move but couldn't. It was as though I were paralyzed. The room spun and I closed my eyes to keep myself from tilting. To keep myself from getting seasick.

Her tongue glided down my leg and I moaned. Despite being overcome with passion, the sleepless nights I had spent awake were finally catching up to me. I could barely keep my eyes open as I quickly slipped into unconsciousness.

The moment I woke up, I knew that something was terribly wrong.

The darkness was profound and heavy around me like a weighted blanket that I couldn't shake off. I tried to reach out but could feel my hand come in contact with a viscid substance and quickly recoiled. I called out for help, but there was no response.

The hairs on the back my neck rose as I realized that I was enclosed in a wet vault.

Panic shot through my veins, my limbs shook with a fear that was primal, not fully conscious. A part of me knew exactly where I was. Although logic seemed to scream otherwise, I *knew*.

I felt a wetness on the side of my neck and I touched where the puncture wound scabs used to be. Now the wounds had been reopened and were oozing with blood.

"No...no...no..." I cried.

And yet, I knew.

Too late.

"I'm sorry," I heard Ariel's voice vibrate loud above me. "But sometimes, I just can't seem to control my appetite." Then her whole body shook with her laughter and I with it.

Outside, I could hear a crow cawing relentlessly.

It was dark in the monster's belly.

# About the Author

Azzurra Nox was born in Catania, Sicily, and has led a nomadic life since birth. She has lived in various European cities and Cuba and currently resides in the Los Angeles area. She has a B.A. Degree in Letters – Classical Studies and an M. Ed. in Secondary Education. She's always been an avid reader and writer from a young age, entertaining her friends with ghost stories. She loves horror movies, cats, dancing, and a good rock show. She dislikes Mondays and chick-flicks. For more info on her writing, visit AzzurraNox.com. She's also the founder and curator of the lifestyle blog TheInkBlotters.com, where she shares her love for makeup, movies, books, music, traveling, and skincare with her readers. You can follow her on Twitter @diva_zura or Instagram @divazura. Her latest works are "Good Sister, Bad Sister," appearing in *Betty Bites Back: Stories to Scare the Patriarchy,* "Baby Teeth," appearing in *Midnight in the Pentagram,* and her anthologies as an editor, *My American Nightmare – Women in Horror Anthology* and *Strange Girls – Women in Horror Anthology.*

# 1,000 Tiny Cuts
Veronica Zora Kirin

I fell in love with her the moment I laid eyes on her. It was an evening gala for the national fundraising awards: not an event I would choose to attend—I didn't have $200 in cash that I could throw away on a ticket—but my best friend Pieter was being recognized as a nominee and, as such, had tickets to share.

I was proud of Pieter and excited to root for him. He deserved the award and had worked hard to fundraise for multiple organizations throughout the year. I'd given five dollars to his fund—nothing in comparison to the ticket cost and size of the other donations he'd received—but I was happy to give my enthusiastic support by attending the event.

Claire was the Executive Director of the organization. She stood on stage glimmering in a skin-toned ball gown thanking us for attending to support nonprofits nationwide. As she spoke of the mission and history of the organization in a lilting British accent, the room faded from my attention. My eyes caught on the way the light shone on her earrings, the loose hairs around her ears which she pushed back with her manicured fingers, the blue of her eyes caught by the spotlight. I think I forgot to breathe for a moment. I willed her to look at me.

The sudden applause shook me from my trance. Everyone around me was standing. I glanced at Pieter and he replied with a look that said *what's up?* I stood and began clapping, smiling and nudging Pieter.

I was dazed for the rest of the evening. Claire was seated at a table in the middle of the crowded room and I could barely see her. I was so distracted I almost missed the queue to cheer when the emcee called Pieter on stage to stand with his fellow nominees. When his name was called as Man of the Year, I screamed, in part because he was the first ever gay Man of the Year, and in part because I knew I'd get to meet Claire.

People buzzed around us at the reception. Pieter glowed from the attention, shaking hands and encouraging others to donate to their favorite organizations, even though the competition was over. Pieter had a heart the size of the moon.

I gulped some air when Claire came over to congratulate Pieter. I tried to smile and say hi between coughs.

"Are you okay?" Claire asked. I waved that I was fine as I tried to clear my throat.

"Is she your girlfriend?" Claire asked Pieter. We were used to the question by now. Any queer best friends of the opposite gender will field that question more than once.

"No, my partner couldn't make it," replied Pieter for me while rubbing my back.

"And I'm single," I managed. Pieter shot me an amused look. Claire smiled.

"Well, we'll need a shot at the photobooth in just a moment. Join us in five minutes? And I'll get you the private dinner details. Will you be attending?" Claire directed at me. I looked at Pieter. I hadn't known of a dinner.

"Um, yes?" I asked. Pieter nodded.

Later that evening, I found myself seated at a table with the entire foundation board, Pieter, and Claire. For some reason, Claire sat next to me. She was way out of my league, my department store dress and awkward table manners betraying my naiveté, but she didn't seem to notice. She plied me with champagne and inquired about my life as a writer. I must admit, I left Pieter quite alone. I couldn't pull away from Claire. Her presence was gravitational.

The weeks following were a whirlwind. On the nights she couldn't see me, Claire sent flowers, chocolates, and little gifts. When we did see each other, it was either an extravagant outing or an evening spent in bed. At one point, I confessed to Pieter that I was experiencing the best lovemaking I'd ever had. There was something selfish about the way Claire drove at me, as if my pleasure fed her ego and reassured her of her talent. After multiple mind-blowing orgasms, I didn't care. Her desire for me drove me mad. I wanted to give her everything.

And so I did. I know it's cliché for lesbians to U-Haul and marry in a few months, but people like me don't let people like Claire get away. She painted for me an irresistible life: a house with a three-season porch (a writer's dream), parties and events at which I was arm candy, and, someday, a family. Mine had abandoned me the moment I came out to them, and the hole left behind craved to be filled.

The night she proposed I cried of joy. The ring was a gorgeous square-cut sapphire set in platinum. It was sitting in the bottom of my champagne glass. Cliché? I couldn't care less.

We decided to marry at City Hall with just Pieter and Claire's friend to witness. My family wouldn't be in attendance and Claire's were in the UK. Afterward, we hosted a massive outdoor reception and danced until the sun came up, sweat and champagne mixing among our friends as the lights and music cast across the lawn. I've never been so tired and happy at the same time as I was the morning after.

The change came bit by bit, so difficult to see at first that I didn't notice. Claire cared for me, loved me, supported me, and I believed she took my well-being to heart.

I admit I never had much fashion sense. What English major does? My head was stuck in books and busy creating my own worlds. No need to spend precious energy on something that didn't matter. So, I was grateful when Claire took the initiative to redress my wardrobe. She was always well put together, and there were constant functions to attend. She was right when she said my style was sullying her arm and she had a reputation to uphold.

Then she started to pick at me about my contribution to the household. Writing doesn't pay well, but I had been doing alright on my own. I also was living within smaller means when single. Claire reminded me that our lifestyle wasn't cheap. I loved the way we lived and didn't want to be a burden, so I sought a professorship at the nearby university. Two classes per semester didn't cut into my writing time too much, and it kept my craft sharp.

That's how things went for the first year. I acted as though the sun shone out of Claire's rear, and her nagging of me seemed a pure reaction to the same intense love. She wanted to see me succeed, just as I did her. That's the definition of a healthy relationship, isn't it?

During our second year of marriage, we set out to adopt a child. Claire didn't want to carry as the physical consequences of pregnancy were deep and permanent, and I had been told it would be difficult for me to conceive. IVF has a price tag of $10k a try, and we decided the money would be better spent at a mission-oriented adoption agency.

The day we brought our six-month old Sammy home was as exciting as the day we got married. Our friends sent flowers, balloons, and weeks' worth of food.

Claire took right to motherhood. She hardly put Sammy down. She'd order me to make a bottle when he cried, frantic to ease his discomfort. She loved putting him in the designer cloth diapers we'd bought. She'd hold him up after changing him and declare, "Look how handsome!"

I admit I didn't mind when Claire went back to work. We decided I could at least take a semester off, and though my writing and friendships suffered, I cherished the alone time with Sammy. When Claire would get home, she would demand to hold and play with Sammy while I cooked, and so the weekdays were our special time together.

Everything made sense. Until it didn't.

One Friday evening, we were up late sipping wine after Sammy had gone down. I could have been more conciliatory, I admit. Claire had had a long day, and she was picking at me more than usual. I was putting the dishes in the dishwasher while she described her day at work when she paused mid-sentence and said, "What are you doing?"

I looked down at the dishes, then back up to her. "What?"

"You're putting bowls on the bottom rack, again."

"Claire, it doesn't matter. New dishwashers can reach all the dishes no matter their placement."

"Yes, but I've asked you many times to load the bowls on top," she stated.

I sighed. "Claire. It's just a dishwasher. You don't have to be in control of this, too." Before I could blink, Claire slapped my face. I dropped the bowl I was holding, which shattered when it hit the tile floor, waking Sammy. Claire glared at me, then turned away to go comfort Sammy, leaving me frozen in place.

I heard her coo to Sammy in the nursery while I tried to process what had happened. I knew she'd had a long day. Why did I provoke her? I turned to retrieve the broom on tiptoe, hoping to avoid cutting my foot, and failed. I paused to wrap the wound in paper towel and swept up the mess.

I was dumping the last bits in the bin when Claire returned. She noticed my poorly bandaged toe and the blood smears on the floor. "Honey, you cut yourself!" she exclaimed and took my hand to lead me to the bathroom. She sat me on the toilet and prattled on about weekend plans with our friends while she cleaned my wound as if everything was normal.

I barely slept that night. I cuddled a pillow and turned our life over and over in my mind. What had happened that made tonight different than the rest? Could I do better? Had I somehow failed as a wife?

The next morning, I woke to the smell of pancakes. The sun was already high in the sky. I'd overslept from the night of worry. I slipped into my robe and padded downstairs, finding Claire and Sammy in the kitchen. Claire was bobbing to music while Sammy played with cups of cereal in his chair.

"Good morning!" said Claire, pecking me on the cheek. "Great timing. We're just about done. Aren't we, boo-boo?" she cooed to Sammy. "Sit down, sit down!" She waved me to the counter stools. I sat and adjusted my robe, not sure what to make of the situation.

Claire hummed as she plated the pancakes, breaking up some small pieces for Sammy. She watched as I took the first bite, then began a one-sided discussion of our plans for the day. I felt dazed. Perhaps I'd made a big deal of nothing.

But Claire had changed. She was more forceful in all things, both in sweetness and cruelty. She no longer allowed me to select an outfit from the clothes she'd bought for events; my appearance was subject to her mood, not mine. She became more critical of my mothering. She created excuses to keep me at home. She'd gotten a promotion so I didn't need to return to work. She picked out the better produce. She needed one-on-one time with our friends. She'd bring home treats as if to reward me for being a kept woman, laughed at how confused a man would be at our "arrangement."

Her anger was like a switch. I never saw it coming, and I began to feel like I was walking a tightrope. One afternoon, I was telling Claire of my plans to see Pieter and Daniel while we went between rooms folding laundry. It had been ages and I wanted the freedom to spend time with my best friends without considering if my behavior was Claire-appropriate. Claire wanted to join for a double date and leave Sammy with a sitter.

"Claire, I really want time to myself with them. It's just been so long since I've seen them, the time alone means a lot." I turned to follow Claire into the bathroom while she put away the towels, reminiscing about the last time I'd seen Pieter and Daniel, but I didn't make it into the room. The door swung into my face. I saw stars as a sharp pain shot through my face and I fell to the floor. I held my nose for a moment, the ache radiating through my skull, and realized my palm was moist with my blood.

"I didn't know you were following me!" Claire exclaimed. I didn't have time to react before she held a clean towel to my nose and ran her fingers through my hair to soothe the ache.

Another incident came while Claire was manicuring my toes. She was giggling about a work story and I must not have reacted the way she wanted. I felt her grip my ankle as the cuticle scissors slid into the tender fleshy nail bed of my big toe, shooting pain up my leg and into my groin. I yelled and tried to pull my foot away but Claire's hand held fast. In an instant, I was bleeding all over the floor.

"Oh, my goodness!" Claire exclaimed as she pulled a handful of toilet paper to pad the wound.

Things would seem normal for weeks, with Claire doting on me after each incident, which is why I always felt blindsided when they happened.

Claire loved being romantic and would sometimes do the dishes with me by wrapping her arms around me. Not helping, but staying close. Sometimes, we'd discuss upcoming plans, something we'd heard on the news, but other times, we were just silent in each other's arms as the water ran down the drain.

One such night, I was washing our wine glasses while we planned our weekend, Claire's arms around me, her hands sometimes caressing down my arms. She wanted to go shopping for a new gown to wear to another gala. I was resistant. Her dresses cost several hundred dollars, and we had Sammy to think about.

"Can't you wear one you already have, hon?" I asked, nuzzling her neck with the back of my head to soften the ask. I knew I wasn't a fashionista like her, but I also couldn't see the logic in wearing a dress one time. Claire's hands played with my fingers while I washed the glass.

"No, dear, I need a new one for each event," she replied.

"It's just so much money, Claire. We need to think of Sammy, too," I explained. Suddenly, her hands clamped down on mine, and the wine glass shattered between my hands, small shards slicing into my palms. We both gasped as blood and glass ran down the drain. Claire held her grip on my wrists, turning my hands to rinse them of the mixture.

"And those were my favorite glasses, too," Claire mumbled as she tended my wounds. Though the glass didn't cause permanent damage, my hands were bandaged and tender for days, making care for Sammy difficult and reminding me to hold my tongue.

I realized things were really bad a year after the first incident, while we were on holiday at the lake with her friends. Claire asked for help with the kayaks, but I wanted to finish my drink. "I'll be along in a moment!" I emptied my glass and followed her to the lakeshore where they were stored.

"Just a second," I said as she bent to pick up the paddles. My new board shorts kept coming untied, and I'd be useless if they fell while my hands were full. I looked down at the laces. Out of nowhere, I was struck in the face and found myself on my back on the ground, my head throbbing.

"Claire, is she okay?" I heard a friend yell from the porch. Claire was already kneeling next to me with her hand on my face.

"We'll need some ice!" she yelled back. This time, she didn't try to act surprised, or even recognize the incident. She'd just clobbered me in the face with a kayak paddle in front of our friends. The illusion between us no longer mattered.

"We always worried that would happen with the kids," they said as they handed Claire a bag of frozen peas. I winced under the cold.

"It was such a weird angle! I suppose I'm just a city girl," Claire replied. They giggled. I held the peas to my face, dazed.

The rest of the weekend I sat on the porch nursing a black eye, my shame for allowing abuse in plain sight, and a newfound fear of my wife. I didn't want to go home with her. I didn't want to be alone with her. I could feel my spirit breaking, so I did what any other good suburban wife would do: I got counseling. All the while, Claire thought I was attending a play-date group with Sammy.

The first therapist laughed at me. "Lesbians don't have domestic violence!" he cackled. "Go home and make up."

The second therapist shrugged. "It sounds like you keep ending up in the wrong place at the wrong time, or saying the wrong thing. Let's talk about expanding your awareness of others."

The third therapist unsettled me the most. "Does she ever hurt your child?"

"No, she adores Sammy."

"It sounds like she's in the clear. She is employed with an immaculate record. You, on the other hand, haven't worked in over a year. If you leave, you leave Sammy, too." I knew she was right. I had to get my life in order if I were ever to make a case for custody. I couldn't leave Sammy with her.

It took me several days to build up the courage to talk to Claire. We were eating dinner, Sammy cooing in his chair playing with his food.

"I've been thinking it's time for me to go back to teaching."

Claire's knife squealed on the plate. She paused cutting her food and looked up. "Oh?"

"Sammy is old enough to be in daycare, and you've said I need to contribute."

Claire sipped her wine. "You do contribute, honey, by caring for Sammy."

I nodded. "I know. But I miss my career, and Sammy is at an age when social interaction with kids his age is important."

Claire set down her glass then placed her hand flat on the table, as if holding the surface down. "I do not want my child playing with those filthy babies."

Claire's reaction made me nervous. I paused to allow the moment to pass and consider what to say next. "With my salary, we could get a nanny."

"What's the point, dear?" Claire replied, her voice tense.

"M-my career?" I muttered as I looked down at my plate.

"Oh, hon! You don't need to teach for that. How about I take Sammy in the afternoon so you have some peace and quiet to write? Wouldn't that be fun?" she said as she turned to Sammy. I felt dismissed, but I feared her reaction if I pressed the issue.

"Sure," I mumbled. Never mind that I'd be too worn out to write by the time Claire got home.

I remained silent while we finished eating, Claire cooing to Sammy. Claire set Sammy in his playpen in the living room as I started the dishes. She returned after a moment.

"Would you like a cup of tea?" There was a note in her voice I didn't recognize.

"No, thank you," I replied. I felt myself hiding inside my body, as if I could make the world disappear. Claire nodded and put the electric kettle on, preparing her tea in its strainer. She claimed that no proper Brit would use a tea bag, though I'd seen her friends do so.

The water boiled just as I was rinsing the dish soap from my hands. Claire stood next to me, filling her tea cup. Then the kettle shifted, and suddenly the scalding water was pouring down my arm and into the sink.

"Claire!" I shrieked as I recoiled several steps back, staring at her in disbelief, her eyebrows raised in response. The throb in my arm demanded attention, and I broke her gaze to run to the bathroom, holding my arm to my chest. I locked myself in, running the reddened skin beneath the cold tap. I stood there for a long time, freezing my arm under the water and crying from fear and from pain. The therapist's words looped in my mind. It was my fault. I provoked her. I'd never be able to get out with Sammy.

This time, Claire didn't come to see if I was okay. I heard her rummaging in the kitchen while I looked at my tear-stricken face in the mirror. I couldn't stay. But I couldn't leave Sammy. My breathing calmed as I became resolved. I thought of Sammy's innocent smile and knew he deserved to keep that smile. I couldn't abandon him like my family had me, and I couldn't leave him with Claire.

I turned off the water and looked at my arm. It had blistered where the boiling water had landed. I rummaged in the first aid drawer of the vanity for some kind of ointment. I found some old burn cream I'd had since college, hoped it was still effective, and tenderly smeared some onto the burn.

I listened at the door for Claire to go to bed, then cracked the bathroom door to peer into the dark hall. The last thing I wanted was to lay next to her, the woman who intentionally caused me pain, but sleeping in the guest bedroom might alert Claire that I'd found my strength. I tiptoed to the bed and crawled in.

I barely breathed the entire night. I lay as close to the edge of the bed as possible with my back to her, not moving so to not wake the sleeping beast next to me.

I let Claire have the bathroom in the morning, pretending to read in bed while she got ready for work. Sammy had been sleeping past dawn, allowing me to remain in the sanctuary of the bed while Claire moved about the house.

When she closed the front door, I waited. When she got into her car, I waited. I waited until I couldn't hear the car anymore, and then I waited to still my heart.

Slowly, I emerged from bed. I looked at my arm, red and angry, and tried to flex my fingers. The fire returned to the tight skin with the movement. It would be difficult to handle Sammy with the injury, but its pain would serve as a constant reminder of my resolve.

Before rousing Sammy, I called Pieter. I held my breath, praying he'd pick up as the phone rang.

"Hey! Oh my gosh it's so good to hear from you. I'm just pulling into work; will you be around today? Can I call you back? It's been ages and I miss you!"

"No, Pieter. Please wait just a second. I have to talk to you, now."

"Okay, hon. Hold on." I heard him turn off the car. "Go ahead." The change in his tone reassured me. After years of friendship, he knew when I had something serious to say.

"I need somewhere to stay. Kind of indefinitely. With Sammy. I know you and Daniel haven't come close to baby-proofing and it's a massive imposition, but Pieter?" I paused to catch my breath or courage or something to hold on to, as the reality of what I was about to say slammed into me. "I'm scared," I sobbed.

Pieter waited while I slowed my sniffles. "Okay, honey. We've got you. Don't worry about explaining everything over the phone. Just get here. When should we expect you?"

"Um," I ran a quick timeline in my head while I wiped my nose. "Probably mid-afternoon. You don't have to leave work early. We'll be fine. I have a few stops to make."

"Okay. Look, you know the office has no problem with me cutting out early. Send a message when you're on the way and I'll meet you at the house."

I nodded against the phone. "Okay."

"Are you safe for now?" asked Pieter.

"Yeah. Yes," I sputtered.

"Okay. Then I'll see you in a few hours. Call if you need anything."

"See you," I replied, then hung up. I thought I'd feel relieved having Pieter ready and waiting, but I felt more butterflies in my stomach. This was it. Now that someone else knew, it was real. I was about to do the hardest thing I'd ever done. Leave my wife. Leave the family I thought I'd found. Another sob escaped my lips.

I took a deep breath and pushed the thought from my mind. There would be plenty of time for that later. I got out of bed and went into the bathroom. I'd read somewhere not to bandage a burn, so I rinsed the area again in cold water, patted it dry, and applied more burn ointment. It stung as it soaked in, another reminder of my mission. By the time I got dressed, I could hear Sammy baby-talking to himself in his crib.

"Hello, little one," I said as I entered his room. He watched me smiling as I pulled his baby bag from the closet and began packing as much of his clothes as would fit.

"We're going on adventure," I cooed. Sammy attempted to repeat the phrase back to me in toddler speak. I set his bag in the hall, picked up Sammy with my good arm, and set him on the floor as I filled another bag with changing supplies and toys. Whoever said it took a village to raise a child wasn't kidding around. It certainly took a village to tote the goods.

Sammy was starting to get fussy and trying to get into things just out of reach. Time for breakfast. I staged the second bag by the first in the hall and took Sammy downstairs to feed him. He was happy and energized by the time we finished breakfast. I placed him in his playpen, ate his leftovers, and prepared the highchair for transport.

Time for a final check. I had Sammy's gear, my own clothes, and my writing archive. I made sure my personal identification papers were handy. I recalled the therapist's words, and I knew I had to get a restraining order on Claire. Though it was just a piece of paper, it could create the precedence needed for protecting Sammy in a custody battle.

It was almost noon by the time I had us packed and ready. I was glad to be leaving the house close to the time for our mom-and-baby group. If Claire inquired with the neighbors, everyone's response would reflect business as usual.

I strapped Sammy into his car seat and thanked the universe for his easy car naps. If I was lucky, he'd be asleep the entire trip. Pieter and Daniel lived 45 minutes across town. On the way was the county courthouse.

Sammy woke for a moment as I transferred him from car to stroller. I rolled the stroller back and forth while we waited in line at the courthouse to maintain his lull. I was already moist from a cold fear sweat. A crying baby might have taken the little courage I had.

"Next!" called the clerk.

"H-hi," I stammered. "I, uh need to file a restraining order against my wife."

The clerk eyed me through her glasses. "Are you okay? Do you two have a safe place?"

"Yes," I replied.

"Okay, hon. Do you feel you are in immediate danger?"

"Um…" I wasn't sure.

"Do you have a lawyer?" My lawyer was Claire's lawyer. I shook my head. "Do you have some time now?" I nodded. "Okay. We can help you fill it out. It will take about an hour." The clerk left the window for a moment. I bent to check on Sammy, tucking his blanket in around him.

"Here you go. Do you know the process?"

"Not really. Just what I looked up before coming here."

"This is your standard form. You'll complete it and then it will need to be served with the court date to the person in the complaint. At the hearing, the judge will make a determination. If you're afraid your wife will retaliate from being served, you can fill out this form for an additional ex parte order, which protects you between now and the court date."

"Why wouldn't anyone fill out both?" I asked. The clerk shrugged.

"Go sit over there and do the best you can. We'll help with the rest."

I wheeled Sammy to the table and sat down. I worried he'd get fussy before I could finish, but I knew that at least the short term ex parte order had to be filed today. I was terrified of what Claire would do when she came home to an empty house.

The forms used a lot of unfamiliar language, and I had to recall in detail many painful events I wanted to forget. I was deep into the form when my phone rang. I eyed the screen with horror. Claire. I couldn't ignore it. She seldom called but when she did, she expected an answer. I didn't want to alert her suspicion.

"Hello?" I steadied my voice.

"Hello, darling. I thought I'd call to see how your day is going."

"Oh, we're fine. The mom-and-baby class is just wrapping up." I cleared my throat. "How's your day?"

"It's going well. We have a new large sponsor we're working with. Another gala is in our future! Isn't that exciting?"

"Yes," I replied. "Hon, they're waving me over. Is there anything you need?"

"No dear, just wanted to check in. Have fun." Claire hung up before I could say goodbye. Was it possible she knew something was up? I took a deep breath and forced myself back to the task at hand, my handwriting suffering from the shock of the call. An hour later I returned to the window.

"All set?" asked the clerk.

"I did as much as I could on my own," I replied. She took the pages and began looking them over.

"Hon, is that your only visible injury?" She pointed to my arm. I hid it below the counter. "This is the precipitating event?" she pointed to my written testimony of the previous evening which felt ages ago. Before I'd decided to leave. I nodded. "It would be best to have photo evidence. Can you take a photo on your phone and email it here?" She handed me a business card.

"Now?" I asked.

"Yes, I'd like to print and attach the photo. Step aside to do it while I help these people.''

I returned to the table. Sammy was starting to fight the stroller. This was far longer than he was usually immobilized. I gave him a handful of grapes from the bag I'd packed and snapped a few photos of the injury I preferred to ignore. For good measure, I held my hand up near my face for a selfie so Claire couldn't argue the hand wasn't mine. I emailed them to the address on the card and returned to the window.

"All set. How much longer will this take? My son is getting restless."

"Just a few more moments." she replied. She flipped through the pages asking questions where I'd left blanks. I rocked Sammy's stroller but he wasn't having it anymore.

"I need to go," I said.

"All I have to do is attach the photos. Sign here while I get them." I completed the affidavit and the clerk stamped the forms. "And now your copies." She separated the carbon pages. "Keep these on you at all times. I cannot stress that enough. I'm guessing you don't want to be the one to serve the court order to your wife?" I shook my head. "Then here's a list of options." She handed me another paper. "Good luck, hon."

I thanked her and left, praying Sammy wouldn't scream all the way to Pieter's.

I only answered one of Claire's calls the evening I moved out. Pieter sat next to me holding my free hand for support. At first, she feigned concern, asking if we were okay. I told her I had Sammy and we were fine, then braced for impact.

"Well, where are you?" she demanded. I repeated we were fine but wouldn't be coming home.

"Excuse me?" she said, her voice modulated the calm I knew held the storm.

"I won't be coming home. You'll have more information in a few days. Goodnight, Claire." I hung up and looked at Pieter. He squeezed my hand, Daniel looking on with Sammy grinning and bouncing in his arms.

My phone rang again, but we'd agreed Claire only deserved to know that Sammy was safe. I turned off my phone.

I threw myself into my writing. I'd written ideas on scraps of paper over the years, hoping I'd get to them at some point. It felt like the stress of life with Claire had drowned my creativity, and now that I was free of her, the dam had broken. It felt good. I felt vibrant. I was starting to realize how much I'd lost, how buried I'd been with Claire. She'd chipped pieces from me so small and gradual that I'd failed to notice until it was too late.

I was determined to be no burden on Pieter and Daniel and began working toward my old teaching role. Though they had space in their three-bedroom mid-century modern home, the importance of my financial empowerment and freedom had come into clear relief since Claire's control. Never again, I thought.

I made a regular habit of keeping my phone's cellular service off outside business hours. I wasn't ready to block Claire's number. We hadn't established an intermediary, yet. Pieter had asked around for a lawyer familiar with LGBTQ divorce and had received several leads, but I feared the price tag.

The protection order hearing took place a week later, and one of the lawyers agreed to attend with me pro bono, for which I was grateful. Pieter volunteered to stay home from work with Sammy so the sight of her son wouldn't trigger Claire at the courthouse. Pieter and Sammy were taking quite a liking to each other. I was starting to hope for the future, of a family of Uncle Pieter and Uncle Daniel, and Sammy healthy and loved.

I expected to feel fear, worry, sadness, or even regret when I saw Claire at the courthouse. Instead, I felt nothing. There was a numb hollow where my love for her had been. It was then I began to accept that I might have the fight in me after all.

Claire held her head high the whole time. I was just learning to stand straight again, but Claire stood as if she owned the courtroom and had no trouble at all with her private life. Her lawyer looked the same.

"Your honor, as you'll see, my client is an upstanding citizen in our fine community with no priors. This is a simple domestic dispute best settled between lovers in private."

"We are not lovers," I mumbled. My lawyer squeezed my shoulder, a reminder to hold my tongue, then took his turn explaining my case. I stared at the carpet in front of us, pretending not to hear the litany of horrors I'd allowed in my life. My lawyer nudged me.

"Approach the bench, show him your arm," he whispered. The judge looked at me. I approached him and pulled up my sleeve to reveal the red and peeling skin.

"And this is your only existing evidence at this time?" the judge said to my lawyer as I returned to the table.

"Ah, yes your honor, though we'll be able to gather anecdotal evidence from some of the events with witnesses."

"Not necessary, not necessary," the judge dismissed the offer with a wave of his hand. I felt relieved. Claire would coach our friends ahead of any interview.

"I'm granting the request. The restraining order is effective until one year from today."

I felt a wash of relief and exhaustion flow over me. It wasn't over, the divorce had yet to begin, but it was a start. I began contemplating the resources I'd need to make that happen.

I felt a harsh grip on my bicep. Claire stood close, breathing on my cheek. "This isn't over," she growled in my ear. Then she was gone. I glanced at my lawyer, but he was preoccupied with the judge's final sign-off. No one had seen. Just like always.

During the next week, my phone remained silent. I wrote, took care of Sammy, and applied to various other teaching roles while awaiting word from the dean of my previous position. Though I preferred my old role, it felt good to apply to others. Each cover letter adaptation felt like another minor step toward who I was before Claire.

The evenings with Pieter and Daniel were joyful. Watching them play with Sammy reassured me. I knew my child was cared for. He'd know connection and love, even after we moved out.

"We missed you," confided Pieter one evening while Daniel played on the floor with Sammy. "We all fell under Claire's spell, but I'm glad you woke up. Daniel and I had no idea how bad it had gotten. We thought parenting had carried you away."

Daniel nodded. "But we're so glad you trusted us when you needed shelter."

"Thank you, both of you." I felt my heart beat a little stronger.

"We decided we want to make sure you and Sammy remain safe, so we'd like to loan you the money to begin the divorce proceedings now." I was stunned to silence.

"Yeah. You and Sammy are too precious to remain in limbo between freedom and Claire's grasp."

I sputtered, "No, you guys. Really, you've done enough."

"We insist," stated Pieter. I looked at my feet, dug my toes into the carpet, processing.

"I'll pay it all back," I whispered. "I want a payment schedule to stick to." They nodded and Pieter gave me a quick squeeze.

I decided to use the same lawyer who had stood with me at the restraining order hearing. Within a few days, the papers were filed. The clock began ticking away the waiting period. The path forward got even clearer.

I braced for Claire to begin calling again, but my phone stayed silent. I thought of her words at the courthouse, recalled the pressure of her nails digging into my arm, but knew there was nothing she could do. She'd want to save face above all. I felt in control again.

Pieter and Daniel wanted to go out to celebrate the divorce proceeding being filed. Pieter got us a reservation at our favorite restaurant; we arranged for Sammy to be with his new daycare family and planned to dress up. We laughed as we sipped wine and approved or vetoed adornments for each other.

Even at the crowded restaurant, in public, we felt we were in our own bubble of joy. We toasted our progress and our new little family unit and anything else we could think of. Soon, my bladder was bursting.

"Guys, guys," I cried through the laughter. "I've gotta go. I'll be right back."

"To bathroom breaks!" toasted Daniel, and we all laughed. I took another sip and prepared to find my legs. I felt warm and light as I walked, concentrating on the straight line made by the tiles to guide me. Perhaps we'd overdone it. I wasn't used to drinking this much. Claire never let me. I smiled. Freedom felt good.

I entered the restroom and chose the first open stall I saw. As I settled into my relief, I glanced at the toilet paper dispenser and found a wisp of tissue stuck to a glue-stained roll. *Shit*, I thought. Just as I began formulating a plan, I heard someone else enter the restroom and the click of another lock.

"Hey, before you go, will you hand me some toilet paper, please?" I heard shuffling and a wad of paper appeared beneath the stall partition. "Thank you," I sighed. "Don't you hate it when that happens?" Still no answer. Some people just hate to talk in restrooms.

I flushed and approached the sink. I could see the other stall closed behind me in the mirror. I turned on the water, which must have muffled the sound of the door opening, of her approach. A cloth wrapped around my face. I sucked in a gulp of the chemical in shock as I looked up.

Claire.

I felt my body go limp, and Claire draped my arms over her shoulder. "Easy, dear. I'm here to take you home."

I stumbled next to her as we maneuvered. Claire unlocked the bathroom door and lurched me forward.

"Excuse me," she said to a staff person. "She's had too much to drink. Is there a back exit so we don't make a scene?" Clever Claire. She'd have known about the exit. A staff escort would clear any suspicion. And who ever suspected a woman of foul play?

I moaned, trying to alert the man, to beg for help.

"It's alright, dear," Claire crooned. "We're leaving." She looked at the staffer.

"Never could hold her liquor. We just wanted to celebrate. You know how it is." My head lolled. I couldn't tell how he reacted. He opened the door at the end of the hall and wished us goodnight.

Claire's vehicle was parked next to the exit. She opened the back door and shoved me in. I tried to push back, but the air felt like molasses, as if my hands had to press through it before they could reach something solid. Where even were my hands? I looked down, befuddled, as the car door shut.

Claire entered the driver's seat and began maneuvering us away from the restaurant and my new family. It seemed my brain's input still worked, despite being drunk, but the output was a mess. I tried to speak again, but only succeeded in drooling on myself. The car's movements tossed me. I had no reflexes. I concentrated on focusing my attention on my surroundings. I couldn't jump from the vehicle in my state, and Claire had engaged the child locks when Sammy had come to us. My purse, cell phone—everything—was hanging from my chair at the restaurant. I hoped Pieter and Daniel noticed my absence sooner than later.

"Your antics have caused a bit of trouble for me. Did you know that?" Claire said. My head rolled and I moaned. "I'm under an ethics review. An ethics review! They're not sure they want someone who has a restraining order on them for domestic abuse and an upcoming divorce to be the face of the organization."

My eyes scanned the car. They locked on a pen on the floor below the passenger seat. Not much of a weapon, but concealable.

"Why did you have to go and do that?" She continued. "It's so unseemly. We could have worked it out. I was so good to you and Sammy. You know, he's my son, too."

Could I reach the pen? I worked to flop my arm down off the bench I lay on. Claire braked for a slow vehicle in front of us and the momentum swung my arm toward the pen.

"Don't fall," Claire warned, thinking my movement had nothing to do with my will. "I want you in one piece." She sped up again, drifting my dangling arm away from the pen. I needed another deceleration. A stop. I wriggled a bit, trying to press the viscous mass of my body into an optimal position. A red light glowed up ahead. Salvation. We slowed, I pressed, my arm swung, and my fingers touched the pen. So close. Suddenly, Claire slammed on the brakes.

"Asshole," she muttered. The car was still. The pen was mine. I pressed it into my palm, fingers feeling like putty, so Claire wouldn't see as she turned to check on me.

"I should have buckled you in," she mused. I groaned. The light turned green, and we took off. I pressed my muscles to move my arm and shoved the pen into my bra.

I knew the familiar sound of the driveway, the garage. She'd brought me home, as she'd promised the staffer at the restaurant. But it wasn't my home anymore. I belonged with Pieter and Daniel, people who saw me and loved me.

Claire turned off the car and got out. She opened my door and yanked on my leg. I tried to kick, my reflexes still dulled from the alcohol and the drug, and she slapped my leg away.

"None of that," she said, pulling me from the car. Then Claire let me go. I collapsed, not expecting to have to use my jelly legs, my face hitting the cement step. I tasted blood.

"Miss Independent here can't even stand on her own." Claire reached for me and pulled me up, dragged me inside the house, my arms once again draped around her neck. My legs tingled. Could I get away? Run if I needed? I tried adding weight to feet that felt foreign. I needed these shoes off. I let myself trip, hoping to annoy Claire into taking them off for me.

"Interesting that high heels, an instrument of the patriarchy, now keep you dependent in your wife's arms." Claire yanked on me. My arm tingled. The drug was wearing off, but I was still drunk. Did Claire know the timing of the drug?

I fumbled toward my breast, groping for the pen.

"Enough, Claire. No more violence." My voice was garbled behind my molasses lips, but it was intelligible.

"Violence? There's never been any violence. You're just so clumsy, my dear." It dawned on me. Was that her plan? To tell the judge I was too clumsy and underemployed to care for my son? Her attacks made to look like my fault, as always? "Just like a moment ago. Sometimes you just fall. Or bump into something sharp," Claire said as we passed the kitchen counter. A paring knife was sitting out, and Claire picked it up as we passed, setting the car keys in its place. She held it at her side in an attempt to conceal it.

I hated violence. My strong sense of empathy made me a good writer but terrible at defending myself from Claire. Yet, when she picked up the knife, I knew I had to act, or I would lose everything.

Still draped over her shoulder, I gripped the pen and jammed it between her ribs then released it. I dropped my body away from hers as the shock relaxed her grip. Claire screamed and spun to swing the knife toward me. It caught my shoulder as I fell. I began crawling toward the stairs as fast as I could, toward higher ground and bedroom doors that locked, arms and legs tingling with the activity.

"Are you serious!?" Claire yelled, the pen still in her side. "I brought you here to talk!"

"Then why'd you grab the knife?" I panted, crawling up the steps.

"Self-defense from being stabbed!" she cried. But I knew what I had seen. She'd grabbed the knife first. I now had no weapon but distance.

As I clamored up, step by step, I kicked off my shoes. I paused to watch Claire examine her wound through the bars of the railing. My heart raced, trying to pump adrenaline and alcohol to my organs and clear my blood and mind.

"Well, this dress is ruined." Claire mumbled, preparing paper towel and kitchen tape, then pulling the pen out with a grunt. Blood oozed from the wound as she patched it. I knew it hadn't gone in far, but it was enough to give me a chance.

"Claire, this is over," I called from the steps. But I'd made a mistake, the same mistake I made throughout our marriage. I underestimated her.

"It's not over until I say it is. I'm the one in control!" she shrieked as she stumbled toward me. I began to back further up the steps, gripping the carpet. "You've forgotten your place, dear!"

Though wounded, Claire still moved faster than me. I turned to scramble up the steps and felt a sting on my foot. Then another on my ankle. Another on my calf. I kept moving, stumbling to get out of reach of Claire's knife.

"Look at you," she said as she sliced at my legs. Another cut stung my thigh. Then my buttocks. My other thigh. "You can't even crawl on your own. How could I have ever loved someone like you?" Slice, slice, slice. I needed a defense. Something. My body rang, vibrating with vertigo and Claire's cuts. She matched my movements, step by step, sweeping her arm past me over and over, cut by cut, as I tried to get away. I yelled for her to stop, begged, cried, but she wouldn't let me go, wouldn't end it.

"You took from me, piece by piece. I gave and gave, and you just took and took! Well, I'm taking it back!" she yelled, punctuating her words with her cuts. My head swam as I fought to focus on a defense. Wasn't she the one who took from me?

I turned to face her, tried to grab her wrist, make her stop. She sliced the knife along my hand. I raised my arm in self-protection. Another cut. Cut. Cut. I tried to grab her; again, my good hand made contact, and I held tight.

"Let me go," she grunted. I wasn't very strong. I'd grown a bit of a mom-body over the past year. But I could hold my grip from holding and pushing Sammy every day. I reached for her other wrist, pressing myself into the stairs, back to the wall, clawing at the woman I once loved.

Claire would not let go of the knife. I would not let go of Claire. I still needed a weapon. This stalemate wouldn't last.

I glanced through the bannister's supports, scanning for a tool that would be too far away. Then I focused on the bannister itself. While I struggled to hold Claire, my back wedged between the steps and wall, I began kicking at the balusters that held the handrail up. Each was the size of a pool cue, which was enough of a weapon in movie bar brawls. I struggled and rolled, our grunts and shrieks matching as I kicked, listening for splinters.

The first crack excited me so much that I forgot my grip on Claire. She wriggled free, now right on top of me, and swept the knife toward my face. I turned to deflect, the knife meeting my upper arm, then crawled toward the railing as the knife stung my shoulder and back.

My hands grabbed the wood and I pulled. I kicked at Claire, trying to make any contact, aiming for her wound. I pulled against the pole for leverage, and it broke free. Claire paused in amusement. I did not. I swung as hard as I could muster, meeting the side of Claire's head. The blow set her off balance, and she stumbled down several steps.

"Stop," I panted.

She staggered toward me. I swung again, but Claire skirted the blow. My hand pressed against the bannister, slipping against my own blood. I leveled myself as I held the piece of wood like a sword. My body ached from the many cuts, blood dripping onto the white stairway carpet. I looked at Claire clutching her side, knife out, ready for the next move.

"Why?" I whispered.

"I have nothing left to lose. You took it all. I want you to feel my pain." I didn't have time to marvel at her twisting of facts. Claire lunged and my staff met her shoulder, diverting her attempt. Her arm swept back to strike again and caught my shoulder as I swung the piece of wood back toward her and made contact with her head. Claire had not yet regained her footing from her lunge and tripped over her feet, falling backward down the stairs. I hobbled a few steps down to better observe her condition at the bottom. She was still. I feared I had killed her, but the overwhelming need for help for my injuries pushed the thought away as I stumbled down the stairs. I either had to find her phone, or get to the neighbors. Both meant passing by her body.

I gripped the bannister, smeared with blood, my hand sticking as it moved. Each step came slow, my breath catching from the pain. I studied Claire for any movement. As I got closer I could see her back rise and fall with her breath, a small trickle of blood on her forehead. My heart clenched, praying she remain unconscious.

One foot on the floor, then the other. I pulled together my strength and let go of the railing. Another step around Claire's legs. I would be okay now. Another step. Pain seared through my Achilles tendon. I screamed in surprise as I fell toward the kitchen, my piece of bannister clattering away from me. I looked back at Claire. She was staring at me, knife gripped in her hand.

"You bitch," she groaned, using on me the label she most hated. I crawled backward, crab-walk-dragging myself away from her.

Claire reached out and grabbed my ankle and I kicked her away, turning to crawl into the kitchen, toward anything that could form a barrier between us. A white-hot pain shot through the arch of my foot. I looked back to see Claire's knife pinning me to the floor. She pulled against the handle, using it as an anchor to drag herself closer. I kicked my other leg toward her, trying to get free. My foot made contact with Claire's head. She yanked the knife from my foot and rolled to her side, dazed.

I reached toward the kitchen counter, using it to pull myself away from Claire before she could reorient herself. I lifted myself onto a stool, then reached for the keys on the counter. I felt Claire's hand wrap around my ankle and pull me down while she sliced at my shin. I twisted with the keys in between my fingers and slashed Claire's face. Claire yelled and reeled back, holding her face.

I jolted toward the garage, using the wall to steady me, leaving streaks as I went. Claire started toward me. I opened the door, the handle slick in my bloody hand, and held the doorframe to step down into the garage. Claire's knife sliced the back of my hand as I thrust myself from the doorway toward the driver's door, grabbing the mirror to hold myself up. Claire grabbed my hair from behind and pulled me away. I reeled, elbowing her in the chest, holding the keys for dear life.

Claire's hold released and I pulled my body weight against the door handle. I thrust myself into the car and fumbled the key into the ignition.

Claire stumbled forward, grabbing the car door as I revved into reverse to get away. The movement sent Claire off balance and she let go. I gunned the car backward, looking in the rear window, and ran something over. I turned to look for Claire, to see how quickly she was coming, but she was on the ground. I stopped the car and slowly crawled out. Claire didn't move. She stared back, eyes bulging without blinking.

"C-Claire?" I managed.

I held the hood of the car as I snuck closer. Claire laid twisted, her shoulders pressed toward the ground at an odd angle, her neck nearly flat. I sank to the cement and held myself weeping against the tire.

"What the fuck? What the fuck?" I repeated, rocking myself. I couldn't stop staring into her eyes, and there was no one behind them to divert their gaze from me.

Claire had finally lost control.

# About the Author

Veronica Zora Kirin is a queer author and entrepreneur whose work aims to unearth within the reader something they may not have known existed. She is the author of the award winning (NIEA 2020 / IBA 2020) *Stories of Elders: What the Greatest Generation Knows about Technology that You Don't* (Identity Publications 2018), which documents the paradigm shift of the high-tech revolution as lived by the Greatest Generation. Her current book, *Stories of COVID™*, is being written in real time to document the impact of the pandemic for future generations. Her poetry has appeared in publications such as *The Poetry Archive* and *New Feathers Anthology*. Learn more at VeronicaKirin.com/books and follow @vmkirin.

# Blessed

George Daniel Lea

A wonderful, terrible thing. This communion. This *rite?* This…

How can I even begin? No word suffices, no analogue in human history or experience encompasses. Falling in love? Oh yes! Yes. Not its entirety, not even close, but a suggestion, a whisper. Also, trauma; the blackest and most soul-shredding, that kind that leaves us in tatters, drifting down into a silt of despair. Break-ups. Bereavements. The end of love and its resurrection. Birth and breaking. Finding and losing God. Revelation of all colors and species.

There. The best I can do without first-hand demonstration. It's what I live for. What I *continue* to live for, long after all other obsessions and appetites have withered, after this wine skin I inhabit should have sundered and bled dry.

My loves. My beautiful boys. My lost children. Men, all; a strange requirement of the process; the sharing of gender, but also a personal proclivity. Call me whorish, narcissistic if you like, but they are my everything. The beautiful, poetic; painted and pierced; the cartoonishly miserable and the absurdly joyous. Their presence, their proximity, swells me, makes me whole, just as their absence sickens, their silence diminishes. My beautiful, beautiful boys.

I don't require ownership, not like most. They don't belong to me, even if they love me back. I'm content to watch them from a distance, to drink their lives without their knowledge. To bask in them, their unknown radiance, the beauty they might never know. There's a reason, I think, that angel motifs feature widely in the sub-cultures they weave.

That need. . .you understand it, don't you? Of course you do. You wouldn't be here otherwise; the *ache* to be among one's own tribe, even if it is one of the *tribeless.* We—what? *Queers?* I always liked that, myself: we *queers* are a species apart. Even from one another; tribes of one, unique and in love with that status. That's what I find, in my *extensive* experience. Self-sewn tapestries, rag-dolls of the strangest and most esoteric components. Often ill-fitting, skewed inside or contradictory without. Broken stained glass windows and shattered mosaics inside our heads. Brilliantly and beautifully broken, as an old flame once put it.

I suppose that's why I seek their—*your* company, barring the obvious:

I can be as I am amongst them; just another pilgrim or sibling in their eyes, a potential lover, one who might wrap them up, call them beauty, profess love, if only for a night, an *hour,* before whatever spell we weave breaks and gray reality intrudes.

Here, in this place; the chemical-sweat scented murk, the hungry, sex-swollen shadows. *I can be as I am;* self-authored, pavonine, predatory. As we all are.

Don't ask me to elaborate, *please.* I don't even know if I can! Have another drink, first; pop another pill before I try. At least that way, you might feel moved to pretend rather than dismiss out of hand.

All right:

Imagine. Imagine *being inside another's skin,* not physically; not as the result of some hideous surgical experiment, but in the manner of their soul. Imagine knowing someone so intimately, it's as though you *are them,* and they you. Imagine a fuck so intense, you fuse nerve to nerve, synapse to synapse, losing the point where you end and they begin.

That's what it's like. Understanding as they understand, operating in a world filtered through their perceptions and experience. The shell of self cracking, flying apart, minds becoming fluid and racing together; a conflux, a new and nameless phenomenon.

It is *everything:* bliss and harm, delight and delirium. Abuse and addiction. Beatification and blindness. Revelation and ignorance. *Humanity.* The ultimate drug, the high and low and everything in between. Heaven, Hell. God and the Devil. *Chaos.*

And it is never, *never* enough.

You see? There it is. I can't even tell you, can I? Not in any way you might believe or understand. Finish your drink. Take the last pill. I don't need it tonight, but you most certainly will, before morning comes and breaks whatever dream we share.

I loved them all. Every one of them. More sincerely than any lover, parent or incestuous collision thereof. More than anyone ever could.

Because I *knew* them, you understand? I knew them, *saw* them in every secret shame, every sublimated disgrace. The fantasies they'd never dare tell, but that I became the living story of. You don't understand; I get that. How can you? Sealed away in your own skin and skull. Straight-jacket and insane asylum all in one. I used to smother likewise, when I was young, before I learned my own story. Twisted and writhing inside myself, born a prisoner. I hurt myself quite badly, once upon a time: slit my own seams, hoping to peel out of myself, to feel the air on naked nerves. To *breathe* at last, even if it was the first and only time.

What? You don't like that? Yeah, suicidal ideation is kind of a turn off, isn't it? Not quite where you expected the story to go? That's okay. If it's any consolation, the ones you tell me without saying a word aren't what I expected, either. It's the same with everyone: the ones I drink on every breath, taste on every kiss and caress, every drop of spit, sweat, blood, and semen. New stories never told or heard before, not in quite the same way. Never the same patterns, despite their common elements.

It's okay! It's okay. I know you want it, though you can't understand, though you're afraid: to be *known* so utterly, in every moment of petulant rage and disgust, every fleeting fantasy of violence and cruelty. For others, for yourself. Here, kiss me and I'll show you; I'll tell you a story that only you know, that no one else could. Will that do it for you? Will that blunt your doubts a little?

What, the taxi driver? Oh, don't mind him. He won't see, won't care, so long as he gets paid at the end. He's certainly seen worse back here; I can taste the echoes of it: atrocities and perversities you wouldn't believe. Is it the crucifix that bothers you, the fact that he's a man of faith? Believe me, he's had it tested so many times here, we're practically invisible to him.

So, come on: one kiss, for the price of certainty? Sounds like a fair trade to me.

Ah! So hungry. So desperate. So *alone*. I taste it, not that I require any capacity beyond the merely human for that. It's there, in the sadness of your eyes, the muted eagerness of your lips, the starved, cannibal writhing of your tongue.

But more, so much more:

A place, so long ago. A darkened bridge, overgrown with weeds, a place you used to walk with friends who are no longer there. Am I right, thus far? Jobless, nearly penniless. An over-educated nothing with dreams of renaissance and revolution that will never blossom. Below, a train track, running to the old mine where your grandfather worked. At this late hour, you can't see the tracks; just darkness, an abyss opening, as though the mine itself gapes in desire of the blood it never had opportunity to claim, the babes never sacrificed to it.

You almost do it, don't you? That black lightning in your veins, a narcotic swell of relief washing your entrails at the imminence of ending. A storm-tossed shoreline inside silver sand, black waters, red sky. You totter on the brink, so afraid, more of another unwanted waking than oblivion.

What stops you? Why do you let the storm inside fade? Cowardice? That's certainly what you think, isn't it? What you've condemned yourself for ever since. Borrowed time, a dead man walking? You've even dreamed of being there, mangled and barely breathing in the dark, waiting for a train that will never come. Is that what you believe? That you're some sort of ghost, a temporal splinter in the eye of God?

Well? Is that good enough? Yes, yes; more than enough. A shock, maybe? I understand. It often is. Don't worry yourself, sweetheart. I'm not like gods or parents. My love is unconditional. I don't care what you or anyone has to confess; stories of failed fatherhood, of miscarriages, of divorce and adultery, drug abuse, destitution. Worse, even. Far worse. Atrocity. Sadism. Genocide. I've tasted it all, drank it so ravenously. A starving child at the wolf bitch's teat.

I'm sure that shocks you. How can I? How can I celebrate as much in cruelty and disgrace as transcendence, revelation?

Because they're all one and the same to me, my love: bespoke feasts. Bring me your broken and sick, your wounded and wild: I will love them, drink them dry when they give themselves to me.

And they do, *they do.* So desperate for some connection, some poetry, to be something to someone, *anyone,* other than a face to pass in the street, a mystery to lament and loathe in the morning. You want it, too. I smell it even now and have ever since you so cleverly snared my eye from the club dance floor. Sinuous, practiced slut that you are.

Do you want this? Do you want us to stop the taxi, get out in the rain and forget one another, come the morning? That's fine; I won't force anything on you. That's not my way. I know there have been others in the past that weren't quite so diplomatic.

Think. I mean, really *think* about it: this is your last night on Earth. As you are, as you understand yourself. After this, things change. *You* change, and so do I. Is it what you want?

Good. *Good.*

So handsome. You're older than you look: I taste that, too. But still so, so handsome. Mid-thirties? Maybe even early-forties. Practically desiccate, by the standards of our tribe. The journey stretches, the taxi carrying us down endless, darkened streets, labyrinths of steel-fronted shops and abandoned homes for rent, for sale. Packs of shadow-things that glare at us with automatic hostility from beneath their hoods, that have known nothing but abuse from the world. Traces and tatters of them reach me; suggestions of scent, whispers of song. Blood and excrement, vomit and burning bone. *Hurt.* Each and every one of them: children of trauma, a generation of the abused.

They can't harm us, not here. This place is ours, for now. A temple, a shrine to our own hermetic faith that can never be violated. It takes you time, I see that; you're not quite there, not quite a believer yet. But revelation is coming, sweetheart. Believe that.

Your gospels flow, flooding me; stories that burst behind my eyes like painted stars, memories and experiences that are as much mine now as they are yours:

Little nothings; the casual flirtations with the young, pierced and heavy-set guy at the local cafe, who always flashes a crooked smile, whose fingers always seem to brush yours over hazelnut lattes. The old woman and her spaniel on the walk to work, who vomits every woe, every snide judgement of neighbors and caretakers and children into your ears until they bleed. The passive aggressive game you play with that bitch at work who wants everyone to think her so sweet, so giving, but is reptilian beneath her smiling masks.

Games. Toys. Books and comics, moments of elation, images behind your eyes. Flashes of fury and desire, unbidden erotic atrocities, mosaics of violence, yearnings for apocalypse.

Trauma. The moments that change you, that cut and sculpt and rip and make you what you are. Those wounds are mine; I wriggle into them, the blood-fattened maggot that gorges on their poison, swelling to the point that I split and sprout wings.

An angel to me, if to no other. Another lost boy.

This place is yours? Yes; small, cluttered, unkempt. Scraps of this and that, papers and poetry, bills and abandoned plays scattered all around. The cases for video games and old DVDs. The smell of dust and dead incense. This is yours and you, the shell you have constructed against the world. It echoes with you: do you know that? A place haunted by your own ghosts; things of old misery and elation, of dead skin cells, dry blood. Phantoms all around us, eager to be heard, to have me drink them into silence.

The young ones, the lovers that seek you out then leave and forget after barely an evening's communion...how you lament them! The perfect, painted, and pretty ones who ache to be so clean and accepted. I taste that, too, with every eager kiss, every bite of the lips or tongue. Not hatred, nothing so intense or consuming as that, but merely a sorrow, a sadness that they don't *attend*, that they flout their own histories and traditions. That it's too easy for them by far; adoration on tap, ephemeral worship barely a few Grindr messages away.

But we, oh we! We know, don't we? We keep the faith. I remember the old ways, even better than you, my weathered and ragged boy. When the clubs and bars were our temples, the sites of our communions and blood-sacrifices. When there was danger and politics to every kiss, anarchy in every fuck, no matter how casual. When we could break the world in our beds and bring civilization crashing down from back-alley shadows.

No more. We are the last, the final keepers of the old and forgotten ways. I know; I *taste* it on them: that need to be part of the world that would crush them for their beauty, to be accepted by forebears who wish them aborted, dead before they could swell to disgrace.

No matter; I already have lovers aplenty, inside my skin, the labyrinths of my soul. Old and young, weary and drunk on the world. Souls enough to spark a hundred renaissances, should I have a mind.

Can you hear them? Can you taste them, as you taste me? I think so. Dimly, distantly, whispering up from depths that no expedition could ever plumb or pierce, a whisper away, yet divorced from us by cosmic spans.

Get used to it, sweetheart. They'll be yours, soon, just as they are mine. Would you like that, huh? To live in me, to be their neighbor, their lover? Yes. *Yes.* They want it, too. Can you hear them singing, clamoring to know you? That's what it's like; to love and be loved by me; to ache for others, to share my appetites. To be lost in the labyrinths, but never alone.

They all live, still, despite what this gray, tattered curtain of a world proclaims. They all live and dream. Within *me.* Isn't that wonderful? Isn't that horrifically *sublime?*

There's still time if you want to stop. To run. Plenty have when they've learned the truth. Too anchored, too addicted to the gray poison of their lives. And that's fine; I won't coerce you. I'm no monster, no matter what others might proclaim. This is all yours: your time, your stories. Drink up, drain the wine, take your medicine. Kiss and tell. *Tell me everything.*

Ah, good. Good boy! Another glass, another kiss, another seal upon the contract between us. Another shard in the eye of the world that demands we be part of it. Why? Why would we ever indulge it, given what it has heaped upon us? Sick, stupid, pointless thing that it is.

Oh, I know, pretty boy. *I know.* Because I remember now, too. Where it started; the self-obsession, the endless wandering of your own interior realms. What are they to you? Primordial wilderness, post-apocalyptic wasteland, a wild wood, a profane temple to elder Gods. You live in them more than you do here, don't you? Always have. Let me take you there, sweetness; we'll walk them and learn their secrets together. Let them become real, *in me.*

More than kisses, more than an embrace. Violent in its intensity, breaking the artifacts you have surrounded yourself with: the lamps and book cases, the statuettes of gods and monsters. Let them go, don't mourn them. If you want, they'll be made anew before the morning. Everything will. But not here, not in this gray desolation.

Give them to me. Confess them, sacrifice them: the child who refuses to die, the reluctant man, so horrified at the world, who's sought a means of stepping out of it his entire life.

Well, here I am, lover.

What? You still don't believe? Ha. That's okay. Belief isn't a requirement. Only consent. Only *surrender*. And I think you're up for that, aren't you? A novel form of seduction, eh? An overly elaborate chat-up line. You're tired of it now? Of course. How silly of me: the night and game both getting old, your bed waiting.

Kisses, kisses, tasting of bitter wine, poisoned honey. A lost boy leading me up the stairs, into familiar darkness, a place where pleasures and atrocities have both been born. Beautiful, each in their own ways; other lost ones seeking some measure of comfort, of belonging, in his alien arms, whatever they discovered there fleeting, ephemeral, some of them dressing and fleeing before it even reaches that phase.

I hear them, feel them all around: ghosts of old love and disappointment, of communions and brutality. Sighs and screams and ragged breaths, sobs burbled through blood.

Yes! No judgement here, lover. No dread or disgust of you. Why would I? Blood is as welcome as milk, pain as exhilarating as ecstasy. My palate isn't discerning, for all of my pretensions.

Kiss me. Undress me. Rake me raw. Cry, if you wish. Cry to be known at last, sob your confessions. I'll take them all, drink every drop of sin you have to give, and more besides. Their names incidental, almost forgotten. But their bodies, their faces, their prayers...

Give them to me, those old loves. Share them with me, in all their languorous loss, their horror and disappointment.

What was his name? The one who showed you, that became the subject of your self-revelation? *Cadmus,* wasn't it (or so he told you)? Nineteen, twenty when you found him, but seeming far younger? Another lost and broken thing, one you recognized on sight as a cracked mirror of your own soul. That you loved from that moment. That you couldn't live without.

So beautiful, a stray lamb courting the attention of wolves, in love with the notion of his own devouring. The taste of him; his lips, his spit, his blood. Can you taste him, still? Can you hear how he moaned, how he pleaded? Not for you to stop, but to *continue*, even when he was open and wounded, peeled back and flowering. Even when blood threatened to choke the hymns in his throat.

Oh, my poor, poor child. Had you forgotten? Had you buried it so deep, hoping never to know again? Such a pity.

Yes! That bolt of black lightning, illuminating the wastelands, cracking them open, inspiring the corpses buried beneath to rise and dance. Give it to me. Let me kiss you open and devour your living heart, lick it clean of every bloody, congealed passion, every defeated, unfulfilled desire.

*Open to me. Let us be a feast for one another, on this last night of our lives.*

Cold sunlight. Dry blood and stale sweat in the quilt. Another dead day. Bones share our bed, bones and ashes. A desiccated smile.

I quiver as I rise, smiling and full, *so full.* Marked by your violence, the love I was happy to endure. A canvas for bites and scratches, an art more earnest than any brush might realize.

I taste you, I hear you: stories that will echo inside of me forever, co-mingling with the rest, becoming new myths that will never be still or silent.

I am the angel you prayed for, in the sweating, febrile reaches of pubescent nights, the shadow-lover you cried out into the night to come and find you, lift you up through your window to sing and sorrow amongst the uncaring stars.

Now, I have come, and the Heaven you demanded is yours, forever and a day.

Feel blessed, my love.

# About the Author

George Lea is an unfixed oddity that has a tendency to float around the UK Midlands (his precise location and plain of operation is somewhat difficult to determine beyond that, though certain institutions are working on various ways of defining his movements). An isolated soul by nature, he tends to spend more time with books than with people, consumes stories in the manner a starving man might the scattered debris of an incongruously exploded pie factory, whilst also attempting to churn out his own species of mythological absurdity (it's cheaper than a therapist, less trouble than an exorcist and seems to have the effect of anchoring him in fixed form and state, at least for the moment). He proclaims to spend most of his time "...feeling like some extra-dimensional alien on safari," which he very well might be (apprehension and autopsy will likely yield conclusive details).

Following the publication of his first short story collection, *Strange Playgrounds* and the follow up collection *Essential Atrocities,* George is currently working in collusion with the entity known as "Nick Hardy" on the project *Born in Blood,* which consists of two volumes of short story collections from *Perpetual Motion Machine Publications (Born in Blood: Volumes One and Two),* multiple volumes of visual work and an independent film (*Hymns of Abarise*), currently in production.

# About the Editor

A member of Horror Writers Association, Rebecca Rowland is the author of the dark fiction collection *The Horrors Hiding in Plain Sight*, co-author of the crime thriller novel *Pieces*, and curator of the horror anthologies *Ghosts, Goblins, Murder, and Madness*; *Shadowy Natures: Stories of Psychological Horror*, and *The Half That You See*. Her short fiction and critical essays have appeared in a number of progressive indie venues, but to pay the bills, she has worked as an academic librarian, high school English teacher, ghostwriter, obituary writer, and copy editor.

Without the encouragement and help from Felice Picano and Louis Stephenson, *Unburied* would never have seen the light of day, and she is eternally grateful to them.

Despite her love of the ocean and unwavering distaste for cold temperatures, she currently resides with her family—animal and human members—in a landlocked and often icy corner of New England. If you visit her at RowlandBooks.com, she promises not to send you junk mail on anything...unless you're into it.

Also From

Available in Print - eBook - Audiobook

Devil's Night, Day of the Dead, and Halloween have been celebrated around the world in one form or another, beginning with the Ancient Celts over two-thousand years ago. For some revelers, it's a time for guising, or dressing up in elaborate costume; for others, it's a time for practical jokes and mischief, and for some, it's a reverent occasion to acknowledge the thin line between earth and the spirit world.

Featuring twenty-one different voices hailing from five different countries and eleven states, *Ghosts, Goblins, Murder, and Madness* is certain to strike a chord with every horror aficionado.

Also From

Available in Print - eBook - Audiobook

**Shadowy Natures**
Stories of Psychological Horror

Edited by
Rebecca Rowland

"The boundary line between instinct and reason
is of a very shadowy nature"

-Edgar Allan Poe (1840)

With its twenty-one stories of serial killers and sociopaths, fixations and fetishes, breakdowns and bad decisions crafted by authors as diverse as their writing styles, *Shadowy Natures* leads fans of psychological horror down dark and treacherous roads to destinations they will be too unsettled to leave.

Also From

Available in Print - eBook - Audiobook

"You are young yet, my friend," replied my host, "but the time will arrive when you will learn to judge for yourself of what is going on in the world...

Believe nothing you hear, and only one half that you see."

-Edgar Allan Poe (1845)

In *The Half That You See*, twenty-six writers from around the globe share their optical illusions in never before seen horror stories of portentous visions and haunting memories, altered consciousness and virulent nightmares, disordered thinking and descents into madness.

www.ingramcontent.com/pod-product-compliance
Lightning Source LLC
Chambersburg PA
CBHW060343030726
47497CB00003B/578